FA'

**EVENTUALLY, EVERI
THE DEMON GC**

An International Murder Mystery

SEQUEL TO ROOM OF DEATH
PART II OF III

by

Sidney St. James

"Nothing turns out quite in the way you thought it would when you are sketching out notes for the first chapter or walking about muttering to yourself and seeing a story unroll!"

-—Agatha Christie

Table of Contents

Fate - Eventually Everything Connects (Demon Gorge Trilogy, #2) 1

Dedication 3

Introduction | The Manuscript is Received...........................5

Chapter ONE | What the Black Rock Cove News Had to Say..7

Chapter TWO | A Day of Tragedy 25

Chapter THREE | A Dark Mystery Still Hung Over Their Heads..41

Chapter FOUR | Reconciliation Between Husband and Wife 57

Chapter FIVE | The Duel to the Death 75

Chapter SIX | Children Drown at Sea.................................89

Chapter SEVEN | The End of the Secret 113

Chapter EIGHT | The Ruined Lighthouse of Demon Gorge...143

Chapter NINE | A Domestic Circle is Found 165

Chapter TEN | It's a Small, Small World 181

Chapter ELEVEN | A Deathbed Confession 201

Chapter TWELVE | The Queen's Anteroom.......................221

Chapter THIRTEEN | Confiding a Secret..........................237

Chapter FOURTEEN | Denouncing Our Savior for His Tender Mercy..255

Chapter FIFTEEN | A Look of Sad Sarcasm......................269

Published by BeeBop Publishing Group
Georgetown, Texas

FIRST EDITION

FATE

The Devil Gorge Trilogy

BOOK 2

Mystery and Suspense

A Sequel to ROOM OF DEATH

This novel's jacket format and design are protected trade dresses and trademarks of Sidney St. James and the BeeBop Publishing Group.

Published Simultaneously in Canada

Library of Congress Cataloging-in-Publication Data

1 3 5 7 9 10 8 6 4 2

AVAILABLE IN EBOOK, PAPERBACK & AUDIO

1

Dedication

This novel is dedicated to my four grandchildren, Haley Dawn, Alyssa Nicole, Dylan James, and Alexandra Leigh!

Waves

Introduction
The Manuscript is Received

No one reads a mystery to get to the middle of the book. They read the novel to get to the end. It's the intention of this mystery to entertain you from the very beginning. In other words, the first page wishes to invite the reader to buy the novel. I trust the story's last page will entice you to go to the next book.

With that said, I believe every reader feels they are a born detective at the bottom of their heart. So, as the story you are about to encounter, as the author, I will, from one chapter to the next, distract you as I scatter clues so as not to let you figure out or solve the case too soon.

Several years ago, I wrote three novels in another trilogy series, "The Storm Lord Trilogy." This is where a small fishing village known as Black Rock Cove got its beginning. Also, the infamous lighthouse and secrets held beneath, and the house of two-time Nobel Prize-winning physicist Johnathan Knight were born in this series.

It's been several years since the writing of that trilogy.

In this international thriller, I bring back the sleepy fishing village, the demon gorge and its large black boulders, and a love triangle and murder mystery that spans the globe and doesn't get solved until my final two chapters in the series.

So, find a cozy chair, begin reading, and see if you can figure out whodunnit!

Happy Reading.

Chapter ONE
What the Black Rock Cove News Had to Say

"**G**o *and find this man!*"

Haley Dawn, the fair and fragile young girl, laid back in a mesmeric trance, her fingers trembling on the torn and ragged edge of the wingback chair.

Victoria Meret, the old crone, and hypnotist waited with her eyes fixated upon the girl. Her real intention was to send the spiritualist in quest of the mortal remains of the late Samuel Knight and claim the reward promised for the discovery.

Victoria had taken out of her pocket a black curl of Samuel Knight's hair and pressed it gently to the forehead of the entranced young girl.

"Go and find this man," repeated the old crone in a low and imperative tone of voice.

"I do," whispered Haley.

"Do you see him?"

"Yes... yes, I see him."

"Where is he, Haley?"

"Wait... I see only his face. There's like a mist before him that hides everything but his face. And his face is also dim and somewhat cloudy to my vision. I do not know it."

"Ahhh, he must be covered by a sheet or something. Watch! Watch closely!" eagerly panted the old vagabond.

"Stop! Stop! You're hurting me," cried the entranced girl.

Victoria slowed down her requests.

"Watch carefully, Haley. He is lying out on a table and covered with a sheet. Watch who comes."

"No, he is not lying under a sheet. He is sitting up. There is something white in front of him. Everything appears to be in a mist."

Victoria lowered her voice to a whisper. "Now, Haley, look steadily... clearly."

"Yes... I know now. He's sitting in a barber shop with a large white towel or sheet over him. He is standing up, and the sheet is falling to the floor. Now I know him. He is Samuel Knight. Wait... he is fading away from my sight."

Victoria let Haley rest for a few minutes. Then, she thought, *"Of course, he is in a barber's chair. I should have known a lock of his hair would have brought him there first."*

She began after a few minutes with her questions. "Go and find this man!"

"Yes. I see him now," said the hypnotized young girl.

"Where is he?"

"He is in a beautiful flower garden. There are tents everywhere and an orchestra playing music. Wait! They all faded away. They are gone!"

"Go and find this man!" she exclaimed, another pass with the steady formula.

"Oh, I see him again. He is in a room full of nicely dressed women and men. I can't make any of them out. But... wait. Now they are all gone," concluded the young girl with a deep sigh.

"Go and find this man!"

"Yes! Yes, I see him. He is in a large room full of books from the floor to the ceiling on shelves. Another man is sitting with him. They appear to be talking."

"Tell me, Haley, what are they saying to each other?"

"I can't hear a word one. Yet, their mouths are moving. There is no sound... wait! The light goes out in the room, and all is dark."

"Go and find this man!"

"Okay. I am following him. There he is. He's in a beautiful bedroom. Large scarlet hangings fringed with silver are around the bed and on the casements of the windows."

"Is he alone?"

"No. There are two other people with him."

"Tell me who those other people are, Haley."

"I am not sure. I can't see them distinctly. For some reason, I can never see anyone else clearly as they are covered with a mist. Samuel is the only one I can see clearly."

"What is he doing?"

"Nothing. But the other two are doing something to him."

"Tell me, Haley, what are they doing to him? Are they killing him?"

"Please stop. You are hurting me... no, they are not injuring him. They are standing on both sides of him while he is laughing"

"You must look harder, Haley. Who are the other two people with him? What are they doing?" eagerly commanded the old crone.

"It is difficult to tell. They are no longer people obscured by a mist. They are now... wait, I can tell that they are men, but they are only shadows. They are tall. That's all."

"Can you tell yet what they are doing to Samuel?"

"I can't tell. But Samuel is getting up. The shadows are following him to the door. The shorter of the two men goes out the door with him, and the other tall shadow of a man remains in the room."

"Samuel is leaving his room?"

"Yes, and the shorter man is with him. The entire room is turning to total darkness now. All is gone."

"Go and find this man!"

"I see him getting on a train at the railway station. The sun is up. There are others with him. But their shapes are only shadows, and I can't make them out. But I see Samuel clearly now."

"Wait! You can see him clearly. Getting on a train in the middle of the day?" interrupted Victoria in bewilderment.

"But, once it was there, the train disappeared."

"Go and find this man!"

"Oh, I see him again. He is on a ship. I can see him quite clearly now. He is standing on the deck and looking out at the Pacific Ocean. His face is smiling and looking out at sea while smoking a cigar."

"Are you sure it is Samuel?"

"Yes, very sure. He is dressed in dirty clothes and a long black beard."

"That can't be, Haley. Look closely. He has no beard and could not have grown one in a few hours."

"Oh, it is Samuel, even though he doesn't look like himself," the hypnotized young woman persisted.

"I don't understand. How do you know it is Samuel if he doesn't look like himself?" inquired Victoria.

"By something surer than sight or hearing," replied Haley.

"What is that?"

"I can't tell."

"Why can't you tell, Haley?"

"Because I don't know what it is. I just can. And, wait... the ship has gone, and everything is black again."

"Go and find this man!"

"I see him again. He is wearing the same old clothes I saw him in, but he has cut off his beard. There only remains stubble on his face now."

"Where is Samuel now?"

"I can only tell he is outdoors somewhere. There are a lot of men, and most are standing on the edge of a river fishing. Many are talking with one another, smoking cigars, but I can't see any of them very clearly."

"What is he doing now?"

"I cannot tell. All is going dark again."

"Go and find this man!"

"I can't. Darkness appears to have swallowed my entire vision."

Victoria repeated, *"Go and find this man!"*

"I can't! It is so, so dark. I can't see him any longer," replied Haley Dawn with a troubled expression on her face.

Victoria watched the girl's face and let it calm before trying to keep her going in her trance. Then, after a few minutes, she rubbed the locked of hair once more on Haley's forehead and said, "Go and find this man!"

"I can't. I can't move. I feel faint! Oh, I'm about to die!" said the tortured young girl with a voice that grew faint by the minute until she fell into complete silence.

All the efforts of the old crone to bring her back to consciousness failed.

She said aloud, "I have overdone it this time, I'm afraid," she said while gently shaking the young girl.

After a while, Haley Dawn opened her eyes. But she appeared to be thoroughly prostrated in vigor.

"How are you, Haley," asked Victoria.

No answer came from the young girl. All she could do was look at Victoria with her dim eyes and sigh.

Victoria got up and walked over to the kitchen cabinet. She pulled out a bottle of Jack Daniels Black and brought it to the young girl, saying, "Come, Haley, drink this. You will feel better."

Haley took the glass and swallowed a mouthful of Jack Black, whose smooth but fiery strength half-strangled her. She began coughing. She became aroused. "Oh, please," she coughed, "can I have some milk, Mrs. Meret. My throat is on fire!" she exclaimed.

Victoria got some milk and gave it to the girl. Haley drank it all down very slowly.

"Now, Hun, are you feeling better," said the old crone while taking the cup from the girl. "Now, do you know what you have been doing?"

"I suppose I have been hypnotized, right? I remember you were going to put me under a spell," replied the girl.

"Do you remember where you went? Or what you did?"

"No, I wish I did. But I suppose I went to look after Lucas. You said you would send me to him."

"Yes, sweetie, and so I did," replied Victoria with a nod.

"Did I see him? Is he well and making lots of money?"

"Oh, yes. He wore the finest clothes but was somewhere a long way around the other side of the world."

Haley's face clouded over. "I wonder... does Lucas still think of me when he's growing wealthy? Why soon he will be as rich as Samuel Knight was himself!"

"Oh, yes, a hundred times richer."

"And richer than Mister Reynolds with his big island?"

"Yes, a hundred times!"

"Oh, I am so worried."

"About what, my dear?"

"Will Lucas still care for me now that he is making so much money?" asked Haley Dawn with a sigh.

"Of course."

"When I saw Lucas, did I see him as he was some time ago or as he is now?"

"Just as if he were standing next to you, Haley."

"Oh, Mrs. Meret, whenever I want to hear from Lucas, I will come here and let you put me in a trance."

"Please do, Haley." She smiled.

"Gosh, if only I could remember what I saw in my trance instead of having to come here and being told by you afterward, Mrs. Meret."

"Anytime, my dear."

"Do you know if going into a trance harms me?"

"No, not at all. What makes you ask?"

"Because I feel weak when I come out of the trance."

"It's nothing. You are only tired as if you went for a long walk. And, if you think about it, it's a long walk to the other side of the world," she said with a gentle laugh.

"Well, I best be on my way. The housekeeper back on Mister Courbis's estate let me off for the afternoon but wanted me back before dark. But the next time I get some time off, I will return and let you put me in a trance again and send to see my Lucas."

She departed.

As soon as Haley was gone, Victoria sank down into her wingback chair, but not before pouring herself her own stiff Jack Black and Coke.

She thought, "Very strange... very strange, indeed," she thought. *"Has this experiment of mine backfired and been a total failure? Or is there some kind of secret under all this show? I have never, in my life, known one of my clairvoyants to go off on a dead end like this girl has done. It would be strange if she was the first to do it."* She paused to go and pour herself another drink.

"I have known bloodhounds who have gone off on a false scent and police who get off the trail, but never have I known a clairvoyant to go off in a wrong direction... never!

The key to all that she told me is hidden somewhere. Let me recall from beginning to end. At first, when I put her in the trance, I sent her off in search of Bernice Luther's body. She followed it. It wasn't to the bottom of Demon Gorge, out into the ocean with the tide, or on some lonesome beach. Nope, indeed. But in a first-class carriage on a train and up to a great city somewhere where she prospered well."

She grabbed a throw blanket and pulled it over her legs as the night was becoming quite chilly. Her thoughts continued to scrutinize the young girl. "That didn't sound like she was drowned in Demon Gorge and cast up by the ocean onto a lonesome beach somewhere. Nope, not one single bit. I have got to figure this out if I am to win the $100,000. Through her trance, I followed him to a lavish mansion and then lost her in Paris, Rome, Sydney, Australia, or even around the bend and up to New York City.

And now, I took her deeper into her trance. Then, sent her looking for a dead corpse, and she took after a living man to who knows where.

I simply can't put my finger on it. What is the meaning of it all? According to the clairvoyant, neither Bernice Luther nor the late Samuel Knight was dead at all... but both were living. She is in some mansion and dressing in the finest of clothes wearing pearls and diamonds, and he is somewhere at the other end of the world. But I've never known one of my clairvoyants to be wrong and get off the trail... but they have. So, it isn't possible that either of them is still living, let alone both.

I know what I will do. I will put that girl off on another search and have her go after Lucas Durano. He might be able to throw some light on all of this. Besides, I want to hear about the poor boy. I should have sent her after him today, only that I was so anxious I could get that reward. It would set me up for life! But unfortunately, she was too weak to do another, so I just have to wait."

With this conclusion to her thoughts, Victoria got up from her chair, made a fire in the fireplace, filled her kettle with water, and hung it over the blaze. Then, it was time to fix supper.

On the evening after Amala Luther was frightened out of her skin by a real or supposed ghost in the gardens at the Reynold's Island Estate, inquiries were immediately made of the servants and their whereabouts at the time. The result was that they were all inside relaxing in the servant quarters, and no one was on the grounds.

Amala was laughed at for her hallucination on the subject. It didn't matter to her. She was sure of what she saw... her mother, as she had stated then and there.

The matter passed out of all discussion and would have been totally forgotten if it wasn't for something that happened a few days afterward.

The music lessons of the day were over. Amala entered the library and browsed the books to find one she could relax and enjoy its quietness.

The library at the Island Estate was a large room running from west to east along the south wall of the mansion. It was pierced by four tall windows. At the end of the room was a bay window with oversized chairs with their own ottomans and the windows covered by scarlet-colored curtains. This window overlooked the thick woods between the mansion and the ocean's shore.

When Amala came into the library, the room was almost dark. All the scarlet curtains were closed. She pulled the cord, opened the curtains, and let in the east sunshine, reflecting the scene of the thick woods and the beauty of the sunlit clouds above.

She then turned away from the window, pulled a detective book by Sidney St. James off the shelf, and took it to the front part of the room. She ensconced herself in a wingback chair near a tall mirror hanging on the wall behind her. No sooner did she sit down and open the book to the first chapter than she got a feeling that she wasn't alone.

Charlotte's oldest daughter, not counting Alyssa Nicole, was sitting on another chair reading a book. She was Amala's prize pupil and was playing so well on the piano. "Oh, Yvon," said Amala," as she opened her novel, "don't let me disturb you, dearest."

Yvon didn't reply as she was deep into her reading and lost in time and space. No other words were spoken by either one of the girls. Both just went on reading while the afternoon sun lower and lower, taking away the gleams of sunlight that penetrated the bay window.

Then, Amala looked up from her book upon the face of the mirror, where the clouds from the outdoors shone and the foliage from the trees could be seen.

"Oh, my God! Yvon! Look! Look!" she gasped, in suffocating articulate tones, as she clutched the young lady's shoulder.

Yvon violently dragged herself from her novel and raised her blue eyes in questioning amazement. She was facing the mirror on the wall and now saw a reflection that her gaze became fixed. It was the beautiful pale face of a woman looking out from the foliage outside the bay window.

With an exclamation of pure astonishment, Yvon dropped her book and ran down the length of the library to the bay window. When she got there, the face was gone.

After a minute of looking everywhere, she returned to Amala, now on her knees with her hands over her eyes. "I couldn't find anyone outside, Amala," said the young lady standing over her music teacher and dear friend.

"But you saw it! Please tell me you saw it!" said Amala in an expiring voice.

"Yes, I saw her, but couldn't find anyone when I looked everywhere. So, who was it, Amala?"

"Did you not recognize the face?"

"I thought I did, but I can't be certain. Whose was it, Amala?"

"It was the face of my dear lost mother, Yvon."

"Oh, Amala."

"It was my dead mother's living face. This is now the second time I have seen it. I don't understand why I shrink away from her vision. I suppose flesh and blood can't bear such sights. If I keep seeing her face, surely, I am destined to die, Yvon!" shuddered the music teacher with bloodless lips.

"Oh, Amala, it could not have been what you think. That's impossible. It was a face that resembled your mother. There must be a stranger on the island. I will tell daddy, and he will solve this mystery. We must finish this. Somebody is playing on your fears Amala," said Yvon.

It was now near the end of the short autumn twilight, and the two girls had left the library.

"Do not talk about this, Yvon. I couldn't bear the discussion at supper this evening," pleaded Amala, still trembling excessively.

"Very well, but the ground should be searched for the intruder," Yvon remonstrated.

"It would be totally useless, Yvon. What does all this mean?"

"Let's not worry about it now. I'm hungry. Everyone is getting together for supper. Let's go!"

Mister and Mrs. Thomas of Ocean View was expected that evening.

"Ahhhh, said Kenneth, "our friends are always so punctual. Not even thirty seconds too soon or thirty seconds late. He was invited for six o'clock, and I'll be darned if it's not six o'clock right now."

The door opened.

"Judge Thomas!"

"Oh, God, Kenneth, why so formal? Jacob! Besides, I will say it for you. I'm fifty seconds late," he said, advancing to his friend with a smile.

"Well, if I'm not more punctual at the Polo Matches tomorrow, let me hear about it then, will you, Jacob," requested Kenneth with a laugh.

One of the main reasons Jacob visited the night before the annual matches were to go over some details of the games connected with the meet the following day.

After supper, all the ladies went to the parlor where the grand piano was made ready for Amala to play some wonderful after-supper music.

The men withdrew themselves and went to the library where they could partake in an excellent Cuban longleaf cigar.

Charlotte asked, "Oh, Misty, how I wish Kenneth would give up this Polo meet. He is getting too old for this nonsense," she sighed while talking to Misty.

Alyssa Nicole answered, "But he never will, Mamma. You know daddy. So, it is of no use to wish," she replied.

"Then dear, if he would at least ride a safe horse in the event. I gather from listening to the men talk that he's going to ride Calypso. It's madness, I tell you," Charlotte anxiously said.

Alyssa turned pale. "Will Daddy really ride that awful horse in the matches tomorrow?"

"Yes. When it comes to his good friend Jacob who is the team captain of the other team, he will do anything to try and win. Those two men might be best friends, but they are both hard-headed when it comes time for the yearly Polo matches," she paused a moment and then continued, "the brute has already killed two men, and Kenneth insists he can break that damn horse's spirit."

Jessica Thomas glanced over to her friend Alyssa. "Your father has been a famous horse trainer since he was a boy. If any man can tame Calypso, he can. I don't think anyone should have fear in what he is doing."

Charlotte sighed. Although she had the highest confidence in her husband's ability, there was a shadow of a calamity coming she couldn't dispel.

Jacob retired for the evening.

Charlotte came to try and persuade Kenneth not to try and ride Calypso in the matches.

He laughed. "I suppose honey, there's still a competitive spirit in me regarding man versus beast. You know the thrill I get from taming a wild horse full of spirit. It's what I live for, besides beating Jacob in the matches tomorrow. Unfortunately, this only comes once a year. But, sweetheart, I will be up early to go to the mainland, so I will bid you goodnight." He stood up, kissed Charlotte on top of her head, and headed to his bedroom.

Charlotte knew that any further remonstrance would be in vain. She sighed, followed his example, and went up to her chambers.

The next morning came early. Unfortunately, neither Kenneth nor his oldest son Michael was present as they had already departed for the mainland and the annual Polo Match.

Charlotte and the others met at the breakfast table. She glanced at the stable's groomsman and promptly said, "Rusty, wait!"

"Yes, ma'am."

"What horse did my husband take to the matches today?"

"The white mare, Cricket, Mrs. Reynolds," he replied.

"Oh, wonderful. Then he left Calypso here at the stables, right? I'm glad," breathed Charlotte with a sigh of relief.

"Ma'am?"

"What?"

"Calypso was taken to the matches, as well. Mister Reynolds plans on riding him today. Michael will ride Cricket."

"Thank you, Rusty. That will be all." Charlotte sighed and left her breakfast almost untouched.

Then, her mind changed directions. A servant entered the room with a telegram from the mainland and laid it next to Charlotte.

The woman glanced over the telegram and saw it was from Oliver Courbis, her son-in-law. She read aloud:

October 25, 1965

My grandfather died here this morning at two o'clock. I will remain here until after the funeral, and I will send another telegram to you when that is over.

Oliver

"So, he is gone. Poor old man," said Alyssa.

"Is the man still waiting for a response?" Charlotte asked the servant.

"Yes, ma'am."

"Tell him to wait, and I will send a response." She got up from the breakfast table and walked into the library, where there was a desk and plenty of writing materials. She wrote a hasty response to the telegram as follows:

"Reynold's Island, October 25, 1965

We have just received your telegram announcing the sorrowful message of your grandfather's death. Unfortunately, Kenneth is absent at the BRC Polo Matches but will be told as soon as possible. We all offer our sincere sympathy and await your next telegram.

Charlotte Reynolds

The message was given to the courier who brought the original dispatch.

Then she instructed Rusty to go to the mainland immediately and tell Kenneth. She prayed he would get there in time before the matches started! It might be a means of saving his life by preventing him from riding Calypso.

She waited and waited. It was almost two o'clock in the afternoon when Rusty returned alone. He promptly presented himself to Mrs. Reynolds.

"Well, did you find Kenneth?" she asked.

"No, ma'am. He was gone."

"Gone!"

"He had finished his first match and was nowhere to be found. I left your message with Michael, who was talking with some friends and came back here for further instructions."

Rusty left the room.

"Oh, God. He got through the first match unharmed. But, oh... where did he go?" She said while walking up and down the floor, wringing her hands.

"Mother, you are going to worry yourself sick. Why are you torturing yourself with unnecessary anticipation of something bad happening?" asked Alyssa, sitting by the bay window reading a book.

"Because I can't help it, Alyssa. I dreamed last night of something bad happening. I can't seem to shake it off," replied Charlotte without stopping her restless walking back and forth.

"Come now, Mother. You are afraid of Calypso. You know that, and I know that. Daddy has been training horses since the day I was born. His horsemanship is unsurpassed in this part of the country. No horse has ever yet been able to beat him."

"That's true, dear. But your father is not a young whippersnapper like he once was in his early days. This is one evil horse! And—-," she stopped her words. "What is that disturbance in the courtyard?" she asked, suddenly turning pale.

"No worries, Mother. I suppose daddy got your message and has come home early. I will be right back," said Alyssa as she departed the room to check. Charlotte sank down on the sofa and waited.

As Alyssa hastened toward the head of the staircase, she heard hasty footsteps ascending them. The next moment she was stopped by her brother, Michael, pale and staring and trembling. "For God's sake, Michael, what is the matter with you? Where is Dad?" demanded Alyssa in sudden alarm.

"That vicious evil—-. Where's Mamma? Go find her and keep her in the room. Do not let her come out until I come and get you. I have sent for Doctor Cantu!" exclaimed Michael.

"Daddy! That horse! Michael, tell me. Has an accident happened? Speak for Heaven's sake," cried Alyssa in a breathless agony of suspense.

"Don't ask me, Alyssa. Go now! Please go! Keep her quiet until Doctor Cantu gets here."

"I can't, Michael. Tell me! I can't go unless I know. Has an accident occurred?"

"Yes, Sis! Yes, it has! Now go to Mamma," said the young man trying to break from her grasp.

"A fatal accident?" she asked, turning pale and tightening her grip on him.

"Oh no, there she is now! Mamma... oh, dearest Mamma!" cried Michael in anguish as he broke loose from Alyssa and ran to his mother, who stood before him.

"Kenneth! Kenneth!" she exclaimed hoarsely but couldn't say any more.

"Mister Reynolds has been thrown from his horse... he has been killed!" exclaimed the voice of a hysterical housemaid hurrying up the stairs on some errand.

"That damn lunatic!" indignantly exclaimed Michael. "Mother! Mother!" he cried while bending toward his mother, who had laid her head on his shoulder. "Mamma... oh, Mamma!"

The heavy form of Charlotte slipped from his embrace limply upon the floor at her son's feet.

Michael and Alyssa worked together to raise her back to her feet. But... Charlotte was dead!

Chapter TWO
A Day of Tragedy

There was no misjudging death in a case like this. In the horrifying hue, glazed and motionless eyes, and the chin that had fallen, the agonized son and daughter both saw the death of their poor mother!

Dazed with sudden sorrow, the two children lifted Charlotte's body, took it into the adjoining room, laid it on a sofa, and knelt beside it.

Amid their despairing endeavors, Doctor Cantu hurriedly, yet quietly, entered the room.

Michael and Alyssa Nicole backed away from their mother and gave Doctor Cantu time to look after Charlotte.

With a mute gesture of acknowledgment, the doctor knelt over his good friend and patient. "It is as I was afraid," spoke Cantu after a short but close examination. "Your mother... I'm afraid your mother is——" began the Doctor.

"She is... Mother is—-." Began Michael in a voice faint and breaking down into a cry.

"Gone... yes, son, she is gone. I have known for years past that she has had a bad heart and that any sudden shock..." he paused a moment. "Michael, look after your sister," he cried, breaking off from his explanation. Alyssa, with a wail of anguish, rushed out of the room.

Michael rushed out of the room, passing Greg Peden, who was coming in.

"What has happened," Greg quickly asked the doctor.

"Never in all my years practicing medicine has a misfortune so swiftly, with such destroying malice, fallen upon such a great family. The father is brought home as a corpse from the polo matches, and the mother drops dead under the shock!"

"How did the accident happen," Greg quickly asked in words scarcely above his breath.

"Kenneth decided at the BRC Polo Matches this year to ride Calypso and—-."

"You've got to be kidding me. That horse is evil."

"You know it, and I know it, but Kenneth was sure that he knew horses and could get the edge up riding that damn horse in the matches today."

"But he has been getting slower over the last few years. His age and all."

"Yes, Greg, you are right. And it was probably because the horse got one up on him and attributed to the tragic ending of his ride today," assented the doctor.

"But how did the catastrophe occur?" again asked the accountant.

"I don't know everything, but the stable groom that attended the matches at the county fairgrounds said that he just finished winning the first match out on the prairie near the head of Demon Gorge. So, Kenneth did as he said and defeated Calypso, and he was beaten. But they were returning to where the horse trailer was and passed by the old lighthouse when Calypso suddenly took fright at the sight of the old crone there, who stood in the path like a witch with her black cloak and hood pulled over her head."

"That woman's enough to frighten even the calmest horse than Calypso," said Peden.

The doctor continued his explanation. "Well, the woman startled him. He reared up and took off in a furious gallop, hoofs thundering on the shaking ground. Kenneth is said to have stayed in his saddle and gave it all his strength to stay in the saddle of the brute until he passed out of view."

"Wasn't there some kind of effort to—-?"

"To do what, Greg? To stop that runaway train... that brute on four legs! Nothing could have been done. Jacob and others went after him, but by the time they caught up with Calypso, they found him lying on the ground near the upper end of the road... dead... quite dead!"

"Oh, my God, that's shocking!"

"The horse was gone—-."

"That is so awful!" Greg added in disbelief. "What about Charlotte?"

"Mrs. Reynolds has had heart problems for years. I knew that a bad shock would be fatal for her. However, even a healthy woman would not have stood such a shock."

"How did you get here before me, Doctor Cantu?"

"One of the men who found Kenneth's body came to me right away in Black Rock Cove. I caught the ferry right over. But, Greg, how did you get here so fast?"

"I was just making a general call on the family when I learned that Charlotte received a telegram this morning from Oliver that his grandfather had passed."

"Yes. It was going to happen. We just didn't know when. Family members seem to have been stricken down today like a bunch of birds by a scattering shot of a double barrel shotgun."

Both bodies were placed in the library on a table and covered with sheets awaiting the undertaker. Then, the two men left the *Room of Death*, closing the door and locking it after them.

The tumult of horror throughout the mansion baffled all description. All the children of the departed parents were brought together in one room. Some were violently excited, as one could imagine, and some quite stupefied with grief.

Amala Luther, striving to keep down her own emotions of grief, devoted herself to being there for the children.

All the servants in the home went about their business with quiet steps, silent lips, and very tearful eyes.

Doctor Cantu, Greg Peden, and Judge Thomas took the complete direction of affairs. They telegraphed the news to Oliver, who was with his grandfather's estate awaiting a funeral there, and a telegram to the nephew, Edmund Richter, in the Seattle Ship Yard. They also sent a telegram to other distant relatives and friends of the afflicted family.

Edmund sent a telegram back to the family and said that he was stricken to the heart with awful grief at this double bereavement. He was getting a leave of absence and starting for the Island Estate immediately.

Another telegram was received from Oliver, who said he was greatly saddened by the news of the two sudden deaths and that he would leave for the Island Estate first thing the following morning.

The following day, relatives and friends began to drop by the home to show their respect. Although he was the furthest away, Oliver was the first to reach the house. No sooner did he arrive than he sent a message upstairs, where the family sat in silence, letting her know he had arrived and begged to see her.

At any other time, Alyssa would have sent an insolent reply. But considering the circumstances, she just said she was ill and suffering and begged that he would excuse her for the time being.

Oliver also explained he was only there to show his respects but that he had to get back to his grandfather's funeral planned for in three days.

The second to arrive at the estate was Edmund Richter, who came on a two-week leave and meant to spend the entire time with his afflicted cousins.

An hour later, Greg Peden arrived to take the head of affairs as Kenneth's attorney and his CPA.

Oliver remained the rest of the day. He departed the next morning without seeing Alyssa Nicole, his wife, who still made her illness a way to not see him and excusing herself from receiving him.

Then, after a day of settling the affairs of his grandfather and holding his funeral, he was back on a plane to Portland and then to his home outside Black Rock Cove. He only stayed there to put his things up, shower, and head to the Reynolds Island Estate.

The funeral of Kenneth and Charlotte Reynolds took place on Saturday.

Near sunset, the remains of Mister and Mrs. Reynolds were lowered into the family vault beneath the small chapel attached to the main house.

That evening, the family gathered in the parlor to hear the reading of the Last Will and Testament.

We have not talked much about wealth, but Kenneth and Charlotte were not wealthy, unlike Oliver and Jacob Thomas. But he did possess a very expensive island estate just a mile offshore from Black Rock Cove. So, in conclusion, he did not have a lot of disposable cash to leave to the family members.

Family and servants were given minimal and modest amounts of cash. It did not stretch very far. As has been for two hundred plus years, the estate was left to the eldest son, Michael.

Jacob Thomas and Greg Peden were appointed the estate trustees and guardians of the minor children.

No one contested the will, and all was as it should be.

After the reading, a large and tasty supper was served with plenty of wine for the adults and lots of Dr. Pepper for the younger ones. After they finished, the crowd dispersed to their respective homes.

The young women of the island estate had not been seen by any visitors. Mostly, they remained in their rooms, and when they did come out, they always had a dark veil over their faces.

When everyone was gone, there remained in the mansion only a few. First, there was the young boy Michael who was now the sole heir of the entire island estate. Also, all his brothers and sisters. Next, there was Oliver and Alyssa Nicole, man, and wife, and then Edmund Richter, a Navy lieutenant finishing his two-week leave, and Miss Amala Luther.

It was the intention of Oliver Courbis to return to his home with Alyssa joining him.

The young heir Michael was to return to the University of Oregon to finish his college education. His brothers were to go to a private school in Portland, and his young sisters, including the youngest, were to go to an uncle in Seattle.

Edmund was to return to the Navy, and Amala Luther...well, now, that's an entirely different story.

She didn't know where she was going or give a single thought to the matter. She was far too absorbed in sympathy with the sorrows of her dear young children.

After almost two weeks following the funeral of Kenneth and Charlotte, and as Edmund's leave of absence was getting close to ending, the question Amala never put to herself just so happened to be put to her by another.

After the morning meal was over, everyone was about to withdraw from the room, and Amala turned to follow them out when Edmund gently took her hand and said in a whisper, "Amala, I would like to take a private walk with you out on the terrace. Will you come?"

"Yes," she said without hesitation.

He walked with her out through the French doors and onto the terrace.

"Amala," he started as they walked up and down in the morning sunshine, "Amala, the mansion will soon be deserted, or only the servants remaining. I know where everyone is going... everyone that is except for you."

"Mine," she replied in perplexity.

"Your plans, Amala? What are your plans?"

"I'm sorry, my plans about what?"

"About your plans for your future home."

"I don't have any plans, Edmund."

"But you know this entire household will be broken up the first part of next week."

"Yes, of course, I know that."

"Well... my question is, where are you going to go when the others are gone?"

"I, uh, actually... I really haven't given that any thought, Edmund, to be perfectly honest."

"Oh, Amala, you never thought once about yourself, and no one ever thought for you!" he exclaimed in sorrow.

"But nobody has had the time to worry about me. They have all been too busy worrying about each other and the family."

Edmund made a gesture of impatience. But then, he said, "Amala, dearest, you realize that I am setting sail for Mozambique at the end of this month."

"Yes... Edmund... I have heard that. I was hoping that was not true," Amala said in faltering tones that betrayed her emotions.

"My uncle would have maybe helped me, but even he has cut me completely out of the will. I fear I have deeply offended him, Amala," he sighed.

"I don't think so. I never once heard Mister Reynolds utter one bad word toward you, Edmund... nothing ever criticizing you," said the girl.

"No, probably not."

"I don't understand. How and why do you think you have offended him, Edmund?"

"By my talk of resigning from the Navy."

"I don't understand. Why would you do that, Edmund?"

"For many reasons, Amala. First, I do not like the Navy. My promotions have been too slow in coming. I would have to wait many years to get my own ship and make enough money to marry and support a family. Then, while in the Navy, I would constantly be separated from my wife at least half the time each year. And, my wife could never accompany me on the vessel."

"You talk like you have already made up your mind."

"Actually, my love, I have. I resigned already and have joined the Army. Promotions come faster. I have many friends who have done this. I can marry at any time, and my wife can live on the base with me, provided she would love me enough to accept me for who I am and not measure me by the size of my bank account. Now, doesn't my reasons sound okay to you, Amala?"

"Yes, indeed I do, Edmund," said Amala with hearty frankness.

"Now, the entire reason I asked you to come out here with me today. Amala... I can take my wife with me wherever my next assignment is," he added with a broad smile. "That is... if she would be willing to come with me."

Amala looked up at his big blue eyes. She understood exactly what he was saying.

He comprehended her silence. He took her hand and whispered her next question, "Amala. Will you be my wife and go with me wherever they ship me off to?"

Amala was silent for a moment as her voice was choked with emotion.

"Amala, if you think about it for just one moment, neither you nor I have anyone but ourselves to consult on this. It only depends on you and me to find happiness together. What do you think?"

After a few seconds, Amala reached up and puts her arms around Edmund's neck. She looked into his ocean blue eyes and said... "I agree, sweetheart. Parting from you now would be the hardest thing to bear."

"Then... Amala, you are saying that we will not part, right?"

"No," she softly murmured.

"You will be my wife and go with me wherever the Army sends me?"

"Yes," she replied clearly and sweetly. "I will be your wife and go with you." Then, after a long, wonderful kiss, she lowered her arms and walked back inside the house.

E dmund strolled into the house after giving Amala a minute to show up without him. Then, he went inside and looked for Michael, the young heir to the estate.

Running through his mind were thoughts of his recent decision and Amala. "I really need to tell Michael at once. I owe him that. I hope the boy will not take our action as any disrespect to him or the memory of his parents."

In a short while, he found Michael walking up and down the hallway all alone, looking very depressed.

"Come, Michael, let's go to the smoking room and have a good cigar together. I've got some important information to talk to you about as you're the new heir to the Reynold's Island Estate," he said while taking his cousin's arm and leading him into the library.

As they arrived, Edmund drew from the corner the wingback chair that was once the main chair Kenneth always sat in and gently pushed Michael into it. He took one of the Antonio and Cleopatra cigars and handed it to him, and took the other and lit it for himself. Finally, he reached his Zippo lighter down and lit Michael's cigar.

"You know, I am sailing out for my next destination with my regiment in four days."

"Yes, I knew, Edmund. I am so sorry for it. If there is anything I can do—."

"I wish you could, Michael. You are the new heir to this estate, but you are still a minor, which does not carry any weight in the service."

"You're right. I know," sighed Michael. "How long do you expect to be away from the states? A year? Two years?"

"How 'bout twenty years."

"I knew when the regiments have been sent abroad, they can stay as long as two years."

"You're right, but it feels like twenty years. Two years is a very long time."

"Edmund, old buddy, we are of the same blood. Therefore, we should help each other whenever we can. If you need money, I can talk to my guardians and have them advance some to you if that will help you stay."

"Thanks, Cus. You are a good friend. But this is not a question of money. It's a question of honor. A soldier never skirts his duty. It would be unpardonable."

"I don't see why, Edmund," said Michael.

"I traded all my seniority with the Navy, resigned, and joined the Army. As a result, my promotions will be faster, and I will obtain a better paycheck each week. But I think I lost your father's confidence when I did that."

"I don't think that's true at all, Edmund," interrupted the young heir to the Reynolds Island Estate. "What can I do to help? Speak up. Is there anything?"

"You can bid me God speed, Cousin. As a matter of fact, I am thinking of getting married and a wife to go with me," he said in a low voice with a slight blush.

"A wife! Wow, I had no idea. Who is this lucky lady?"

Edmund's flush deepened as he replied, "Amala Luther."

"Are you serious?"

"Yes. I have laid it all out for her. She prefers to get married instead of waiting until I return. She will go with me."

"Wow, I am so happy for you, Edmund, and Amala, too."

"The only other circumstance that needs to be considered is—-" Edmund stopped his words.

"Is what?"

"I must marry Amala before we ship out if I am to take her with me."

"I would think so. What else?"

"I was worried that you might think it is too soon in respect to the memory of your parents, my uncle, and Aunt, for us to marry so quickly," Edmund gravely explained.

"I do believe that all the circumstances justify your speedy marriage. I have seen the way the two of you look at each other. I know there is deep love by each of you for one another. I think you should put the ceremony off until the day before you sail. Then, you can have it performed as quietly as possible. But Damien and Yvon must lead the way for you and Amala to the altar. And, I will give away the bride," he said with a broad smile. "Furthermore, again, dear friend, if there is anything I can do for you, surely you will let me know."

Edmund reached out and grabbed his cousin's hand and held on to it a moment, then said, "Only one thing in which I will feel grateful. I wish you to break the news to Alyssa and Yvon and make them understand the necessity of our case."

"Yes, of course. Anything else?"

"No... accept Michael, you are a dear good friend and Cousin!"

"Okay, Edmund. But I think it will be my sister's job to help her find the clothes to get married in and her new traveling wardrobe for the honey and voyage to your next destination."

Edmund once more reached out and grabbed Michael's hand in silent gratitude, who arose with a smile. "The sooner I speak to Alyssa and Yvon, the better! When my sister was looking for her marriage dress, it took her four months of preparation, and she didn't have to travel out of the country, either."

"Ahhh, but yes, Michael. However, Alyssa was destined to become the bride of the wealthiest man in this part of the country. And I, well, my beloved is only a curate's orphan about to become a poor lieutenant's wife," Edmund replied with a smile while getting up from his chair and wasting no time searching out his sisters.

He found them all sitting around in Alyssa's bedroom in the attached sitting room. He took a chair among them and told his news.

They were astonished at the prospect of Edmund and Amala's impending marriage, although they were off to some long-away country after getting married.

However, now that the news has been broken, Alyssa asked, "Isn't this place in Mozambique a wild and crazy place that Edmund is assigned? Aren't there lots of terrible people and evil spirits? Isn't there a prison colony there?"

Before Michael could answer, Yvon said, "Oh, my, we can't send our dear friend, our sister, to live among people in that environment."

"She will not be in the mining communities where she might see people of unquestionable motives. Instead, she will be in an area that is normal working people and clean living."

"Well, I'm glad the place she is going has families of respectable people and not one so dreadful as Yvon, and I think it might be."

"Very well," said Yvon. Since we really can't prevent Amala from going, the next best thing is to go out and have some fun with her finding her wedding dress and clothes for the voyage."

"Sensibly spoken, baby sister!" exclaimed the young heir and head of the family.

The plan was approved by everyone. Michael bent down to Alyssa and said she had all the funds she needed to help Amala.

As Michael left the girls, he passed Amala, who was coming in. A glance at her happy face proved that she didn't suspect him of knowing her secret of the upcoming marriage. He gave her a nod and continued.

No sooner did Amala enter the room than all the girls greeted her with the largest of smiles. It was unusual as none of the girls had smiled since the passing of their parents. However, these smiles no doubt aroused her suspicions. "My goodness, what is it with all the big smiles?"

"Ahhh, Amala, my dear. You know very well why we are all smiling," said Alyssa Nicole, springing up from her chair and wrapping her arms around her good friend's shoulders. "We have all heard about it! Sorry, but Edmund couldn't keep his happiness to himself! He had to tell Michael. And you know, Michael. He had to tell us. So, tomorrow morning, you and I are going to town to find you a wedding dress and lots of new clothes for your voyage."

Oliver was called back to his grandfather's estate to take care of some loose ends associated with the estate he had just inherited there. He would be gone for about ten days.

This circumstance was good news to Alyssa as she was still very cold toward Oliver and most distant. She continued receiving Oliver's notes but had them returned to him unopened.

Oliver thought, or he knew that by Reynold's Estate being broken up, Alyssa Nicole had no alternative but to rejoin him back at his mansion and home and conduct herself more rationally.

Alyssa was still resolved to maintain aloof from her husband until she had an opportunity for a legal separation from him. However, now that Kenneth and Charlotte had passed and the home was shut down, she scarcely knew what the next steps should be to secure her legal separation.

She continued to give a lot of thought to what to do. For example, should she accompany her sisters to their new home with their uncle, or should you join Jessica at the Thomas residence off the Portland Highway? But, on the subject of returning to the Knightwood or now what is called the Courbis Estate... she was resolved never to return to that awful place!

But, for the time being, Alyssa put all of that out of her mind as she had happy thoughts about the pending marriage of her good friend, Amala.

The next morning came early. Alyssa, Yvon, and Amala drove to Portland and got rooms in a nice hotel. Michael tagged along and had the checkbook. After a nice lunch, they headed to a specialty bridal shop and lots of nice traveling clothes for Amala.

After trying on numerous clothes and assuring the right size, Alyssa and Yvon spared no expense. First, they checked off the most delicate bridal gowns and traveling clothes in the whole place. Then, they asked that they be delivered to the Portland Hotel and the bill with them.

After finishing up with the bridal clothes, they went to Parkland Outfitters, the best shop in the city, to find trunks to pack the clothes and belongings.

They continued. Finally, they found themselves back at the Portland Hotel, where Michael joined them for supper. Their orders were filled by the second day in Portland, and their business was done faster than anticipated. The next morning, they returned to Reynold's Island Estate.

Edmund received two letters back regarding assistance from friends who had also taken their wives with them. It was highly recommended that it was essential to carry a maid or helper person as any help once there would rip them off.

The necessity hadn't occurred to anyone concerned before.

Edmund mentioned this matter to his older cousin, Alyssa Nicole, wife of Oliver Courbis, who at once summoned the housekeeper. They had to find a suitable young woman to travel with the couple to help her when Edmund was in the field on assignment.

The following morning, Amala got a message from the butler that a woman in mourning was at the door and apparently in deep trouble and wished to see her.

"Who is she, Thomas?" asked the young lady, thinking that it was someone who wished to inquire into the maid position.

"I really don't know, ma'am. She's a stranger to us all. When I asked her what her name was, she said it was of no consequence. Shall I go back and tell her that you are busy with other matters right now?" Thomas asked.

"No, it's okay. Show the woman into the parlor. I will come down."

Chapter THREE
A Dark Mystery Still Hung Over Their Heads

A slender girl in deep mourning came into the room, nodded respectfully, and drew to the side her black veil. It revealed a thin white face, hazel gray eyes, and the blonde hair of Haley Dawn Johnson.

Amala arose quickly and held her hand out to her former maid, exclaiming, "Haley! Haley Dawn, my dear girl, I'm so surprised and happy to see you. Sit down, child. There's no need to stand. Surely you didn't walk here from the Courbis place, did you?"

"Oh, actually, I did. I didn't have the money to get a taxi. I'm somewhat spent, to tell the truth."

"Then, please, quit standing and sit down and take a load off your feet," she added kindly.

Amala waited until her friend sat down. "Now, tell me what I can do for you, Haley?"

I suppose you've heard that I've lost my stepmother, ma'am," said the young girl quietly, raising her eyes to the face of Amala."

"Oh, yes, Haley, I did hear of it. I should have come to see you in your trouble, but for the double burial here at the estate that afflicted this family at the same time, it kept me here," said Amala with a feeling of compunction at the very thought of having neglected the poor orphan in her time of sorrow.

"It's okay, Amala. I knew you would have come if there was any way. I also knew of the two deaths at Reynold's Estate. So sad.

Besides, my mother's death was a sudden heart attack. Doctor Cantu said it was, and it was all over so soon... the funeral and all."

'I'm really sorry, Haley."

"Thank you, Amala. She was only my stepmother, and a stepmother isn't like a real mother, right? I once thought she was unkind to me, but then I realized she was my only friend and person who protected me from harm. Now... she's gone. Death opens our eyes sometimes. It makes us feel so much different towards them once they are gone."

"It does, indeed, Haley. I know that, too, from my own experience. The worse part of our grief for those who have passed away is frequently remorse... or, at least, regret. Anyhow, Haley, back to why you are here. What can I do for you?"

"I have heard word that you are looking for someone to be your maid on your voyage overseas."

"Yes, of course, Haley. My only objection might be that of your state of health."

"Doctor Cantu was saying to me that a long sea voyage would be the only thing that can cure what ails me. He said I should try to get a position for someone going to the Indies and that it would make a woman out of me. That was before I even heard that you were looking for someone."

"Were you ill and called on Doctor Cantu for medical advice, dear?"

"No, ma'am. When the doctor was called in to see my stepmother, he saw me and pulled me over the coals for looking so dang badly, Amala."

"Well, I would have to agree with the doctor. What have you been doing to make you look so weak, Haley?"

"I'm not sure unless it is the trances," sighed the young girl.

"The, what?" questioned Amala in perplexity. "The——."

"Yes, ma'am, the trances. I am sure I have grown weaker whenever she puts me into a trance."

"What trances are you speaking about, Haley?" asked Amala.

"The ones Mrs. Meret from the Lighthouse near Demon Gorge does to me."

"I'm not understanding. Victoria Meret put you in a trance?"

"Yes, ma'am., Ever since the first one, she has done a dozen more. Maybe you might not believe it, Amala, but I am a clairvoyant," whispered Haley with a mysterious expression on her face.

"A clairvoyant, Haley? How did you become a clairvoyant?"

"I'm not sure. I never thought I was such a person until the old woman convinced me I was."

"What did she do?"

"She puts me in a trance and makes me follow—-."

"Follow whom, my dear?" demanded Amala.

"I was to follow a friend of hers," replied Haley with a flushed face.

"Haley, that old crone is an impostor! She ought to be taken up and put in jail," exclaimed Amala.

"I'm not so sure of that. She puts me into these trances and makes me follow anyone she likes, even if it is to the other side of the world. Then, she gets me to tell her where they are and what they're doing. Then, after I come out of my trance, I can't remember anything about what I have seen or told her. My body is very faint. I am so sick to my stomach."

"And you will become weaker in mind and body if you keep this charade up. It is suicidal nonsense," said Amala with a feeling of resentment against the old vagabond.

"There is no satisfaction to me in these trances. I can never remember anything. Then, when I am awakened, I don't remember anything, and I'm so weak. And besides, Amala I—-," her words stopped, and she hesitated.

"Besides what, Haley?"

"I am starting to fear the woman. She has this power over me, Amala. Even back at the estate, I can feel and hear her calling for me. Sometimes, I fall into a trance when she isn't near me at the mansion where I work," the young girl whispered while trembling.

"Nonsense! My decision is made. You shall go on this voyage with Edmund and me, Haley. What you have just told me settles that point. I would be so wrong to leave you here at the mercy of such a terribly dangerous old swindler. I am getting married in one week and then traveling immediately overseas. Can you be ready to leave with me on that day or sooner?"

"Oh, thank you so much, Amala. You have made me the happiest girl in the world. Unfortunately, I must work for two more days and pack my bags, what little I have. I can come back on Monday, if that will be okay, Amala?" she stood up, ready to depart.

"That will suit me perfectly, Haley Dawn. I'm happy that you will be going with me, dear."

Haley Dawn left the room.

It was a subject for great congratulations from all the ladies in the Reynold's Estate that Amala would be accompanied by her former maid overseas after she was married.

Later in the evening, Oliver retired to the bedroom he had occupied since his wife's illness. Before going to sleep, he sat at a writing desk in the room and began a letter to Alyssa. When finished, he sealed it in the envelope. "I think if I know Alyssa Nicole, this letter will bring her to terms." Then, he undressed and went to bed.

Oliver walked down and entered the breakfast room. All the family was assembled except for his beautiful wife, who remained in her own room.

Although he waited until the table was cleared, Alyssa never showed up for breakfast.

Then, Edmund recognized the absence and asked, "What's wrong with Alyssa that she's not able to attend breakfast this morning Oliver?" the lieutenant bluntly inquired.

"Alyssa is indisposed," coldly replied Oliver.

"Sorry to hear that, Oliver. And, just as you have come home, too. She was doing well yesterday," he blurted. "Nothing serious, I hope," he carried on.

"Nothing serious," replied Oliver, rising up from the table.

After taking a few steps from the table, he said, "Here, Victoria," and handed her a letter. "Will you please take this up to your sister?"

Victoria took the letter and ran upstairs to take the note to Alyssa.

Alyssa was sitting in a wingback chair reading a book by the bay window, looking out over the ocean nearby.

A rap came to her door. "Can I come in, Alyssa?"

"Certainly, Vickie," replied her oldest sister.

"Have you not finished your breakfast?"

"Yes, I'm finished. What is it, Vickie? Does Amala need something?"

"No, It's not about Amala. I was told to give you this," said her baby sister. She laid it on the nightstand and ran out the door.

Alyssa took the blank envelope and drew it from within. Immediately, she recognized the handwriting, frowned, and almost threw it away in the blazing fireplace had not a few words caught her eye, just like Oliver knew it would.

"IMPORTANT MESSAGE FOR MY WIFE – A PROPOSAL FOR THE ADJUSTMENT OF OUR DIFFICULTIES!"

Alyssa had thrown all past letters in the fire and gave no response. But this one grabbed her attention. She continued to read,

"Reynold's Island Estate

December 5, 1965

To Alyssa Nicole Courbis.

Madam.

Your sudden anger, continued resentment, and obstinate silence as to why my offense has almost discouraged me from seeking an explanation with you. But such an explanation is necessary and something you and I owe our friends and family.

You have, or you believe, you have a just cause of offense against me. But, unfortunately, the true nature of this offense, real or false, I remain totally in the dark.

So, the reason for my letter is to ask you if there is a common justice in condemning me without hearing me out? I feel I have a right to know the nature of the charge against me so that I might defend myself. Even the worst criminal in the world has a right to an open trial and a full opportunity for a fair defense.

All I am asking you is my right to a fair trial, and I levy my protest against being condemned without being heard.

Do not ask me to beg, Alyssa. Give me an interview, and if I plead guilty or should be proven guilty of any offense for which I should forfeit your love, I will submit to any penalty in the form of separation or divorce that you may please adjudge.

I await your answer and remain your most obedient husband, Oliver Courbis."

Alyssa dropped the letter face down on the nightstand. The sun was dropping on the horizon out over the Pacific. She stood in the window and watched it slowly melt away on the blue waters by the minute.

"That is the most reckless letter I've ever read!" she exclaimed in a whisper while staring out the window. "Does Oliver not know why I will no longer associate with him? Doesn't his conscience warn him? I have little courage for such an ordeal. Does he really desire to visit with me for an explanation or only pretends that he does? Does he think I'm afraid to make one and that he will put me in an uncomfortable position? Oh, enough is enough, Oliver Courbis. You shall have your wish! I will prosecute you before me to answer for the murder of Samuel Knight!"

A lyssa walked over and saw one of the maids walking out in the hallway. "Would you please have Thomas come up here?"

"Yes, ma'am."

Within only a few minutes, Thomas stood at Alyssa's door. "Thomas, would you see that my breakfast tray is returned to the kitchen and then ask Oliver to come to my room? I wish to see him," Alyssa said in a low tone of voice.

"Yes, ma'am," Thomas said and withdrew.

Alyssa walked over and turned her wingback chair around, so the back was up against the bay window. Then she sat down so that her face was in a shadow. She was doing the best she could to hide any emotions she might portray.

The door opened. Oliver entered. He took the chair Alyssa pointed at in front of her for him to sit down, only three feet away from her.

The setting sun's light shone fully upon Oliver's face and revealed a disturbing expression. Neither of them spoke. They both looked at each other with pale and grim looks in their expressions.

Oliver was the first to finally break the silence. "You have sent for me, Alyssa," he said in a low, monotone voice.

"I have sent for you at your request, Oliver. You wanted an explanation," she replied.

"Yes, I want an explanation."

"Upon what subject?"

"Upon the subject of your sudden and strange offense against me for almost three months. Plus, your continued persistent estrangement from me since."

"You want an explanation. Then, you shall have it, Oliver Courbis. Take yourself back fifteen months ago to the very night the late Samuel Knight was murdered?" inquired Alyssa in a low and stern tone. Her eyes were fixed on his.

"I have never for one blasted moment forgotten that awful night," he answered in a whisper.

"I should suppose not. You may also remember the illness that struck me down and prevented any testimony at the inquest?"

"Yes, I remember."

"I wasn't even called as no one thought I could throw any light on the mystery of Samuel's death... his murder!"

"Yes."

"Well, the truth is that I was in the hallway late that night or early in the morning looking for my lost necklace. I was returning from having found my necklace to my bedroom," said Alyssa slowly, maintaining eye-to-eye contact on Oliver's face while she spoke.

"Well," he gasped.

"I saw Samuel alive and well and heard him speak on dismissing two men, Lucas Durano and Johnny McLean, from his room that night. I know they left Samuel alive and well. Therefore, neither one of those two men killed Samuel Knight."

"No!" exclaimed Oliver.

"Now, the question is, who murdered Samuel Knight? Do you know, Oliver?" she asked while her eyes were fixed on the man sitting three feet away from her.

Oliver didn't reply.

"Your silence Oliver most definitely speaks louder than words. You do know who killed Samuel. And, knowing that, you understand why I can never tolerate your presence again. So leave me now and let all future correspondence between you and myself be through our attorneys," Alyssa said in a cold and demanding voice.

Oliver stood up. "You are so very wrong, Alyssa. Cruelly wrong. I feared from your sudden and intense hatred that you suspect me of the murder, but the thought was too monstrous to be entertained! I actually dismissed it all as an impossible theory! Yet it is true... you do suspect me, don't you? Your husband! You say that—-."

"I have not accused you, Oliver. But a guilty conscience doesn't need an accuser," interrupted Alyssa with a scornful expression.

"You said I knew who murdered the late Samuel Knight, my cousin!" he exclaimed vehemently.

"Do you not know?" she asked.

"No! As the Lord is my judge, I do not know!"

"What? You say that you don't know who killed Samuel?"

"No, I do not."

"Then, I do," solemnly declared Alyssa Nicole.

"You?" Oliver faltered in a fainting voice.

"Yes, I!"

"Explain."

"Very well. I will speak plainly. Let's go back again to the night of the tragedy, fifteen months past. I told you that night I was standing at the end of the hallway and saw Samuel dismiss Lucas and Johnny from his room. He then shut the door after them."

"You did."

"That was when I headed downstairs to look for the lost necklace. It was around four o'clock in the morning. Are you listening to me, Oliver?"

"With all my heart and soul."

"After two long hours of looking, I finally found it and was returning to my bedroom. I saw the real murderer slipping out of Samuel's bedroom when I was upstairs. I didn't recognize the man then. I only saw a man in a dark dressing gown and thought he was another guest staying in the house. It wasn't until the following day, when Samuel was found dead, that I remembered seeing the man in a dark nighttime robe earlier.

Well, now I come to my point," continued Alyssa severely. "On the anniversary of that tragic night, you and I returned. It was nearly midnight. I couldn't sleep. I grew nervous and left my bedroom to go look for you. I came again to the bachelor's quarters. The moon was full and shone through the windows and lit the place up. It appeared just like it did on that dreadful night Samuel was killed. I stopped and looked, and a man was leaving the room that was occupied by Samuel Knight. The man I saw leave the room had the same black robe and a gold tassel on the sleeves and stood in the same light as the murderer on that fatal night twelve months before."

"Well... go ahead."

"I was so spellbound with amazement and shock that I couldn't move. Everything was the same as it was the year before. I froze as the man came toward me... came right up to me. Oh, for God's sake... I recognized the assassin," Alyssa dropped her face into the palms of her hands.

"Now we're getting somewhere!" exclaimed Oliver. "Charge me with the murder, Alyssa. Charge me distinctly! Say that on that fatal night of the tragedy, you recognized me... your husband!"

"You know that I did," quickly snapped back Alyssa in a hollow voice.

"You speak the truth, Alyssa. It was me that came from my cousin's bedroom on the night of the murder. But, Alyssa, I swear on a stack of Bibles that I'm not guilty of my poor cousin's death!"

Alyssa stared at him with the utmost intensity. Then, she said slowly, "Is it... is it even possible? Can what you say be true?"

"As the Lord in Heaven is my witness, I swear again that I am guiltless in Samuel's death! But, for a husband to find it necessary to deny such an accusation from his own wife...."

Alyssa's stern white face changed. The color came and went away. The young woman became greatly agitated.

"Oliver, I beg your forgiveness since I have wronged you terribly. But, unfortunately, I don't know anything more I can do to ask for your pardon," she muttered in a broken voice.

"I do. Say no more about this, Alyssa. Let my kiss seal our reconciliation," he said while stooping and placing his lips upon hers.

Alyssa said no more and broke into tears and sobbed deeply. She had never really loved Oliver. Her marriage with him had been a conventional union entered into for the purpose of making her parents happy. It would also bring her great wealth and a residence that was not more than thirty minutes away from them.

Oliver, unlike Alyssa, loved her as much as he was able to love anyone. He had won her affection during her early weeks of marriage. This affection between the two got stronger until the discovery of his crime, from which date Alyssa's entire being revolted with him with great violence.

She thought of her husband only with great horror and hatred for several months. She consented to allow his visit this morning only because she saw a way to begin arrangements for a final and permanent separation between them.

All this was too much for Alyssa's fragile nerves, whose sobs shook her gentle frame as though they would have shaken it to the termination.

"Alyssa, why do you cry so bitterly? One might be tempted to suspect that you're sorry to find out that it wasn't your husband who did that terrible deed," whispered Oliver.

"I am overwhelmed with sorrow and disgrace!" she continued to sob. "How can you forgive me, Oliver? How can I forgive myself?"

"Sweetheart, you didn't willingly think I was guilty, did you?" he gently asked.

"Of course not."

"Then how in the world are you at fault? You were deceived by circumstances and suffered more so than I."

"There's one thing to be learned from this, my love."

"What is that?"

"Never keep suspicion from a friend. Always discuss your concerns, and don't let them eat you up inside."

"Right? How could I have spoken on such a subject of murder with you? I would never have spoken of it if you didn't draw the words from me by force!" Alyssa sobbed.

"Alyssa, although you were so sure of your suspicion, why didn't you impart this to anyone? Why did you keep it to yourself?"

"Never! My knowledge of this almost suffocated me to death, but I would've rather died than have told the horror to any human being... even to my mother, Oliver. No one ever suspected the reason for my seizures. They thought I was losing my mind," she said earnestly.

Oliver leaned over and kissed her on top of her hair. He didn't reply.

"Tell me something. What took you to your cousin's room at that unusual wee hour of the morning when your presence caused an almost fatal delusion?"

"I don't mind telling you at all, Alyssa. There should be no more secrets between you and me. I went to Samuel's room as you first saw me that night of the tragedy. As you know of my heart problems, I had chest pains and went to him to discuss."

"Yes."

"A good shot of brandy seems to always calm my heart down and relieves me."

"Yes, I know."

"I didn't have any in my room. And, at that hour of the morning, the butler and all others were asleep. I knew my cousin always kept some in his room and went out to go see him. I went there and—-." Oliver paused a moment and appeared somewhat disturbed.

"I understand. How simple it seems now that you explain it all to me. I was crazy for ever suspecting you, Oliver."

"You were frightened, dear."

"Explain something to me, Oliver. How did you find your cousin at that hour in the morning? It was almost six o'clock when I saw you at the door. The murder must have occurred after six then, right?"

Oliver became agitated. His face was pale. He was in shock. "Shush," he whispered. "Samuel was not alive and well when I saw him in his room that night! I never wanted to tell you, but I see that I must do so. Please take a deep breath before I relate my story to you."

"Yes. I can be strong and calm," replied Alyssa.

"Very well. I will tell you more of the secrets from that night. When I left my bedroom in my black robe to go to my cousin's room, I walked by the grandfather clock and heard one bell that got my attention. It was five-thirty in the morning. As I was walking down the hallway, the entire house was quiet. Finally, I reached Samuel's room and gently tapped on the door. No response came. I knocked again, but louder this time. To my great surprise, it swung open, showing that it had never been locked. I took a few steps inside and called Samuel's name, but I didn't receive an answer.

Some of the moon was shining inside, so I stood there to let my eyes adjust to the glow. I saw that the furniture was in disarray and tossed about the room.

I walked over to his bedside. I placed my hand on him to gently wake him up without scaring him. Oh, God, Alyssa—-"

"You found Samuel dead! You were the first to find him. You!" gasped Alyssa.

"My hand came into contact with an ice cold and stiff face. A clammy substance got on my hand and had a sickening scent of blood. I knew immediately that Samuel was dead... murdered by a midnight assassin's hand!"

"What did you do?"

"I have no memory of how I left Samuel's room or how I got back to my bedroom. Instead, a panic of horror paralyzed my mind and body."

"Why in Heaven's name did you not give a statement to the authorities? Why didn't you wake the house? The assassin might have been caught. Samuel's life might have been saved."

"Actually, Samuel was quite dead! His body was cold and stiff. There was no way he could have been recovered."

"Still, the murderer might have been caught. Why didn't you wake up the house?"

"I was rendered for a few hours incapable of any action. I was breathing hard and in total panic mode. Then, when I was able to go and wake up the house, I thought that I would place my own life and honor in deadly peril. I left Samuel's body to be discovered by the servants later in the morning."

As Oliver finished talking, he attempted to take Alyssa's hand. She withdrew it gently and said, "For all of that, I wish you would have wakened the house when you first made the discovery."

Chapter FOUR

Reconciliation Between Husband and Wife

The reconciliation between **Alyssa and Oliver was** but a superficial one. She agreed with Oliver's proposal but in a calm and uncaring manner.

She agreed to return to the big mansion.

On the outside, Alyssa was civil and kind to Oliver. But, on the inside, she was still full of suspicion and uneasiness. Something just didn't feel right in all his explanations of that fatal night.

Alyssa had discovered what seemed to her to be proof that Oliver was the assassin of his cousin, and simultaneously with this discovery, she took a horrible antipathy to him. With that terrible secret in her heart, she had withdrawn from society without giving one single reason for doing so.

The truth of the matter was that she couldn't explain her conduct. It was a crime that was awful to think of and impossible to talk about... the crime she thought that Oliver himself was guilty of.

To her amazement, he had completely vindicated himself from the crime of murder.

Oliver had gone to Samuel's room to get something to calm his heart ailment and pain. Having seen him at the door of Samuel's bedroom, looking somewhat pale and agitated, she suspected him of the murder. Did a wife wrong her husband with this observation? What could she do to make up for such an injury to him?

Still, on her mind, day in and day out, was why he didn't rouse the house immediately on the discovery of the murder as anyone else would have done. Alyssa Nicole knew that Oliver was no coward. But, knowing this, why then had he suffered from being overcome by pain or panic at the time? These questions in her mind bothered her once, and she would not let them bother her again... at least not for now.

Since Oliver was proven to have been not guilty of Samuel's death, she would do everything she could to atone for the terrible treatment she shone him by suspecting him of the murder.

T he wedding day dawned!
It was as lovely of a day ever formed by God, although it was a day in the winter when it was usually very foggy and cold.

At an early hour, the Reynolds Island Estate was astir.

Everyone breakfasted together. Then, they began to prepare for the ceremony.

In honor of Kenneth and Charlotte, the wedding was to be a private one. None but the nearest relatives were to be present as witnesses.

There wasn't even a wedding breakfast for the ceremony was to be quietly performed at the Presbyterian Church in Black Rock Cove. Then, in conclusion, the newly married couple were to drive to the railway station and take a train to Seattle, where the lieutenant's regiment was preparing to embark.

Amala was up early, as were her friends.

She sat down in a low chair before a tall dressing mirror and submitted her beautiful head to the tender mercies of Alyssa Nicole, who, in addition to her other qualifications, was a great hairdresser.

As she was fixing Amala's hair, the door opened, and in came newcomer Haley Dawn Johnson, who, in honor of Amala's wedding, exchanged her black dress for one of gray cashmere. She walked over to Amala.

"You are very punctual, Haley. Are you still quite willing to leave the country and all your friends to go with me to the other side of the world? If you have any regrets, it's never too late to change your mind," said Amala.

"I have no friends here, Amala. I'm leaving to go with my only friend."

"Then I am delighted. It will be a great comfort to me, Haley, to have a person helping me from my childhood in a distant land where everyone will be strangers."

After she was dressed and awaited to be called for, everyone left to go downstairs to prepare for the trip to the church.

Amala looked at a package sitting on a side table and picked it up. Then, Thomas came to the door.

"Oh, your timing is wonderful, Thomas. Here is a keepsake that I wish to leave with you."

"Thank you very much for thinking of me, ma'am," replied the butler as he began to unwrap the package.

It contained a red leather-bound Bible in large print. It also had a pair of gold-rimmed reading glasses in a red walnut case.

"These are wonderful, ma'am. I will treasure them as long as I live in your memory," he said while raising her gloved hand to his lips.

"I am delighted they please you, Thomas," replied Amala.

"And now, Haley Dawn," said the butler turned to the young maid, "go and join the other ladies. They await you. Let them know the bride is ready."

"Yes, sir," said the meek young girl as she left the room.

A few minutes pass, growing ever so close to the time to depart. Then, finally, a flutter of footsteps was heard in the hallway. Ivon and her younger sisters and small brothers came into the room.

"We are all ready and await your arrival downstairs to depart to the church."

"Oh, I am so happy that the children are coming with us. It will defer the parting for some hours longer," said Amala as she kissed every one of them, one after the other.

"Yes," Yvon said, "they will all be adults when you return, Amala."

When her dress was smoothed out from the kids jumping in her lap and hugging her, she said, "Well, they are waiting for us downstairs. Shall we go?" she paused and walked over and hugged Thomas. "Goodbye, Mister Thomas," said Amala, who never once was not kind to the humblest of her attendants.

When she reached the door, she stopped and looked back at her bedroom that she had lived so long and which she would not see again for many years... or might not see again forever. The looming sadness of separation was already starting to cloud the sunshine of her bridal day.

Everyone awaited her at the foot of the grand staircase.

Oliver drew Amala's arm within his own and led her to the ferry landing. He said, "You and Yvon are to go in my car with Alyssa and me. We will be your church parents for this occasion," he said with a smile.

The bridegroom with the new heir to the Island Estate, Michael, and two of his younger brothers, filled the next car.

There were no bells and no flowers and no gathering of servants. Instead, it was a short drive to the ferry. Three cars drove onto the ferry, crossed to the other side, and then through the small fishing village of Black Rock Cove. Halfway through the town, they arrived at the Presbyterian Church.

A small group of people in the churchyard caught wind of the celebration. Three of these were the inevitable, the ubiquitous Randall, Henry, and Jack.

The church doors, which were locked to keep out the curious, were opened to allow the wedding party to enter.

Oliver walked up the aisle with Amala holding onto his arm.

The bridegroom escorted Alyssa. Then, they were followed by Michael with Yvon. And finally, all the small brothers and sisters followed.

On reaching the front, the procession broke.

Oliver led the bride to the altar, where she kneeled on the cushions. Then, with a gentle nod, the bridegroom dropped Alyssa's arm and knelt on the right-hand side of Amala. Behind Amala stood Yvon as a bridesmaid. Behind Edmund stood the young heir to the estate, Michael, as the best man.

The rites began.

It was the usual solemn exhortation and prayer and proceeded normally. But, during its progress, a few people were observed to steal quietly into the church and scatter themselves among the empty pews.

One slender and graceful woman in deep mourning noiselessly came and sat down on the back pew near the church's stained-glass windows. She had a clear view of the bridal pair. But, because of her dark veil covering her face, nothing distinctly could be seen of her.

The wedding ceremony was completed with the solemn words, "I now pronounce you man and wife." The bride and bridegroom, who had stood for the vow, kissed, turned around, and began hugging friends and family.

They began to break up the group as the new bride and groom followed the minister to his office to sign the official papers of their marriage. They walked to the back and passed the last pew in which a solitary woman in mourning sat in the shadows. She stood up and came closer to Amala, gazing at her for a moment through the thick folds of her black veil.

This happened so fast that only Amala noticed it. However, the effect of this passing encounter on her was startling. For a single moment, the bride stopped and was suddenly stricken with paralysis. She couldn't walk. She reached out and grabbed Edmund's arm. They continued to the minister's office.

They gathered around it to record the official marriage of the two love birds. Edmund looked down upon Amala, saw her pale face and trembling frame, gave her a broad smile, and drew her closer to him.

Her family and friends joined them and gathered around as signatures were made. This was when the deadly emotion of the bride was noticed and commented on by her friends.

The bride had not been agitated by the wedding ceremony. What then could have so profoundly disturbed her since its conclusion?

As Edmund was signing the register, Alyssa walked up beside Amala. "What's wrong, Amala? Something is troubling you?"

Amala replied in a low and expiring voice. "Oh, Alyssa, I have seen it again!"

"Seen what, dear?" she whispered.

"My mother's face! My dead mother's face!"

"Where did you see it, Amala?"

"Here in the church! On the back pew. There was a lady dressed in black and wearing a black veil over her face."

"I didn't notice."

"I didn't think so. I am the only one who saw her, her own daughter, to whom she has appeared for the third time," said the bride in a trembling voice.

"Nonsense, my dear. I thought you were above such superstition. This woman you saw in mourning probably only resembled your mother."

"Mrs. Richter, your signature is needed here," the minister said.

Amala signed the register.

Everyone gathered in front of the church, got in their cars, and began driving to the railway station. However, they arrived five minutes late and would have to wait an hour for the next train headed north to Seattle.

Oliver walked up, who was lingering outside to buy a copy of the BRC News, which had just been dropped off by a truck. He walked up with the paper in his hand, exclaiming, "Edmund, do you know the honors in store for you?"

"I don't know what you mean. I know the honors I am enjoying now," he said while proudly looking at his new bride.

"Well, then, listen to this," said Oliver.

"The marriage of the Honorable Jessup Austin with Dianne Smith, daughter of the late Reverend James Henry Smith, and grand-niece and heiress of the late Sabrina Covington, is scheduled for the twenty-eight of November.

Jessup Austin has recently been appointed as Ambassador to Mozambique and will set sail overseas with his bride from Seattle on the first of December."

"There, Edmund. What do you think? You and Amala will not only have the honor of the Ambassador's company but the delight of the woman who, by refraining from matrimony during her aunt's life, deprived you of the largest private fortune in the country. Now, what do you think?"

Everyone was struck with amazement from the reading. "I am glad, Oliver, that they are going on the same ship and Amala and me. I am curious to see the beautiful woman who could withstand all the overtures to matrimony until she had secured this immense wealth. Then, not only that but wait until her later years in life to take up with an old Ambassador of feeble health and impecunious condition. I really don't care. I have all the fortune I covet in this world," he added, taking his bride's hand, and bringing it to his lips with a smile.

The conductor's voice cried out, "All aboard to Seattle, Washington!"

Hasty and earnest goodbyes were exchanged.

Almost before Amala could collect her faculties, she was seated in a first-class carriage with her husband beside her and her maid in the chair in front of them... all being whirled onward at fifty miles per hour.

There was nobody else in the carriage. Edmund would gladly have dispensed with Haley Dawn's company so that he might have been able to enjoy a tete-a-tete journey with his bride.

"I'm sorry, Edmund."

"Sorry for what, dear?"

"I have Haley Dawn in here with us because whatever she might be in years, she is only a child. I don't trust people to have her travel alone in the second-class carriage. You don't mind, do you, dear?"

"Not at all, sweetheart," he replied with a smile.

"Haley Dawn wasn't born yesterday. Instinctively she felt like an intruder on the newlyweds and seated herself as far away toward the front of the carriage away from the couple. She shrunk down and looked out the window at the Pacific Ocean beside which the railroad ran for miles.

The trip to Seattle was uneventful.

On arrival, they stayed in the Freemont Hotel for the next five days, awaiting their ship's disembarkation.

Amala exchanged letters back home with Alyssa and Yvon, who were now at the Courbis Estate. But unfortunately, none of the letters gave Amala any insight into the strange woman in mourning who had frightened her so much at her wedding. If she ever existed in the flesh, such a woman had never been seen around the area.

On the last day before the ship was set to sail, Edmund took Amala onboard the great ship. She was filled with wonder at how large it was and the comfort of its accommodations for passengers.

As she was given the tour, she could peek in at the cabin and staterooms of the ambassador and his new wife, the heir to the estate of Sabrina Covington. It was like looking at large luxury apartments lined up side by side. It was truly magnificent.

Then, finally, she was taken to her stateroom in the front of the ship, which was cramped but clean.

Leaving the ship, Edmund said, "What do you think, sweetheart?"

"This ship is truly a marvel. It is gigantic and just unbelievable something this large can float in the ocean," she said with enthusiasm as they departed and returned to their hotel.

"You will get intimately acquainted with the big boat. You will be on her for at least a month, if not more."

"I will like that, Edmund."

"I hope you don't get seasick."

"I hope not, too. Pray don't suggest such a thing, Edmund," laughed Amala.

The next day, the final day of embarkation of the regiment and the big ship, a large gala was held in Seattle on the wharf where the vessel was docked.

That early morning, Lieutenant Richter took his beautiful wife Amala and her maid onboard, saw them safe into their quarters, and left them there to return to his duty with the regiment.

At straight up noon, the regiment marched together onboard the vessel. All the community showed up for the festive hour of the day.

Not long after all the soldiers were onboard, Ambassador Jessup Austin, his family, and attendants came on board. All the ladies in the fore cabin crowded up to the rails to see the new ambassador and his bride as they came onboard, walking on the main entrance.

They pointed at the splendid older gentleman with a piercing complexion and piercing blue eyes. His eyebrows were heavy, and he had iron-gray hair and a mustache.

One of the women said, "My, is he not a handsome one... so distinguished."

The other women agreed.

For his new wife, who he had just wed, they were not so well able to judge. They saw a very tall and elegant woman hanging onto his arm. She wore an emerald green jumpsuit, trimmed with silver fox fur and a green veil that hid her face. She also had on black gloves and carried a royal blue cashmere shawl on her arm.

She passed without any of the women getting a glimpse of her face.

But, one of the women, Amala Richter, began to tremble. She reached up to her heart with her right palm pressed against her chest and whispered under her breath, *"Oh, no, it can't be happening. Am I going mad again? Oh, good God, I am going mad! Why am I seeing my dead mother's living form under every disguise I see? Her living face shadowed forth under that veil. Mad! Indeed... I must be going crazy!"* She wasted no time and followed the other women to the officer's quarters at the front of the ship and entered her stateroom. Haley Dawn was busy putting everything up in their drawers and unpacking valises and trunks.

"Haley, did you see the new Ambassador's bride as she passed?" she asked as she sat down on the sofa.

"No, ma'am, I didn't. I was at the foot of the ladder and only got a small glance at her shoes and blue jumpsuit."

The ship shook, and noises were heard creaking throughout, telling the passengers the ship was getting underway. Her door was open as the other ladies were talking in the hallway about going up on deck to watch the shoreline go out of sight... their last look at the homeland for who knows how long.

Amala joined them and looked upon the receding shoreline of North America, which she might never see again. She departed from the other wives and attendants, leaned over the bulwarks, and fixed her eyes upon the fading shoreline, determined to watch it until it was entirely out of sight.

She gazed as though she was in a dream until suddenly, she was awakened by an incredible thrill that shook her entire body.

The ambassador and his wife passed close behind her, brushing up against her with their bodies as they went by.

Amala turned around and watched their progress.

The ambassador took a chair and pulled it up to the railing for his wife to sit. He wrapped a shawl around her shoulders and then, after a few words, departed to meet some of the officers who had come up on the quarter-deck.

The bride of the ambassador, who had kept her veil down as she walked onboard the vessel, now raised it so that she might look toward the east as the ship got further and further from shore.

The ocean breathed slowly, her surface rising and falling with rhythmic ease. The waves became her pulse this day. Her thoughts were back onshore as the ship got further and further out to sea.

Her face was turned from Amala, who, with lips apart and dilated eyes, was staring at the woman's form.

Amala couldn't stand it. She didn't know what possessed her, but something commanded her to get up and walk in the direction of the woman sitting by herself, staring back at the homeland.

The lady felt her presence and turned.

The girl stood still.

Their eyes met in one long, fixed stare of amazement, and then they both spoke, "Amala!"

"Mother!"

"My child, how in the world did you—-!"

"Oh, my God! Mother! Mother! Mother!

With that agonized cry of mingled terror and amazement, Amala sank down at her mother's feet and dropped her head in her mother's lap.

However, Amala was not so utterly overcome by the shock of what she discovered because the apparition that had startled her on three separate occasions had also prepared her for this very moment in time.

The silence was so deep they might have heard each other's hearts beating, and then the older woman spoke in a voice full of tears.

Bending down over the kneeling girl, she put her arms around Amala's shoulders and laid her face upon the sunken head until her lips touched the soft, dark hair and said in a voice broken with her crying, "Amala! Amala! I thank God for this meeting. It might bring me to ruin or dishonor, or even death. I don't care. But, oh, Amala... it is my baby girl!"

"Mother," said Amala in a faint tone but said nothing more.

"Oh, my child, my heart has hungered for you. I never knew just how deeply I really loved you until I had left you that day at the Reynold's Estate."

"Oh, Mother, what made you leave me?" asked Amala.

"Necessity, my child," said Bernice in a deep sigh.

"What necessity should part the widowed mother from her only child?"

"I can't tell you where we might be overheard," said Bernice.

"But you married the new ambassador to Mozambique, Mother. We read in the newspapers that he was marrying Miss Dianne Smith, the millionaire heiress of the late Sabrina Covington. This is a fact,

Mother. So how did you suddenly marry him at the last moment instead of Miss Dianne Smith?"

"I'm sorry, Amala, but I can explain nothing here and now. I have reasons why, as I've told you."

"Mamma!" she murmured in a voice full of pity.

"Hush, honey!" said the woman in a low and frightened tone that caused Amala to turn her head. She saw the ambassador returning toward them.

He said, "Ahhh, if it isn't the newlywed bride of Lieutenant Edmund Richter. I must congratulate ma'am. I hear from your lieutenant husband you two were just wed back in Black Rock Cove."

Amala, trembling excessively, bent her head to acknowledge his words, then timidly raised her emerald green eyes to her stepfather's face. How strange was the thought of her having a stepfather? One who has never known a father her entire life. And, how strange it was to talk to the ambassador who had no idea he had a stepdaughter!

She raised her head and stood by the railing before the tall older man of over sixty years of age with iron-gray hair and a mustache.

The ambassador looked at Amala, saw her disturbance, and attributed it to the bashfulness of a new bride. He smiled his keen, blue eyes at hers. Amala felt her heart drawn out to love and trust him.

"Mrs. Richter is a dear love of mine, whom I've known since she was a baby. And now, I think I must carry her off with me to my cabin and catch up on all the time we have lost in seeing one another," said Bernice with a composure that filled the newlywed with wonder.

Amala thought while smiling, *"What does Mamma mean by what she just said? Why doesn't she just introduce me to my stepfather as her daughter? She will need to do it at some time... why not now?"*

"Please, Jessup, will you help me back to the cabin with Amala? It is hard keeping our feet on this deck."

The large vessel was now beginning to roll heavily.

Just before passing into the cabin, Edmund glanced at the ambassador and smiled as he passed by with both women in his arms. But unfortunately, he failed to see that his wife was one of the two who hung onto the ambassador's arms.

Mrs. Austin led her daughter once down below to her cabin, opened the door with a key, and led her inside.

No sooner did she close the door behind her than she threw off her veil and then threw her arms around her daughter. She gave way to a burst of tears that made her shake and tremble like a tree in a high wind. Her excessive emotion distressed Amala, who sought to calm her down with tender words. "Oh, Mother, don't cry so. Why are you grieving? Something is troubling you. Your new husband is an ambassador and a fine and handsome man. I liked him the first time I met him and am sure he will make you very happy. I am glad you married him... Miss Smith," said Amala.

"Oh, Amala, you just don't know... you simply have no idea!"

"Then tell me, Mamma, what I don't know, please."

"This meeting with you on this ship has filled me with great joy and despair. Oh, sweetheart, when I came onboard this vessel, I thought I should never see my child again on this side of the grave. And now! Just when I thought that I had lost you from my sight forever as if a coffin lid had closed on top of you... now to have you by my side for the entire voyage and that you will be living in the same country as me... oh, dear, although this prospect is full of perils of exposure and even death, yet in the middle of all the despair I can only rejoice!"

"Oh, please start from the beginning, Mother. I am so confused."

"Very well," said Amala's mother, still sobbing, "tell me just how much you remember. It will help me to tell you my story."

"I remember when we lived near Portland, and my father got very sick and passed. I don't believe I can remember anything before that. I only remember seeing my father sick in bed with very black hair and whiskers on his face. After that, I vaguely remember his funeral."

"What next?"

"I remember our journey to Black Rock Cove and bringing Mrs. Johnson and her daughter, Haley Dawn, with us."

"And then, Amala?"

"Then, I remember everything else very clearly. I remember living in Shaw's Bend from the day we got there in that old solitary mansion until the sad day when I missed you waking up with me and having breakfast. Oh, Mother, I still don't understand. Why did you leave me?" she asked, still sick from the memory of that terrible and frightening day when she got the news that her mother had died.

"From necessity, dear, as I have explained to you before," said Bernice with a shuddering sigh.

"Oh, Mamma, I thought you were gone forever. Everyone thought you died in Demon Gorge. But, then, Hugh Jackson, the nightwatchman, saw you on the bridge in the early morning hours in the darkness before the sunrise. A fisherman found fragments of your dress caught in the brier bushes halfway down that awful abyss. Later on... later on, they found—-." Amala's voice broke down into a sobbing tone.

Her mother finishes her sentence for her. "A body which was supposed to be mine and which was buried for mine. Yes, dear, I read all about it in the BRC News. I also read how that old crone, Victoria Meret, and Hugh Jackson, the nightwatchman, got the reward. I did, in fact, read all about it at the time and have even been to the cemetery and have seen my tombstone."

"Ohhh, Mother, how can you bear to talk of it?"

"Why not? It was so kind of Kenneth to put it up. When was it that you think I saw it, dear?"

"Oh, Mother, I don't know." The sigh that left Amala's lips was slow, as if her brain needed time to process everything happening.

"I was there the day you got married. I was in the church, sweetheart. I heard of my one daughter's approaching marriage and was definitely not going to miss it. I had on a dark veil and sat on the back pew. You walked right past me when you went to the registry with the minister. You almost recognized me, child."

"Oh, but I did recognize you, Mother. I believed in the reappearance of departed spirits when I walked so near you. That was not the first time I saw you since your getaway, Mother! Another time was while I was on the terrace looking out over the ocean and once at sunset while looking out the bay window in the library."

"Yes, dear, that was me on all three occasions. But, oh, Amala, I was trying to get a glimpse of you one last time before I left the country forever with my husband!"

"No one believed me when I told them I saw you. Everyone thought I was hallucinating."

"And you, dear?"

"I thought you were a spirit that had returned from the dead. What else could I possibly think? This was the first time in my life I began to believe in the reappearance of departed spirits. What else could I believe, Mother? I don't understand how it was that I could recognize you and no one else?"

"Because no one expected to see me. And, I kept my veil down all the time except when looking out from a safe point of view for you."

"Where have you been sleeping and eating, Mamma, all this time?"

"In my home in Black Rock Cove, where I was not known as I did not frequent out much."

"Except when you made the journey to see me each time."

"Yes."

"Oh... poor Mamma."

"Okay, Amala, let's return to our subject... your reminiscences. You have seldom heard me talk about my girlhood, but you surely knew my maiden name, right?"

"Yes, your maiden name was Smith, I know."

"A very common name, right? The commonest name in America, probably."

"Yes."

"And how many Smiths do you know, Amala?"

"Oh, there is the gardener at Oliver's estate named Smith, a fisherman in the village named Dewey Smith, Dr. Smith the dentist, a lawyer name Smith and the Miss Smith, the heiress to all the riches in the big house in Black Rock Cove who was reported to be engaged to—-." Amala stopped her words. She reddened. She continued, "Then there was no truth in the newspapers that the ambassador was engaged to the great heiress," she said.

"Yes, sweetheart, there was perfect truth in it. He was not only engaged to that woman, but he married her."

"Wait! How can that be, Mamma? The ambassador married you. You are that heiress?" asked Amala with a puzzled expression.

"Yes, I am the wealthy heiress, and I am that Miss Smith," said the lady in a low tone.

"Come now, Amala, don't be a foolish girl with what you are thinking. I was Miss Dianne Smith, indeed. That was before I married Arthur Luther, your father."

"Wait, I am very confused, Mother. I have been led to believe that Miss Smith never married. That her inheritance of the great estate of Sabrina Covington was made conditional upon her remaining unmarried as long as Mrs. Covington was alive," Amala said gravely as she was wondering how her mother could survive such a criminal affair of fraud.

"Amala," said Bernice, "you have told me, per my request, all that you remember of our joint lives together. Now, I will supplement that by telling you everything I remember of mine."

"Thank you, Mamma. All of this is still confusing to me," she sighed deeply.

Chapter FIVE
The Duel to the Death

"**You know I was the only child of the late** Reverend Henry Smith of the Presbyterian Church in Black Rock Cove. And, I lost both of my parents in very early childhood."

"Yes, I have heard you often speak of that, Mamma."

"Well, when I was left as an orphan, I was placed in a private school where the cost was paid for by my only living relative, Sabrina Covington. She was my grandaunt. I met her for the first time when it came the summer, and all the students went home to their relatives. I went to her grand estate in Black Rock Cove, where she was almost seventy years old back then. She lived all alone in that magnificent place."

"When I was young, I had your beauty, my dear. All the servants were unreserved in their admiration of the little beauty or, as they called me, the little heiress, as they were fond of calling me. I didn't think much of it back then. They said I would surely attract a man with great wealth because I had all the qualities if you know what I mean," she lightly laughed.

"Anyhow, the mere babble of the servants reached my aunt's ears. Well, a woman almost seventy years of age was as jealous and selfish as she was suspicious. All the servants talking about my beauty and how I would attract the, as they said, the rich and famous, caused her great rage. I have never known a woman in her senior years become so jealous of a person like me... little ole me, Amala." Finally, she paused and reached over and drank a small glass of Llano

Moscato wine taken onboard from the finest of vineyards near Fredericksburg, Texas.

"I was sent back to my school after that and never came back to the large mansion on the city block downtown Black Rock Cove. Instead, I spent my holidays and summer vacations at the school." She paused and looked at the wine bottle and the extra glass. Amala's mother poured another drink and handed it to her daughter.

She then continued, "I was educated to become a music teacher. When I was eighteen years of age, I graduated. That is when my Grandaunt Sabrina summoned me to her presence for a short visit. When I arrived, I found her confined to a wheelchair as both of her legs were paralyzed. She suffered from this for the remainder of her life. Then, she gave me a good preaching to," she said while pouring another glass of wine.

"She told me that I needed to go out in the world and work hard to earn my keep, just like she had to do as a youth. Now, this is when she said that if I remained unmarried, honestly laboring for my living until her demise, I would inherit the entire estate... and an immense estate it was. But, if I were to marry during her lifetime, I wouldn't inherit a single dime, and the property would be given to her nephew, Edmund Richter."

"To Edmund Richter, my husband," said Amala.

"Yes, the only man who was the brother of Kenneth Reynolds married and had only one son. But, of course, I didn't know any of these particulars beforehand. I only learned of them when I showed up to take control of the estate after my grandaunt passed away."

"But," Bernice continued, "my grandaunt thought she gave me fair warning of what I could lose if I were to marry. But she didn't know. That fair warning came a little too late. I was already married to your father."

"You married when you were just out of school!" exclaimed Amala.

"No, dear, I married while I was still in school. You see, the boys had their own teacher while in school and took a young boy named Arthur Luther. Our classes met together for meals and Sunday School and Choir almost daily. Arthur was the only boy that I cared for. You may still remember your father on his deathbed, my dear. You will never know how handsome and sweet that young man was when I first met him. Whatever chemistry was there, it mushroomed as I took for him, and he took for me. After a while, he and I gathered our clothes in each suitcase and met at the railway station. We took a train to Portland, got married, and returned to Black Rock Cove before we were ever discovered missing.

You can imagine how I judged my dismay on going to Aunt Sabrina's mansion after I graduated that summer and was told by her that my inheritance of her entire estate was conditional upon my remaining unmarried.

"But Mother," said Amala in a piteous tone, "I don't understand, and I want to understand. Isn't it wrong to elope and have a secret marriage, and even worse if the man you married is a man of God? But, please, don't misunderstand what I am asking. I am not criticizing you or father at all. I only want to understand."

"Actually, such conduct is not looked upon favorably by society and especially for a minister of the cloth. But Arthur was not a pastor then. He was only a theological student in Portland in college. And he was madly in love with a pretty schoolgirl who didn't have a mother or a father to consult. So, there was no reason that we should not have gotten married, except that he and I were almost entirely broke.

Arthur was nineteen years old, and I was seventeen when we were married.

When I graduated, I taught music at Black Rock Cove Music School. The principal was Miss Smith.

While there, I wrote back and forth with my husband finishing his Theological Degree in Portland under the name Miss Dianne Smith."

"Oh, Mother, let me stop you a moment. I just wish to say thank you for opening up to me about your childhood. I feel like I've finally got to understand everything about you. But I want to hear more."

"Well, while my grandaunt was confined to a wheelchair, she asked me to come up for three months during the summer on school vacations and then two weeks at Christmas and one week during Easter... or four full months during the year.

During these times, I went to see her, I liked what my aunt offered me and, of course, Arthur. Then, I conceived the idea of keeping my marriage a complete secret from all the people as long as Aunt Sabrina still lived. It was decided that Arthur and I would perform the marriage ceremony again, as if for the first time. Another thing was that our marriage was simple without a ring, license, or witness. It was perfectly legal, except neither of us could have proven it today without the minister who performed the ceremony could be produced.

"Did you ever tell my father of your arrangement with Sabrina Covington?"

"Actually, no. I never told him once of the cruel condition of my aunt's will, which would disinherit me for marrying during her lifetime. So, I decided that I would never tell him. For the time being, I decided to manage my plan alone. During the early days, it was easy to manage. But in the future, I saw many difficulties," she paused, swigged down the glass of wine, and filled her glass again. "Oh, Amala, please don't judge me so harshly."

"My heart doesn't judge you, Mother. It only hurts for you," murmured Amala in a broken voice.

"Well, my first difficulty came when he was ordained and was given his first church. It was the Presbyterian Church in Black Rock Cove."

"Where you attended school, Mamma?"

"Yes, where I went to school and where I met your father and from where we departed to go and get married secretly in Portland. He was expected to enter on his duties early in the ensuing month of September. He asked me to make all the arrangements for his return and joining me at the church school."

"Did you ever tell my father about Sabrina's last will and testament?"

"No. He who never had a bad thought in his mind would never have consented to deception like I was doing. But I told him my aunt was in poor health and cared for her. I further told Arthur that my grandaunt was violently opposed to my marriage during her life, which was very true. I also said that the shock might kill her if she was ever told of my marriage. Although that wasn't wholly true, Arthur believed it."

"What was the plan," Amala interrupted.

"Well, we talked about it, and he agreed. I would live with him in the pastor's home, but every summer, Christmas, and Easter vacation would go and stay with my aunt, Miss Dianne Smith.

Our plan worked. You were born, and my grandaunt never suspected anything. She even started sending me two thousand dollars allowance each quarter because I was skin and bones on one of my visits. This was very helpful for several years. Then... well, your father was stricken with Cancer, and I lost him. So, from the date of my loss and yours, your own memory will supply," she paused and topped off her wine. Never had she sat down with her daughter and had such a long chat.

She continued. "After your father died, I had to leave the pastoral residence for the church to make room for the successor to your father. I did have the allowance my aunt gave me, which helped you and me when I moved to Shaw's Bend. My health went down after your dad died, and Shaw's Bend was wet and damp initially, which didn't help. But we got by, sweetheart.

Do you remember when we moved to Shaw's Bend, we brought two attendants, Haley Dawn Johnson and her mother, Betsy Johnson?"

"Yes, I do, Mother."

"Well, for years, my aunt got older and older. Finally, I discovered that I couldn't depend entirely on her for our future support. So, after about a year, I began to think seriously about marrying for wealth, in your interest as well as in my own. I had beauty and felt like I could wed wealth, be independent, and not need my grandaunt's millions of dollars.

It never happened. Then it was that momentous morning at the Reynolds Island Estate where Kenneth read from the newspaper about the death of my grandaunt. That's where the shock was too much for me, and I fainted."

"Yes, Mother, I remember."

"Well, the hours that followed my recovery were the most distressing time I think I have ever had in my life. My crisis and fate had come. If I didn't claim the property left by my aunt, I would also lose the allowance, which was our only means of support."

"I think I understand, Mother."

"This, at that time, meant absolute destitution for you, Amala, and for me. I was required to simulate my death as Bernice Luther so that I may never be sought after again. I would once again be Miss Dianne Smith."

"But, Mother, what about me?"

"Sweetheart, that was the biggest kink in my plans. For this to work, my greatest trial for me to endure was giving you up as my child, forever! Yet, even for your sake, no less than for mine, it seemed absolutely necessary that I should give you up. To have remained with you would have doomed you and me to the most abject poverty." She paused to catch her breath.

Bernice continued, "I decided to go through with the plan. I went and finished up with Charlotte and arranged for you to join her family and be the music teacher for their kids. Then, having secured that position, I returned to Shaw's Bend for a short while. Do you remember that night we spent together there, and you couldn't understand my anxiety... my distress?"

"Yes, Mamma, I remember that last night as if it was yesterday," replied Amala with a sigh that appeared to upheave her heart.

"Well, that distress I was feeling was because it was the last night you and I would spend together. So, no sooner did you go to bed than I went and wrote a note to you that said I was going back to the Reynold's Island Estate. But, in fact, I went to the headwaters of Demon Gorge, where I staged my accidental drowning, which fooled even the coroner's office.

In the course of my plan, I met Hugh Jackson, the nightwatchman for the area who was on his beat. He shined his flashlight on me and, in the darkness, saw that I was not a suspicious person, begged my pardon, and passed me out of sight.

"The next day, I was just in time to attend my grandaunt's funeral and the reading of the last will and testament, which constituted me her sole and only heiress. I entered the undisputed possession of my great fortune... millions upon millions of dollars."

"I took over the undisputed possession of the total estate," continued Bernice, "and yet I held it not in a peaceful way. On the contrary, I was haunted every day by the fear of someone recognizing me. I saw these people when I spent time with her for the Christmas parties and whom I might have met at Easter or whenever."

"Two circumstances were in my favor. The first was that neither my grandaunt nor I mingled much in the Black Rock Cove Society. We had all we needed and remained behind the tall brick walls surrounding the property. The second one was that I would stay inside the walls for at least a year in mourning. No one would question that.

Then, I was determined that I wanted to see some of the world. I shut down the whole place except for my attendants and left for Rome. I met Jessup during this time, and we returned to Black Rock Cove and got engaged to be married.

Finally, we had a festive day of our marriage and only invited people we knew didn't know me as Bernice Luther. It was a grand time, but one that I was still not happy about. I wanted my daughter to celebrate the big occasion with me."

After I was married, I would make trips to the island and places I knew would be to just see you. You didn't always see me, but I saw you over the next several months. During this time, I heard lots of gossip about people seeing my ghost." Finally, she stopped and walked over to close the porthole on the ship. The breeze was getting chilly during the nighttime voyage.

"Amala, I sent you money in a blank envelope twice. Did you receive it?"

"Yes, Mother, I did, but I had no idea who sent it, but it was greatly needed. Thank you."

"I also read the account of Oliver Courbis and Alyssa Nicole and how they traveled overseas for a few months on their honeymoon. Later, I read that they returned.

It happened that Jessup got an appointment from the President of the United States to be the ambassador to Mozambique off the eastern coast of Africa. He was pleased to find me so willing to share his exile, as he called it.

Jessup and I arranged to be married on the day we were in Portland. Afterward, we traveled to Black Rock Cove and agreed to only have a skeleton staff man the estate. I went to the BRC First National Bank and put $100,000 into your account. I had a notification sent to you. Yet I suppose you never got it."

"No, Mother, but thank you very much, all the same."

"You never got it because you were already on your journey to Seattle to the wharf for this departure overseas. I didn't hear of your marriage until the day thereof and rushed down to the church and found a spot on the back pew of the empty church. It was the same day I put the money in your account.

What is amazing is that I had no idea that he belonged to the traveling regiment with my husband on the voyage. Our meeting on the deck was just as much of a surprise to me as I am sure it was to you... So that's my story, Hun."

Amala exhibited signs of uneasiness.

"I trust, sweetheart, that you will keep my secret as long as it may be possible for you to do," concluded Bernice.

"Oh, Mother... I'm sorry, but how can I keep such a secret? I couldn't keep it even if I would. And, I ought not to keep it if I could," said the confused young newlywed.

"What are you saying, Amala? Why should you not keep my secret to yourself?"

"Mother, how in the world can you ask me such a question? My husband, Edmund Richter, is the rightful heir to the entire estate you hold through your secret," said Amala.

"No, that is not true!" exclaimed Bernice angrily. "Edmund Richter is not, never has been, and can never be the rightful heir of Sabrina Covington's Estate. He is not even of her blood! No! He is not a rightful heir to the Covington Estate," concluded Amala's mother with the most passionate vehemence.

"Then, Mother, if he is not the rightful heir, he is certainly the legal heir of that property you unlawfully hold! I am sorry to say this, Mother, but Edmund is my husband. Even if he wasn't, how dare you ask me to be a party to such a—-."

"Oh, Mother, you don't understand, but I would have rather died than to know such a secret," moaned Amala.

"What are you going to do, Amala?"

"I don't know! I just don't know!"

"All I wish to know is are you going to keep your mother's secret?" demanded Bernice vehemently.

"Let me ask you this, Mother. How can I look my own husband in the eye, knowing your secret, and keep it from him? I love him!"

"Well, dear, you take the strongest against the weakest... the husband or the mother, the man against the woman," bitterly answered Amala's mother.

"Not true, Mother. I take the side of right against wrong... as I must! As I must because God in Heaven help me, I can't do otherwise!" Amala said while crying with her face buried in the palms of her hands.

Bernice contemplated what her daughter said in gloomy silence for a short moment. Then, she said, "Listen to me, child. Let us reason this out together, mother and daughter. Keep my secret just as long as I shall live, and I will give him one-third of the entire estate and leave you two-thirds. What do you say to that compromise?"

More at a calm, she replied, "Mother, I have no right to compromise with you or to conceal all of this from my husband."

"Then, let me get this straight, Amala. In bitter indignation, you will not keep this secret?" demanded the woman.

"I have no right to keep it, Mamma."

"You will betray my secret and deprive me of all my newfound wealth?"

"I know, Edmund. He is a good and kind man. He would never impoverish you, Mother. Never!"

"The loss of my wealth wouldn't be the greatest of dangers of you divulging my secret. I would lose my esteem, my reputation, and my liberty! Yes, and loss of life, for surely, I wouldn't survive these losses, Amala."

"What are you saying, Mother?" demanded Amala in an agony of terror.

"Are you even considering what the law might do with knowledge of this secret?"

"The law? It would simply give it all back to Edmund," answered Amala.

"Not true. The law would consider what I have done as a felony. That means time behind bars."

Amala threw her hands over her ears and said, "Oh, please, Mamma, don't!"

"Yes, my dear... a felony! Are you ready to send your mother to prison? Are you? Condemn me to a felon's fate?"

"Oh, my God, if I could only die!"

"We can wait no longer. Give me your decision. What do you intend to do? Send me to prison or seize at once a third of the wealth in the estate and receive the rest on my death, sooner or later?" asked Bernice with a bitter smile.

"Oh, please, Mother, trust in Edmund. Let me tell him your secret. Let me tell him!"

"Never! My secret must be kept," vehemently exclaimed Bernice.

"Mother, you just don't understand. Even if I could keep your secret, others would discover it. Two others on this boat know you as Bernice Luther and would recognize you on sight."

"I have changed everything about me. I wear better clothes. I cut my hair really short. I even dyed my hair red. They might see my strong likeness of me, but they will never recognize me. Still, who is this person who might recognize me?"

"Haley Dawn Johnson!"

"Haley Dawn... she is here!" exclaimed Bernice in trepidation.

"Yes, Mother, the girl who has grown up since a child in your service. She will surely recognize you."

"Then I must avoid seeing either she or Edmund face-to-face. You must help me, Amala."

"I can't, Mother. I can't be a party to all of this. I just can't!"

"Then there is only one thing I can do," said Bernice slowly and solemnly.

Amala looked at her but made no reply. She sat there, posed in a picture of despair.

"One thing only... I will bury myself and shame beneath the waves of the Pacific Ocean!"

"Mother!" she stood up with a sharp cry.

"I will surely do it as I live now! I will do it when I find out you have betrayed my secret!"

"Oh, God, help me decide what to do," breathed Amala in distress.

"Listen, child. Give me a little time. Don't tell anyone yet. I am your mother. Please, don't tell anyone today."

"Very well. One day."

"And, before you tell it, give me a few hours warning. Will you do that?" persisted her mother.

"Okay. I will not reveal your secret without first warning you."

A rap came to the door. Bernice walked over and cracked the door open a few inches, "What is it, Jessup?"

"It's time to go to supper."

"I don't want any supper. I couldn't eat if I did. But, thank you, dear."

"Not seasick, I hope?" asked the ambassador in a voice of concern.

"Yes, Jessup, deadly seasick," sighed the woman.

"Very well, honey. Oh, Edmund is here looking for his new bride."

"She is here. He can have her," answered Bernice. She turned to her daughter and said, "Go, dear."

Amala rose, trembling with emotion, and passed out into the hallway where the ambassador and Edmund were standing side by side.

"Hello, love. I hear you have found an old friend onboard. That is so charming. But Amala, what is wrong? You are so pale and trembling. Are you seasick, too?" he asked, looking at her anxiously.

"I suppose I am," she answered with a feeble smile.

"I tell you what works. Walkabout, talk and laugh and eat and drink as though there was no sea on this planet earth!"

When Amala reached the dining room, her new friends, the lady wives of the regiment officers, awaited her. They sat down at one table where they showed very little of an appetite as the motion of the big ship affected all of them.

Amala was pleased with the excuse she could use to retire to her stateroom, where not even her husband intruded upon her.

For several days from this time, Amala was confined to her stateroom in the front of the ship with severe sickness.

Chapter SIX
Children Drown at Sea

More than ten days passed before Amala saw her mother again. She remained in her berth, prostrated with a nervous condition from the stress of having to decide.

There was no doubt the young woman was suffering more in mind than in her body. However, as far as everyone else was concerned, she was ill from seasickness.

Bernice, or Dianne Smith Austin, sent her own attendant, Mrs. Landry, every day to see Mrs. Richter and inquire about her health.

Amala could not return the compliment by sending Haley Dawn with respectful inquiries about Dianne's stateroom. The first reason was that she was also very ill from seasickness. And second, she would recognize her former boss, and the secret would have been prematurely exposed.

Finally, the seas calmed, and it was smooth sailing for a week or more. Amala received a standing request from Dianne Austin to come to her as soon as she should be able to leave her stateroom.

Amala, feeling much better, took her leave of her cabin and went to see Ambassador Austin's wife. She found her mother stretched out on a sofa in her room with ashen skin and very thin as though she hadn't eaten for days.

"Oh, my love, you have been very ill. I'm so sorry. It is still written on your face. Sit down beside me," said Amala's mother, taking her daughter's hand and gently drawing her toward the chair next to her.

"And you, Mother? You must have also been here suffering like I was. You look worse than I feel!" said the girl with unintentional, cruel frankness.

"Yes! I have been pretending to be worse than I am. I have come up with all kinds of excuses to stay in my room so that I don't run into your husband or attendant, Haley Dawn, on the deck."

"Since I was laid up in my bed for almost a week, I've been thinking. I don't think Haley Dawn's recognition could hurt you."

"Why do you say that?"

"Because she knew nothing of Sabrina Covington or of Miss Dianne Smith. And though she would undoubtedly recognize you as someone she attended to for so many years as Mrs. Bernice Luther, she wouldn't ever dream you went by any other name until you married the ambassador. But she will be curious how you jumped from the Demon Gorge bridge and died and are now here very much alive.

Still, no worries. She will be perplexed about how you should be a living person when you are a deceased widow, but she will not mention it and keep it to herself.

Now, as far as Edmund is concerned, your danger of recognition by him is much greater. He knew you well as Mrs. Bernice Luther, and he also knew the terms upon which Miss Dianne Smith inherited her grandaunt's great wealth. And he knows that Dianne Smith married the ambassador. He would then understand it all at a single glance, Mother!"

"But Amala, my circumstances have changed. I have different colored hair now. I have cut it very short. And I wear my makeup altogether differently. Edmund would not recognize anything more than a remarkable likeness between myself and the late Mrs. Bernice Luther. But you are right. I must remain in my room during the day and only come out at night. I must do this for the rest of the voyage."

"But, Mother, that will be very difficult. Your health is already suffering from your one-week confinement," said Amala in a tone of tender sympathy.

"Amala, may I ask? You have been thinking, of course, of your resolution while you laid ill in your cabin these last several days. The pillow is said to be a good counselor."

"I don't understand, Mamma."

"My secret, dear. You will not reveal my secret now. Are you going to accept my terms for keeping it? One-third now of all my wealth and the rest will be given to him at my death?"

"Mother," pleaded Amala, in a low and tender tone... "Do you not see that it's not for me to consider this proposal? I can only see myself telling my husband. I owe him the truth."

Bernice Luther (Dianne Smith) looked at her daughter long and wistfully before saying anything. Then she asked, "When will you tell him?"

"I don't know. Each day I keep this secret from him, I feel like I am doing him wrong! I still say you can trust Edmund with your secret. You can make this same offer to him. It would come with so much more grace from you than from me. All you must do is explain to him what you explained to me. He will understand. You won't find him a harsh judge. You will find him just and merciful!"

"Answer me something, Amala. How can I expect either justice or mercy from my son-in-law when I can't get them from my one and only daughter?" bitterly inquired Amala's mother.

"God, Mother! I wish I could die! I am in a grasp of a destiny... a torture engine from which there is no way to escape!" moaned Amala, burying her face into her hands.

"Very well, Amala. There is only one choice. It must be made. Listen carefully if you feel compelled to tell your husband my secret."

"Yes, Mamma?"

"I repeat. Within one hour after I hear that you have made this revelation to Edmund, I will bury myself and all my sorrow and dishonor in the depths of the Indian Ocean."

Amala muttered a low cry of anguish.

"Oh, Amala, I wish to live a little longer. All I ask is for a little longer life, that is all... a little respite from this dreadful death by suicide!"

"Mother! Mother! My heart is breaking! I'm dying! Do you hear me?" the young woman moaned faintly. "All of this talk is making me a raving maniac!"

"Calm down, honey. Defer telling the secret until we reach Mozambique a month from now. Consider this. The ship may never reach port. She might go down in a terrible storm. Who knows? In either case, I might be saved from a crime of suicide. And, you will be saved from the crime of having driven your mother to such a desperate deed. Just forbear until then, dear."

"Very well, Mother. I will keep your secret until we land in Mozambique," she replied in a voice so faint that her words could scarcely be heard.

Before Bernice could reply to her daughter, she got up from her chair, left the stateroom, and went back to her cabin like a drunken man, where she fell across her bed, insensible.

A few hours more in the day, Edmund dropped by to check on Amala. He found her in almost a delirious condition and on the verge of another life.

Edmund, Doctor Sanders, and Haley Dawn attended to the poor sick girl. Bernice sent her attendant two or three times a day to inquire after Amala and express her sympathy for and anxiety for the sufferer. However, she never attended. How could she? She dared not meet Edmund nor Haley Dawn in fear of recognition.

There were moments when Mrs. Austin thought she might brave such recognition and their firm conviction of her death and their established faith that they would see two different people... Miss Smith, the great heiress, and Mrs. Bernice Luther, the poor widow, to be two distinct people.

However, she deemed it best that being cautious was the thing to do and stay on the safe side.

Mrs. Austin began to suffer the severest penalties for her long life of fraud. She was tormented with anxiety for the suffering daughter whom, through all her own making mistakes in life, she had dearly loved and to whose bedside now she couldn't go and visit.

Amala might just die from her inflicted illness brought on by her mother. She might die from a nervous breakdown that she, her mother, had thrown her. And, if so, the knowledge of the terrible secret would pass with her.

But, would the ambassador's wife be then safe? Actually... no! She would be in more danger. Edmund Richter and Haley Dawn Johnson would be sure to recognize her, and then there would be exposure and dishonor. Without Amala to mediate between her and Edmund, it would be impossible to avert the worst consequences of her fault.

Whichever way Bernice looked, the ruin was surely going to follow.

If this occurred, the relationship with Jessup Austin, whose esteem and affection she now possessed, would be gone. But, on the contrary, she had grown to love and honor him.

Oh, God, to lose them! To forfeit the place she held in her husband's heart! Yet, she felt this must be the penalty she must pay for the fraud she committed.

Her threat of doing away with herself was not an idle threat. She would not survive dishonor.

Bernice had begged her wronged and unhappy daughter for a delay until the vessel reaches port. But then... what happens then? She didn't know. She knew she had a reprieve, which was getting shorter as the big ship neared its final destination. In the meantime, Bernice was an unhappy woman who was a self-condemned prisoner in her stateroom.

Under the appeal of seasickness, which no longer existed, she kept to her chambers as long as the sun was up, scarcely daring to go out of her cabin lest she might be recognized by one of the two persons who had known her back in Black Rock Cove.

She never ventured out to the dining room and took all her meals in the stateroom.

She did visit the deck to get fresh air and look at the vast ocean they traveled. She was always heavily veiled and looked out to sea when she sat near the railing.

The voyage was more than half over before the sickness of Amala illness passed. She was finally declared by Doctor Sanders clear of any danger.

One day, while sitting comfortably in a lounge chair on the deck, she was joined by Edmund.

"Hello, sweetheart," she panted after reviving from her dizzy spell. How long will it be before we reach Lourenco Marques?"

"Maybe ten more days or so if we don't hit rough weather. Cheer up! We will soon be pulling into port," said Edmund, who thought his wife was weary of such a long voyage at sea.

Amala sighed profoundly. Edmund didn't know the truth. To her apprehension, the end of the sea voyage was the end of peace, hope... the end of love, and life!

Amala was a good Christian girl. Reared in the Presbyterian Church but now found the closer they got to shore, the more her faith was passing through a fiery trial at this very moment.

To demonstrate how terrible an influence her mother's fault and her own dilemma had upon this shy girl, it is only necessary to say that there was some hope that the ship would run into a storm and never reach land.

She thought, *"Oh, God, what should I do? I will never, never own up to this hope, far less than express it. I would be terrified to hear another human being express such hope. To wish a ship with over a thousand people on board should sink in a storm at sea to save one guilty and three interested persons from shame and sorrow! But, please God, why do I even have such horrible and monstrous thoughts?"*

Wait! Was there a dark cloud rising on the distant horizon? Was a whisper of stormy weather ahead said from people walking the deck?

Amala continued her thoughts. *"Hush! Come now, Amala, whisper not this hope. But if the ship should founder, I will not be compelled to reveal my mother's dishonor and drive her to her death below the ocean waves!"*

At Sunday morning services in the main cabin, Amala made a discovery that filled her with self-horror, far too great for tears. From listening to the pastor, she could only, in deep humiliation, recognize and acknowledge the secret evil that was inside her. She prayed to the Heavenly Father to take it away.

After her prayer, there came a strange trust. She couldn't see any ray of light... no ground of hope, but she trusted in the Lord and found some peace.

The ship was nearing Port Lourenco Marques, the capital of Mozambique.

It was cold, and icicles hung from the railings of the vessel as it got closer and closer to shore. Christmas had just been celebrated onboard the ship, of which she took no part in the festivities.

Early in the morning on the day before New Year's, that word began to spread like wildfire across the cabins that land was within sight.

A few hours later, all the passengers who could leave their cabins were assembled on the deck with binoculars which they passed from one to another... anxiously viewing the rocky coastline.

Amala, who remained on the deck all wrapped up, went below as the temperature dipped with the setting sun and visited her mother. She stayed with her for several hours, describing the terrific scenery of the coastline she had seen through some binoculars another woman loaned her to look. But unfortunately, she didn't mention one time the subject that was uppermost in both of their thoughts.

Later in the evening, utterly exhausted from all the sightseeing and her visit with her mother, she retired to her own berth and slept soundly until the following day.

The following day she found herself all alone as Edmund was off doing his soldier duties early. She began to get dressed warmly for the day. While doing so, she noticed the slow motion of the big ship had entirely ceased and that it was moving along as swiftly and smoothly as a steamboat on a river cruise.

This circumstance, taken in connection with all the hustle and bustle in the hallway outside her door, revealed that they had entered Espiritu Bay and were very near the port in Lourenco Marques. It meant the passengers were preparing to depart soon and go onshore.

Aloud, while looking out the port hole in her room, she said, "The day of judgment has come!"

Amala hurried through her getting ready and headed up to the deck. What a remarkable change! What a delightful scene met her view.

The ship was being made ready for departure. It rode at anchor in a beautiful cove at the head of which began Lourenco Marques, the capital city of approximately one million people. In the distance could be seen richly wooded hills beyond were lofty mountains whose blue summits towered up into the clouds.

One could not ask for a more glorious morning. The bright sun had just come up in all its dazzling splendor. It dispersed the few clouds that now floated, white and rose-colored, over a deep blue sky. The surface of Espiritu Bay was as smooth as glass and blue and brilliant as a sapphire.

The sandy beach on both sides of the long dock where the ship was anchored was as bright as the sapphire bay and glistened in the sun's rays until its sands appeared golden and its sand pebbles amber.

Amala stood and watched all the seamen working to moor the ship, tying ropes on posts up and down the long protruding dock from the mainland. She gazed at the scene with complete surprise and delight that made her for just a second blind to the crowds of friends from the ship covering the deck... and, oblivious to the fact that this, to her, was the "Day of Doom!"

There came a touch on her elbow. She turned and saw a woman wrapped up tightly wearing a veil standing next to her. It was her mother. She hadn't seen her on the deck for several weeks, and now, at her touch, she trembled and involuntarily backed up.

"It appears the ship is anchored. We will soon be departing, love," whispered her mother.

"Yes, we are."

"Yonder, there is the great big city of Lourenco Marques."

"Yes."

"We have spent our last night and eaten our last meal onboard the ship."

"I suppose we have, Mother."

"They will be opening the exit gates to the dock at any moment."

"Yes."

"And, the 'Day of Judgment' has come, has it not!"

"Yes, it has, Mother."

"Yes... yes.... Yes!" angrily whispered the woman. "What do you mean by 'yes'?"

"I am only agreeing with you, Mother," replied Amala.

"Since you are being so truthful this morning, tell me, Amala, do you intend on telling Edmund of his right to the Sabrina Covington estate today?"

"For the past several weeks, I had done nothing but think about what I needed to do when we reached the shore. So, to answer your question, Mother... yes, I must inform him. I have already kept this secret from him for too long. And, as you know, I would rather die than tell him, but I must. I simply must!" sighed Amala.

"You will be a *matricide*! As I've told you, I will not outlive such a dishonor," the woman hissed.

"Oh, Mamma, please... Don't say such terrible words. They make my blood run cold!"

Before another word could be said, Ambassador Austin rushed up and took Dianne by the hand. "Come dear, they have opened the gates. We can depart now."

Dianne placed her hand in the bend of her husband's arm and began to depart the ship.

"Come, Amala, take my arm. I am allowed an absence from my regiment to help you off and to our hotel in the city."

"But everything is still in our chambers on the ship."

"They will be perfectly safe for now, dear. But, come, we must hurry."

Walking down the plank to the main dock, they looked a hundred yards away and saw another ship. "What is that other ship, Edmund."

After a quick look, he replied, "It's the Dethardt that was scheduled to sail here ten days after us, and here she is already here before us. It probably made the fastest passage between Seattle and Mozambique in all of history. This is kinda funny, dear. We will have the news from home more than a week after the news we are bringing with us," laughed the lieutenant.

A canon is heard onshore. The sound echoed from the downtown coastline buildings. It again sounded in a welcome for the new ambassador to their country from the United States.

A large crowd was standing up and down the wharf to welcome the new ambassador and his newlywed wife.

Once they reached the shore, Ambassador Jessup Austin led his wife out to a limousine especially waiting for them but was met by many dignitaries gathered to receive him. They were compelled to exchange handshakes and greetings before they were allowed to take a car to their next stop at the capitol building.

Amala sat in one car with Colonel Palermo's wife, Vittoria, Doctor Sanders's wife, Gabriella, and the minister's wife, Cassandra Kennedy.

The vehicles reached the capital in a bustle of reception. It was difficult, but they made their way inside the building.

The ceremonies welcoming the new ambassador were most uninteresting but brief. A few forms were signed, a few speeches made, and it was over as fast as it had begun.

Edmund Richter was kept on duty this entire time and sent his wife, Haley Dawn, with a friend and fellow passenger, to the Ocean View Hotel, where rooms had been engaged for her until his officer quarters at the barracks could be made comfortable for her reception.

Nightfall came. Amala sat in her hotel room, waiting for her husband's arrival. Her wait was not that of longing for Edmund but with dread. Amala sat by the window high up in the hotel, looking out over the ocean. She prayed and prayed that some kind of deliverance might come to avoid all this trouble. She hoped that her prayers might be answered.

She believed it was her duty to tell the awful secret to her husband at the first opportunity she got. It was his right to know, and she should tell it this very night before either of them was to go to sleep... unless something would make it impossible for her to keep her resolve.

A rap came on her door.

"Who's there," she replied.

"A messenger from the barracks, ma'am, from your husband."

Amala opened the door, took the message in her hand, and returned to her chair by the window. She opened it.

"Dearest Amala. I feel terrible that I can't get leave for tonight to return to you at the hotel. I will be off duty tomorrow morning and will be there right away. Keep Haley Dawn in your room with you tonight, and make sure your door is locked and you are secure. You need not be afraid of anything. You are quite safe in that hotel. It is the finest in the city. God Bless you, sweetheart! Edmund."

"Another respite!" Amala thought to herself as she made a deep sigh... not of disappointment but of relief. She then replied with a message and gave it to the waiting messenger for her reply.

"My dearest Edmund.

Do not give yourself another thought about your delay. It is your job. You must attend to it. I'm not afraid to stay here with Haley in this well-filled hotel. If circumstances permit, I would like to never be parted from you for even an hour. God Bless you, too, Edmund.

Amala."

After handing the note to the messenger, she sat down in a chair and was able to breathe again.

No sooner had she sent her message back to Edmund than there came another rap on the door. She was confused but slowly cracked the door, thinking it was the messenger who had forgotten to tell her something. But, instead, it was the bellhop from downstairs who was delivering another message, this time from an unknown person.

Amala took the letter and knew right away when looking at the handwriting on the outside that it was from her mother. She opened it trembling with fear for what she was going to read. She read,

"Dearest Daughter.
I know your husband has been occupied all day at the barracks, and
you have had no opportunity of confiding in him the dreaded secret you
and I have with one another. But nevertheless, I know you feel it is your
duty as a wife to tell it, even at the price of your mother's life and
reputation.
I am alone in my private quarters in the penthouse suite as the
ambassador is busy with some gentlemen this evening. I must have a
chat with you dear this very night. I received correspondence from the
Dethardt with startling news from Black Rock Cove. It profoundly
affects your and my life. I must tell you the information right away
before you have any discussion with your husband. Come up and talk
with me right away. With love, your Mother."

Amala folded the note and put it in her pocket. Then, she summoned Haley Dawn from the other room adjacent to hers. "Dear, I am going up to visit the ambassador's wife. I shall not be long, but be sure to lock the door behind me. Okay?"

"Very well, Amala. I will be fine."

Amala grabbed the elevator and went to the top floor. When she got off, two armed men were outside the penthouse doors. They had already been instructed to let Amala pass.

Amala entered the room. The malachite clock on the beautiful Italian marble mantelpiece struck seven o'clock as their hands met.

"I thank you for coming, daughter. I suppose if you got the chance to tell your husband today that I kept him out of the Covington Estate by fraud, that if brought home to me, would be a felony, punishable with many years in prison."

"Mother, what terrible words you say. I can't see it in that light. I would have never put it in that way!" Amala exclaimed with a shudder.

"Come, dear and sit down," said her mother as she led Amala to a scarlet red satin sofa, pushed her gently upon it, and seated herself at her side.

"Mother, you must listen carefully to me. I do love you... with all my heart. I would much rather die at my young age, happily married, than tell that secret whose disclosure must bring you sorrow, terror, and humiliation. But, Mother... it is still my sacred duty to tell," said the girl with a sobbing voice.

"It is no longer your duty to open your mouth on the subject, Amala," the ambassador's wife curtly said.

"I don't understand what you're saying."

"I told you that I just received news from Black Rock Cove by the Dethardt's mail pouch, which sailed over a week for Lourenco Marques after we did but got here two days earlier than we did. I guess they didn't run into storms like we did. Who knows?"

"Yes, Mamma."

"Well, the news was from my attorney. It changes everything. It relieves you from all responsibility regarding Edmund's fortune."

"Oh, Mother, this is a blessing from God if what you say is true. Can light have truly arisen in this deep darkness? Hope in all this despair? What is this news, Mother?"

"You need to hear Doug Gibson's letter, my attorney. That will tell its own story. I just got the letter delivered not more than ten minutes ago. No sooner did I read the letters than I wrote that note to you to come and visit with me. I wanted to share the good news."

"Come, Mamma... that news?" eagerly exclaimed Amala.

"Listen, darling."

"My dear Madam.
I fear the announcement I'm about to give you will bring you as much
of a surprise as it did for me when I first discovered the facts.
You might remember that on the first time we read the last will and
testament of Sabrina Covington, I informed you that I hadn't been

employed to draw up that particular will and that my father, my
predecessor, had drawn it up under the verbal instructions from
Sabrina Covington. The custody of that Will came to me for
safekeeping after my father had passed.

When I brought the Will from the stack of documents I maintained in
a safe, I hadn't the slightest suspicion that a later Will existed.

Last week, however, on opening a box containing some older oil leases
to which I wish to refer, I found, to my great surprise, a will dated some
ten years later than the one under which you inherited all the property
and the assets of Sabrina Covington.

This latest last will and testament, which was drawn up and witnessed,
the entire estate, property, and wealth, is to be bequeathed equally and
unconditionally to you and to Edmund Richter, share and share alike.

In closing today, the last will and testament are valid in a court of law,
and the nephew, by the marriage of the late Sabrina Covington,
Lieutenant Honorable Edmund Richter, inherits half of everything.

I am very sorry, Dianne, for this on your account.

I await your instructions on the premises. I am madam, your obedient
servant... Douglas Gibson"

"There, Amala," said her mother, "that's the lawyer's letter. I have the legal right to one-half of my late aunt's estate. Edmund has a legal right to the other half and no more.

So, isn't this wonderful? Now you don't need to denounce your mother to your husband," concluded the ambassador's wife.

"No, I have not! I can't tell you how much I thank God for answering my prayers!" exclaimed Amala, bursting into tears and sobbing for joy.

"Of course, I do have a confession indeed, which this new Will at once forces upon me," said Bernice in a grave tone.

"Mother, however it ends, you will feel much happier for making the confession. It has got to be a terrible cross to bear throughout life for so many years in your bosom a secret from a confiding and loving husband," murmured Amala, now with her arms around her mother's neck. She pressed her lips to her mother's cheek.

"Ahhh, you've found that out in just these last six weeks' experience, my poor child!" sighed the woman returning her daughter's caress.

"Yes, I found that out in the last six weeks when I kept a terrible secret from Edmund," breathed Amala in an inaudible voice.

"Now, Amala, you must return to your hotel room. I am sure Haley Dawn is wide awake, jumping at every sound she hears," she said with a light laugh. "I will make a full explanation to the Ambassador and trust in his generosity and affection for forgiveness."

On reaching her room, she walked inside and found Haley Dawn watching television. No sooner did Amala walk in than Haley used the remote to mute the tv program. "Amala, how far are we from Australia?"

"From Australia?" repeated Amala musingly. "Let me see. No more than a week's travel, I suppose."

"Oh, so far. I didn't know that," she added, falling into mournful silence. How was she to find her sweetheart so far away from where they were located?

Amala instructed Haley to go to her own bed. She switched on the lamp next to a table near the window, sat down in an easy chair, and kicked off her shoes. She was greatly relieved of the terrible necessity of denouncing her mother to Edmund. The second will of the late Sabrina Covington had given Edmund an equal share in the estate... all that he had a legal right to expect. Her mother couldn't wrong him out of a single penny.

The fraud she committed was now an affair to be settled between the ambassador and her mother. Since it no longer affected the interests of Edmund, Amala was exonerated from the responsibility of enlightening him on the subject.

But what a task her mother had laying ahead of her... to confess the fraud of which she had been guilty to the noble-hearted husband who had loved and worshiped his wife as one of the kindest and most remarkable women in the world!

Amala thought, "I fear to think what might result from Mother's confession. Would the ambassador's affection for his wife survive the shock of seeing her fall off her pedestal of honor, which his faith had completely enthroned her? The man can't possibly honor her as he had before. Can he even continue to love my mother?" Amala shuddered at the doubt that crept inside her heart.

She began getting ready for bed. Amala felt no further compunction about keeping her mother's secret. Since her secret didn't affect her husband's interests, it was not strictly a matter between her mother and her stepfather. But nevertheless, she felt bound to respect it.

Amala went to bed. It had been a very long day.

It wasn't until after breakfast the following day did Amala see her husband.

She had taken breakfast in her room. It was half past eight when Edmund arrived. Edmund threw off his coat and pulled out a packet of letters in his hand. "Well, you are a lucky girl. There are numerous letters for you. There's one from the Thomas Estate, one from Oliver, one from Alyssa Nicole and Victoria, one from Jessica Thomas, and one from Doctor Cantu. Quite a pile, Amala. And they are all dated a week after we departed."

He handed the letters to his wife, opened a Black Rock Cove newspaper, and started to read it. "Oh, my goodness, Amala. Right here on the first page. I have come into an unexpected fortune," he said, adding, "Hello?"

Amala looked up from her stack of letters.

"Sweetheart, I've unexpectedly come into a fortune!"

"What about it, dear?"

"Listen!" He read,

"It is rumored that a second will of the late Sabrina Covington has been found, one of a later date than the one which was read after the funeral, which it supersedes. By this will, the enormous wealth of the deceased Sabrina Covington is bequeathed equally and unconditionally to her grandniece, Dianne Smith, now Dianne Austin, wife of Ambassador Jessup Austin, and Lieutenant Edmund Richter, who is her nephew by marriage."

"I'm afraid Edmund, I have heard the news."

"You have heard it before, Amala?"

"Yes, Edmund. The ambassador's wife requested I come to the penthouse so she might speak with me. She had just received a letter from her attorney, Douglas Gibson."

"Then all of this must be true, then! Under what circumstances was this last will found?" asked Edmund.

Amala answered him.

"Oh, Amala, this makes our life together so much better. Why didn't you tell me this since you already knew it? I would have thought you would be bursting with excitement on bringing me the news," demanded Edmund with serious eyes.

"I don't know. I was waiting for my moth-—I was waiting for the ambassador's wife to make the communication with you. Also, you gave me very little time to say anything coming in here and throwing those other letters at me and started reading the paper," she paused to catch her breath and tried to change the subject. "Edmund, tell me. How long will I remain in this hotel separated from you?"

"Only until they are finished constructing the officers' quarters at the barracks."

"How long will it take to finish the work, Edmund?"

"Maybe a week. But now, about your letters. Have you read all your mail?"

"I have skimmed over them."

"No one has married or died or were born since we left?"

"No one, sweetheart."

Haley interrupted the two. "There is one of the soldiers from the ambassador's office to deliver a message to you, ma'am," she said while walking across the room and laying the note in Amala's lap.

Amala opened it and read,

"Amala, my dear. All is over. I had a full explanation with Jessup this evening. He has forgiven me. However, I am overwhelmed with sorrow and humiliation! I now know how great my sin has been through the deep grief it has caused him. And, although he is deeply grieved than angry, and though having forgiven me, he will never, by word or by look, reproach me with my fault, yet I fear I have fallen so far beneath his esteem that I can never be instated in his life!

Oh, how bitter it is, my dear.

The harshest thing he said to me was, 'Since you were married under your maiden name, to which you had no further right, we must be quietly remarried by our minister, Pastor Kennedy, under your proper name. We must also not let the guiltless young people suffer for our misfortunes. Send for your daughter and her husband. You see them alone first. It will be less embarrassing. I will see them later."

"Yes, Amala, those were his words. I never loved and honored him so much as now. He has gone out and left me here to receive you and Edmund. Come at once and bring him with you. Your Mother."

"p.s. – You should show Edmund this letter so that he is prepared for his visit here this morning."

Amala continued looking down at the letter and folded it up.

"That sure is a long letter, my love. Who is it from, and what is it about... if you don't mind me asking? You don't need to answer unless you want to," said Edmund in a bantering tone.

"It is from my moth-—from the ambassador's wife. She wants me immediately up at her suite in the hotel. Will you accompany me there, if you please, sweetheart," said Amala with some embarrassment.

"Certainly! I shall be happy to meet this woman who married the ambassador. I have never yet once set eyes on her face?"

"Yes, I know," replied Amala.

"But, my love, I wonder why is it that your thoughts are running so much on your mother this morning? You have said 'Mother' twice and corrected yourself by substituting the ambassador's wife."

"Because, Edmund, there was a very good reason for that slip of my tongue, which I will explain to you as we go up to the hotel's top floor," she replied in a grave tone.

"Is Mrs. Austin like your mom in appearance?" he persisted.

"Yes, you might take her to be the same woman," the lieutenant's wife answered.

"I thought so, too."

"Thought what?"

"That everything about that woman... her form, her mannerisms, the way she walks were strikingly suggestive of your mother."

"You will see her face to face this morning in a matter of minutes, dear."

The two got on the elevator as Edmund pushed the Penthouse Suite button. As soon as the elevator began to go up, Amala reached over and pulled the red stop button out. The elevator came to an abrupt stop. She then put her mother's letter in Edmund's hand and said, "Please, my love, read this letter before you make any more comments."

Edmund took the letter and began to read.

Amala never once took her eyes off his face as he read. But, on the contrary, she watched with the greatest of interest.

He read the letter, backed up, and read the letter another two times before looking up. Then, he raised his bewildered eyes to meet those of his beautiful but fatigued wife. "What in Hell is this letter about, Amala? I am beside myself! Mrs. Austin appears to be your mother... an impossibility, you know."

"The letter is exactly as it appears, Edmund. Mrs. Austin is, in fact, my mother, the one and only Bernice Luther."

"Mrs. Austin, the ambassador's wife, is your mother?"

"Yes," she breathed in her response.

"Who then was Bernice Luther... your foster mother?" demanded Edmund in a distraught tone.

"She is my mother. She married the ambassador."

"No! This is totally incomprehensible! Your mother died in Demon Gorge. They found her body and buried it in the Presbyterian Church cemetery. Dianne Smith, the niece of Sabrina Covington, co-heir to her great estates."

"Yes. My mother was Miss Dianne Smith before she was Mrs. Bernice Luther. Her first marriage was concealed from her aunt and all persons except her few close friends. When Sabrina passed away, she simulated her death as Bernice Luther so that she might appear as Dianne Smith and claim her inheritance of the entire Covington Estate," Amala explained.

"So, under the name of Dianne Smith, she deceived and married Ambassador Austin? Is that what you're saying, Amala?"

Amala didn't reply verbally and only nodded her head.

"And this is what she was talking about when she confessed to the ambassador?"

Again, Amala nodded her head.

"How long have you known about these facts, Amala?"

"Only since I came onboard the ship. I recognized my mother looking back at the mainland. It was such a shock! I thought, just like you, that she was in Heaven. I was going to tell you right away. I didn't wish to keep the secret from you, Edmund... not for a single day. But my mother pleaded with me not to tell anyone until we reached Lourenco Marques. She took an oath in front of me and swore she would throw herself off the ship and end her life if I told. Oh, Edmund... Edmund. I need you to understand. She is my mother! I had to keep her secret but wanted to tell you so much. It caused me to have a nervous breakdown and remain in my cabin for so long. I was going to tell you yesterday, our first day after landing, but you didn't come home until this morning."

"Tell me, Amala, what induced your mother, at last, to divulge the secret to Ambassador Austin?"

"The news of the discovery of the second will, and also the knowledge from me that it could no longer be kept hidden," said Amala.

Edmund said nothing and reached over and pushed the stop button, allowing them to continue their walk to the ambassador's suite on the top floor.

Chapter SEVEN
The End of the Secret

Amala's heart was throbbing violently in her chest.
"Oh, Edmund, please," she whispered, "remember in the midst of justice... remember mercy! Please do not wound her by words or your look if you can do so. You have no idea how much she has suffered."

"Remember? In the middle of all things, dear, I will promise that I will not say anything nor do anything that would hurt your mother more than she already is," replied the young husband.

Two armed guards received them at the suite's double doors on the top floor. The door was opened, and one of the guards announced, "Mister and Mrs. Edmund Richter," and returned to his station and closed the door.

The couple found themselves in a large elegant parlor, upholstered in rose-colored silk and adorned with ornate mirrors on the wall, paintings, and numerous vases made by the natives from different places in Mozambique.

A few steps away, Dianne Smith was on a sofa in a beautiful white cashmere dress. Her face was so pale it was a toss-up which was whiter, her skin or the cashmere fabric of the dress. She attempted to stand up and receive her daughter and husband but sank back down onto the sofa, half fainting.

Edmund rushed over and caught her arm to help her sit down.

Mrs. Austin attempted to address them, but her voice waned into total silence. Finally, after catching her breath, she said, "Please, dear, you and Edmund sit down."

Edmund grabbed two chairs and placed them close to the sofa for him and his wife to sit.

"Amala has told you all," said the woman in a low tone, turning to Edmund.

"Yes, ma'am... all," he answered.

"What do you think of me, Lieutenant Richter?" she asked in a low, monotone voice.

Edmund didn't know what to say at first. He hesitated in answering.

"You may go ahead and say what you're thinking, young man. What do you think of me?" repeated Dianne.

"I think, Mrs. Austin—-."

"It is Dianne. I am your mother-in-law."

"Uh, very well. I think," he paused a moment, "Dianne, you have suffered and yielded to an almost irresistible temptation."

"Yes, indeed, a quite irresistible one for sure. I couldn't help myself, Edmund. No woman was ever placed in so horrible a dilemma as I was put in by my aunt's first cruel last will and testament. She had no right to make my celibacy the sole condition of my inheritance of that estate, which should have been mine unconditionally and right at her death. What do you think?" she suddenly demanded defiantly and aggressively.

"No, ma'am, she had no right to make such a will with those conditions, " Edmund replied without hesitation.

Amala watched Edmund answer but added nothing.

"I was very young, Edmund. Everyone said I had great beauty and was extremely warm-hearted. I had already fallen in love and was secretly married when Aunt Sabrina told me the unnatural and cruel terms of her first will. I can't tell you just how shocked I was. I was terrified beyond all measure. I was always told that since I was the only blood relative, I would unconditionally inherit all her possessions at her death... that they were mine by right. But, again, Edmund, was not my assumption a normal one?"

"Yes, ma'am," replied Amala's husband.

"What could I do? I was still in school at the expense of my aunt. My young husband was still at college at the cost of his father. When we were married, we were separated and only to be consummated when we could move back in with one another. What was I to do? Confess my marriage to my Aunt Sabrina and be turned out on the street to beg and starve? And to bring down the anger of my husband's father on the man I loved. Again, Edmund, what was I to do?" demanded Dianne again, turning fiercely from Amala to Edmund, who sat beside her.

"Nothing," sighed Amala reluctantly.

Edmund remained quiet.

"That is precisely what I did... nothing! I made no confession of my marriage at the time and went back to school. When I graduated, I moved to Portland with my husband but still came and spent my summer vacations with my aunt and Easter and Christmas holidays with her.

I kept my secret throughout my short-married life and my time as a widow. However, the death of Aunt Sabrina brought my affairs to a crisis. I could no longer live my life as two different people. I had to die as Bernice Luther to live as the heiress of the Sabrina Covington Estate. As you would agree, I committed an unpardonable fraud," added Dianne. She then paused and waited on a reply from Edmund.

"Dianne, you suffered a horrible temptation," gently retorted Edmund.

"A very irresistible one, as I have told you before," Dianne said emphatically.

"Yes, Mother, it was hard," Amala sighed.

"The alternative that I had was, on the one hand, the inheritance of the enormous wealth, my own rightful fortune, at the price of the suppression of my marriage, which was nobody's business whatsoever. But, on the other hand, the loss of my just inheritance with absolute destitution for myself and you, Amala. Do you see?"

"Yes, we see," answered the couple simultaneously.

"I simulated death as Bernice Luther. I claimed and enjoyed my rightful inheritance as Miss Dianne Smith. Let me ask you, did I do so very wrong? Please, I need both of you to answer me," said the woman.

"Dianne, I am not your judge," replied Edmund in a quiet and grave tone.

"I understand the hidden censure of your words, Edmund," said Dianne coldly, and then, turning to her daughter, she asked, "What do you say, daughter?"

"Oh, Mother, please... please don't ask me. It's not for me to criticize you," said Amala as a crimson tide swept across her face.

"Very well. I can see in your faces and the words you use that you are sidestepping my question. I can tell that in both of your hearts, you judge me unjustly! I was not selfish in what I did. I made a provision for my one and only daughter! I founded a place for homeless men and women. I made large donations to nearly every charity in Black Rock Cove. And, Edmund, I was only waiting for a favorable opportunity of dividing my wealth with you... not because I recognized your right to any portion of it but because the entire amount had been willed to you on a certain contingency. Do you both believe this"

"Certainly, Dianne. It would never occur to me to doubt one word you have said," replied the lieutenant.

"My marriage to Jessup made no difference in my plans. I explained to him that I wanted to divide my wealth with you, Edmund, the grandnephew of Sabrina's husband, who was the person she inherited her wealth from. Jessup told me that he approved what he termed as justice of my intentions."

"And they were just, Mother," said Amala, who appeared anxious to seize any good opportunity of agreeing with her mother.

"Ahhh, but the unexpected meeting with my daughter on the ship's deck the first day. Naturally, I pleaded for and obtained a delay of my concealment until we should reach Lourenco Marques. But, listen carefully, your wife... had she told you about my secret yesterday evening, I would have ended my unhappy life by killing myself before the news of the second will arrived. Yes! I see it in your faces. How stupid that would have been. But I assure you I would have died by my own hand!" said Amala's mother solemnly.

Amala began to shudder intensely. Edmund placed his arm around her waist to support her and comfort her.

"That second will, conceived and executed in the spirit of justice, makes everything right. However, there was one exception to it all... one bitter exception. That will be my punishment for life. The man I fell in love with and will honor to the ends of this earth has now lost all respect for me. He is very merciful and affectionate, but he is no longer confiding. In his high sense of honor, he looks at my faults in all of this with great severity. This is while at the same time treating me with wonderful tenderness. It is so difficult to lose the esteem of so good and noble of a man," said Dianne.

"Mother, you may recover his esteem," said Amala with great emotion.

"Never, my dear!" exclaimed Mrs. Austin. "I have his love, but it's not the love of an honorable man for an honorable wife. It is the love of a compassionate man for the erring woman who is legally bound to him! My husband does not find impending destitution and irresistible temptation any excuse for my behavior. I really don't know if I can bear my punishment."

Neither Amala nor Edmund knew what to say. They sought their thoughts but said nothing. They both knew too well that what she said was the truth.

She took a handkerchief, wiped away her tears, and shouted, "Willie. Bring our refreshments in here to the coffee table, please."

Within a few moments, the butler brought an arrangement of cakes, pies, and some other delicacies native to the country and spread them out before the guests. "Go ahead. Eat and enjoy. The ambassador will be here presently. Amala, have some hot chocolate. I find it an excellent sedative to the nervous system," she said with a faint smile.

While the three of them sipped on some hot chocolate, Dianne, in some embarrassment, continued with a further explanation. "Well, let me continue now that we have some refreshments... those that help our nervous systems, my wonderful husband, thinks that since I was married to him under my maiden name of Smith, to which I no longer claim instead of my widowed name of Luther, he wishes to make our union legal and asked the minister that traveled on the ship with us to remarry us to make us legally married. So, he and the regiment's chaplain will attend us here in a short while. The ceremony will be held in this room quietly with only two witnesses... you two newlyweds."

The butler came and cleared the table.

In five minutes, Jessup Austin and the Chaplain, Jeffery Kennedy, walked into the room. Jessup walked over, took Dianne's hand, lifted her into his arms, and gently kissed her crimson brow. Then, he lifted Amala up and kissed her ever so gently on the cheek as he knew how much humiliation the girl suffered for her mother. Then, he stuck his hand out and shook the hand of Lieutenant Edmund Richter.

Jessup and his bride-to-be, again, stood at the table side by side. On the bride's left stood Amala, and on the right-hand side of Jessup stood Edmund... as the two witnesses. The officiating minister, in plain clothes, stood before all of them with a small Bible in his hand. It wasn't long, and the second ceremony was done and witnessed by Edmund and Amala. Finally, the new marriage certificate marrying Jessup Austin to Bernice Luther was finished. Everyone signed on the bottom lines.

Amala had the time to observe her stepfather. She quickly saw how heavy of a blow he suffered and deprived him of respect for his beloved wife, her mother. He appeared to have aged ten years since she saw him sworn in at the capital only a day before. Now, he seemed to be a careworn and sorrow-stricken older man. However, his manner was calm and controlled, and his demeanor toward his guilty wife was tender, and toward his daughter and son-in-law, kind and considerate.

"I regret to break up this wonderful moment, but I must be back at the regiment very soon."

"Oh, I am sorry to hear that, Edmund. But, since you go on duty now, perhaps you might be able to join us for supper this evening? We will dine at seven o'clock. Will you join us then?"

"Yes, sir, Mister Austin. I will return after I am off duty."

"And, Edmund, when you are in my presence away from the public, please call me Jessup. I am, after all, your father-in-law," he said with a broad smile.

The ambassador added, "I have a meeting with Colonel Palermo. Therefore, I will share your taxi with you, Edmund."

"Yes, sir."

Jessup walked over, lifted Bernice's hand respectfully to his lips, and bade her good morning. Then, he turned and looked at Amala. "Goodbye for the present, my dear. Do your best to cheer your mother while we are gone," he gently pressed her hand and departed the room.

There was not much cheering that went on for the remainder of the day. It was perhaps the dullest day Amala had ever passed in the entire course of her life.

Amala was thrilled when the hour came that brought the ambassador and her husband back for supper.

Later in the evening, several visitors dropped by the suite. The ambassador introduced Amala as his daughter, Mrs. Edmund Richter, and his son-in-law, Lieutenant Edmund Richter.

Since none of the visitors knew any different, they took the introductions as fact and not mere courtesy.

At eleven o'clock in the evening, Edmund and Amala took leave and returned to their rooms down in the hotel.

A few days later, the housing for officers was completed. Amala joined her husband at his quarters in the barracks. They were nicely done up and comfortable.

Amala depended much on the friendships of the ladies of the regiment. There were quite a few who stayed in the officer's housing.

Amala found the opposite side of the world more habitable and enjoyable than she had ever imagined. The officers' quarters were very nicely done. The other officers' wives quickly became friends with daily socials at someone's place.

All was going fine for Amala, but not so for her attendant, Haley Dawn Johnson. Since their arrival at the barracks, her spirits had drooped and continued to sink.

One day, while attending, Amala said, "It gives me a lot of distress looking at you so depressed in spirits, Haley. Are you unhappy here? Can I help? Tell me what's wrong... I am your good friend. If you wish to go home, I will help procure passage on the next ship to take you home."

"No, Amala, I am not depressed and missing home. I came here with you because I had no friends back home. And, because you, my only friend, were leaving the country, I wished to come with you. So why should I wish to return?"

"Then, Haley, if you're not homesick, what is the matter with you, girl? Tell me your troubles, and I will help you. That's what good friends do," Amala said in a kind tone as Haley suddenly broke down and burst into tears.

Amala gave her young friend a moment to collect her composure and continued. "Then, if you're not missing home, what is wrong? I will help you if only you let me. Tell me what's wrong."

"Okay. Do you remember Lucas Durano, the man falsely accused of killing Samuel Knight? He knew no more of the crime than I did."

"That tramp? Yes, I remember his name."

"Amala, he was very well educated and kind as could be. But everyone did call him a tramp. You might disagree, but when a wealthy man walks all over the world, people praise him and talk highly of him. But, on the other hand, if a poor man walks in the same steps, people call him a vagabond, or as you say, a tramp, and commit him to homelessness! So please forgive me for speaking so freely, ma'am."

"I can readily excuse you for defending your friend, Haley Dawn. But what about this man... Durano?"

"Well, Amala... he and I were engaged to get married."

"Haley!" exclaimed the woman in dismay.

"Lucas had no bad habits except he wandered back and forth picking up odd jobs here and there. But he promised to stop that, get a permanent job, and settle down once we married. So... yes, we were engaged."

"Oh, my goodness, Haley. I am so sorry. I didn't mean to say he was a tramp. So, where is he now, Haley?" asked Mrs. Richter.

"He is in Australia now. But he could be anywhere, and the cities are so far apart on that big country that I would never find him."

"Yes, they are."

"I am as far away from Lucas now as if I had just stayed back in Black Rock Cove," she paused to catch her breath and added, "at least if I had stayed in Black Rock Cove, he would know where to write to me. Now, he doesn't."

"I am afraid that finding him will be difficult. He is in hiding, I am sure. Have you forgotten that a warrant for his arrest is still outstanding for the murder of Samuel Knight?"

"Yes, I can't forget that, but he was falsely accused of that horrible crime. I thought he would be safe in Australia since it is across the world from Black Rock Cove."

"I am so sorry for you, Haley Dawn. The only thing I can recommend to you is to trust in Divine providence," said Amala and a sympathetic tone.

"I will do that, ma'am. Otherwise, I think I might go mad," said the girl.

Amala began to allow Haley in on her daily strolls around the woods and the nearby lake. When Edmund was off, they would take a ride in the jeep into the countryside. The scenery was some of the most beautiful and picturesque that could be imagined and gave great delight to both Amala and Haley.

On one occasion, a larger party of the regiment picked up two jeeps consisting of Edmund and Amala, the Reverend Jeffery Kennedy, and his wife, along with their daughter and a good friend, Terrence Adkins. They set out to explore the backcountry into the mountains only jeeps could climb.

They all ate breakfast at dawn and left the barracks at half past sunrise. They passed the prison camp where the country's largest prison camp was located and saw that the prisoners were already breaking stones along the roadside.

They rode deeper into the mountains for hours, passing beautiful scenery as seen by the leaves changing colors during the fall. Finally, at noon, they reached the base of Mt. Ramses. After an hour, they broke out lunch, partook, and continued their adventure for the day.

After a while, the road ended with the dense thicket of scrub woods and thorns, rocks, and briers, where nature defied them.

It was obvious that Mt. Ramses, whose savage fastnesses had never been visited much, was presenting an impenetrable front to the adventurers.

Edmund said, "This is the magic wilderness of 'Sleeping Beauty' from the fairy tale. It would take the magic horse and lance of the prince to break through it."

"Yep, you hit it on the head this time, Edmund."

"What?"

"You observed, did you not, that this wilderness was kinda like the impenetrable woods of *"Sleeping Beauty,"* did you not?"

"Yes, but what of it?"

"This thicket, my friend, is a wilderness surrounding a great palace of an enchanted beauty. I've known it since we arrived several weeks ago."

Jeffery Kennedy, the minister, said, "Now, Terrence, you are speaking in enigmas."

"Not at all, Pastor. I am talking about the truth. I will prove it. It will be rough, so Edmund, hang back and make sure you are in low gear four-wheel drive. The way through here will be bumpy and rough. Plus, it is not safe." He started his jeep and led the way down a dark and deep ravine that might have appeared as though one was entering the *"Gates of Hell."* Deeper and deeper, the two jeeps descended. They seemed to be leaving the daylight behind them as the forest got thicker and thicker.

Then, the sunken ravine wound around the base of Mt. Ramses for almost a mile and began to wind upwards towards the light. The jeeps climbed the mountain's steep sides until they started to catch glimpses of the blue sky above.

Higher the two jeeps traveled. They finally reached the mountain's summit upon a plateau, from which a vast panorama of marvelous beauty was spread out before them.

Everyone simultaneously said, "Wow!" The adventurers continued to gaze in a trance. Was what they were looking at part of the earth, or was it a heavenly planet with divine scenery?

Amala asked, "How in the world did you come about this magnificent view, Terrence?"

"Just by chance. I was out exploring one day all by myself and found it," answered the young officer, lifting his ballcap.

Everyone continued to stare at the magnificent view when Casandra suddenly asked, "Wait a minute, Terrence. Where is the palace if this is the woods of Sleeping Beauty?"

"Ahhh, Casandra, take your eyes as you are drawn far away at the views and look straight down the mountain below where we are standing."

Everyone did as Terrence instructed.

Halfway down the rough side of the mountain was a vast flat terrain surrounded by the woods. On the plateau was a magnificent palace glistening like white stone... right in the middle of nowhere.

"Whose place is that?" asked the chaplain.

"Not just that, but how does one get to it?" asked Casandra.

"Who lives there?" questioned Amala.

Edmund continued to stare with his eyes riveted upon the scene. "I don't believe in what I'm seeing poised in what seems like mid-air! It is nothing but a mirage... a hallucination. It is not real!"

"You have shown us the palace, but where is the princess?" asked Myra, the chaplain's daughter.

"Well, I suppose she is hidden deep in the castle, sound asleep, waiting for the prince to awaken her?" retorted Terrence.

"Do you have any idea who owns that place, Terrence?" asked Edmund.

"I only know what the town folks tell me. Supposedly, the man who owns the palace in the middle of nowhere is Serafin... Viktor Serafin, if one can believe in rumors told on the streets. He arrived here three years ago with no wife, no family, a few servants, and a boatload of money. But nevertheless, he selected that out-of-the-way place on the plateau to build his home."

"Why would a man with such means choose such an out-of-the-way place like that when there are so many beautiful places we passed getting here and more easily reachable?"

"I don't know. Yet you can't deny Edmund the paradisial beauty of the place. It is magnificent," replied Terrence.

"But how in the name of magic could the building materials be shipped up there? The entire mansion looks to me like black magic," Edmund replied.

"I have your answer, good friend. There was a pass from the base of the mountain to that plateau. It was narrow and tortuous. Serafin entered an agreement to pay the state's wages for the convict labor out of the prison camp near our barracks to make and widen a road from the bottom up to the plateau. Everything was carried up by that road."

"I wonder if the place's interior is as magnificent as the exterior."

"From what I know, there hasn't been a soul to step inside the place," Terrence replied.

Myra quickly interjected, "What about the enchanted princess? What about her? You mentioned earlier it was only the man and his servants who lived there."

"There is a rumor that the sleeping beauty or the young lady that lives there is as beautiful as any woman could possibly be, but really, I'm sure I can't tell you for sure. Only town talk," laughed Terrence.

"So do the people have any communication with the outside world, Pastor Kennedy asked.

"None whatsoever, with one exception. Once a week, when a ship arrives with mail, a servant named Winston comes to Lourenco Marques and does business such as buying goods, getting the mail and any parcels sent to them, and returns. No one else from the place is ever seen."

"Oh, Terrence, please... tell us more about the young lady... the enchanted princess or the sleeping beauty as you call her," persisted Myra.

"I'm sorry, that's all I know. If I had any imagination, I might make up a story about her," laughed Terrence.

Pastor Kennedy looked up at the sky and said, "Whoa, time is getting away from everyone. The sun is getting low. Shouldn't we turn the jeeps around and head home?"

"Oh, yes, you are right, dear," chimed in Casandra. "I don't wish to be out in this wild country after dark... not even for a million dollars," she laughed.

The adventurers descended the tortuous mountain pass, winding in and out. The sun was only thirty minutes from sinking below the horizon when they reached the barracks.

Amala, fatigued with her day's adventure, left Edmund with the other men, and retired to her room.

A surprise awaited her when she arrived.

Haley Dawn was sitting in a chair staring at the door as Amala entered. She was pale as death. Her face was stained with tears.

"My dear girl, what is the matter, Hun?" asked Amala. "Have you heard some bad news?"

"Oh, Amala, I saw him! I saw him!" exclaimed the young girl, breaking into violent sobs.

"Seen whom, Haley?"

"Him! Oh, God, it was him! Lucas!" gasped the girl.

"Lucas Durano?" asked Amala.

"Yes, ma'am. Lucas Durano! Oh, my poor Lucas!" Haley continued to sob heavily.

"I don't understand, Haley. Try to calm down for a moment and tell me what's happening. Where have you seen him?"

"Oh, Amala, after you left this morning, I went for a walk in the area you and I always stroll. This morning I was walking, after my work was done, and I saw Lucas! He was in a chain gang working on the side of the road," gasped the young girl amid suffocating tears and sobs.

"Lucas Durano, a convict on the chain gang on these roads in Lourenco Marques?" asked Amala with incredulous amazement.

"Yes, ma'am! Yes! I definitely saw him. Oh, my God, my heart is broken!" wailed Haley Dawn, wringing her hands.

"My goodness, Haley, I want to believe you, but this is quite impossible, dear. You couldn't have seen him. It had to be somebody else that resembled Lucas that you saw."

"Oh, how can it be? You say that as if I did not know my own dear friend, my fiancé, Lucas Durano! How can you say I could mistake him for any other man?" moaned Haley.

"Come now, Haley. Think. When we left Black Rock Cove a few months ago, Lucas hadn't been arrested, though there were warrants for his capture. There were also large sums of money paid for his apprehension. How could he have been caught and tried in a court of law and found guilty? And, if he were, he wouldn't be sent to a prison outside Lourenco Marques. He would have been sent to the electric chair."

"Oh, Amala, I don't know how it could have been. I stood face to face with him while he was in the chain gang on the road," persisted the tramp's sweetheart.

"Haley! I'm so sorry you went near those terrible convicts. It was no place for you to be. But, tell me one more thing. How did you get so close to him that you could recognize him working on the road... right here in Lourenco Marques?"

"After I finished my work, I went for a walk and headed a short way out of town to look at the leaves changing colors on the trees. That is when I came up on the chain gang. All the convicts had bright yellow clothes on. I got closer and stopped and stared. I wasn't sure if I should walk around them or turn around and head back. That is when one raised his head. Oh, Amala... I almost dropped dead on the spot where I was standing... it was definitely my Lucas!"

"Impossible, Haley! It was someone who looked like Lucas."

"Did he look up?"

"He started to, and a guard hit him over the head with his whip and began cursing him."

"The brute—-" said Amala.

"He dropped his face and never looked up again. Finally, the guard came over and told me to turn around and return, or I would be working on the chain gang, too."

"What did you do?"

"I came home. I was so afraid. I have been crying ever since I got here."

"What do you want me to do, Haley?"

"Well, I could never go home now that I know my poor Lucas is in prison here. I will remain and see him from time to time, even at a distance. I don't want to go home. I have no one there, ma'am!

Do you think they would let me talk with him? Maybe you wouldn't want someone like me who was on speaking terms with a lawbreaker?"

"Oh, Haley Dawn, I don't know the prison rules. I can't really answer any of your questions."

"Then you wouldn't mind if I went to see Lucas in prison and take him some things if I can?"

"Certainly not, Haley. But really, think about it good. Way over here on the other side of the world. I don't think the man you saw was Lucas, only someone who looked much like him."

"Oh, Amala, do you really think I would be face to face with a man and not recognize he was the man I was engaged to? Besides, he did not have a familiar face."

"Yet, there are other men that look like him and even have been taken for him. Do you remember all the contradictory reports back home about the places that Lucas was seen by people who knew him well?"

"The three Lucas Duranos! Oh, very well!" replied the girl with a broad smile.

"The three fishermen. Dylan James Stark, Rusty Simms, and Thomas Davison are all good men. All honest men. They had known Lucas since he was a young boy and testified on the morning of the murder, they had taken him in the boat and took and dropped him off at the wharf in Seattle. They left him there and said they weren't sure where he went from there."

"Yes, I know they said that, but Amala... they were mistaken."

"So thought the Reverend Quentin Clair, a gentleman. A man with unimpeachable veracity, who was Lucas's Sunday School teacher and Bible study teacher for years. He testified that on the morning of the murder of Samuel Knight, he got on the train out of Black Rock Cove and rode with him to Portland."

"Yes, I know. But the pastor was equally mistaken, as were the fishermen," said Haley Dawn with an unusual smile.

"And, what about Doctor Cantu, a man of his word... a good man said that two weeks after the death of Samuel Knight, he was coming by Shaw's Bend, our old home, and recognized the young man, who he also knew since boyhood, and told him to surrender to the authorities, but only got laughed at by Lucas. Haley Dawn, the good doctor, was just as confident as the others that he encountered the real Lucas Durano!"

"I still all the world is mistaking the man, except the one woman who loves him and will marry him. I am not mistaken that I saw him face to face on the chain gang."

"Maybe it is true. Maybe the man you saw was your fiancé. He might have gotten in trouble over here and be suffering a sentence in prison."

"Oh, Amala, would you talk with your husband? Could you find out for me and let me know? Please!" pleaded Haley with her hands clasped together, and her eyes turned to the heavens in prayer.

"Absolutely, Haley. If the man should prove to be your Lucas Durano, whom we knew at home, and the crime he has been charged with is not a heinous one, we might pay his fines or whatever and set him free. Maybe the ambassador could use one more attendant."

"Oh, ma'am, if you would do that, I would be eternally grateful!" exclaimed the girl. A shadow of despair passed over her face. "I know Lucas could not have been found guilty of any offense that should have condemned him to such a fate!"

"Very well. I will try to help, and so will Edmund, I know," she said, failing to remember any public notice of him will get an arrest warrant served on him for the murder of Samuel Knight.

Amala was perplexed.

Finally, it was decided that Amala would speak on behalf of the prisoner. But now, she needed to get dressed for supper.

With Haley's assistance, she was dressed and went to the living room, where she was soon joined by Edmund for supper. After supper, they sat at the table and began to chat.

"Edmund, do you remember from stateside a young man by the name of Lucas Durano?"

"Of course. How could I forget him? He was the vagabond who lived in the old lighthouse on the Knight Estate. The poor guy was falsely charged with the murder of Samuel Knight and his only friend. Yes, my dear, I remember him well," said Edmund.

"Then you do believe he was falsely accused?" exclaimed Amala, eagerly looking into his face.

"Of course, I do," Edmund said and continued, "I felt positive he was not guilty of that murder even before I heard Alyssa Nicole's statement of what she saw in the hallway that night. It should have settled the question forever as far as poor Lucas was concerned. It was a shame that the warrants for his arrest that were scattered on the FBI's most wanted posters all over the world weren't withdrawn after Alyssa's statement. Poor fella! He grew up with us. The man didn't have a vice except for his hatred of restraint."

"I am so glad to hear you say this, Edmund... because I have a problem to solve now regarding Lucas Durano. I need your advice and help."

"Lucas Durano? Why do you need my help now, and where we are now?"

"He is said to be here in Lourenco Marques," replied Amala. She didn't mention where he was, however.

"Here in Lourenco Marques! What in the world is he doing here?" abruptly inquired her husband.

"He is said to be working on a new road outside town."

"A new road! No one is there that I know of, except the convicts who work on a chain gang breaking rock."

"Yes, I know. He is said to be among them," replied Amala in almost a whisper.

"Who said that?"

"Haley Dawn."

"Haley Dawn Johnson?"

"Yes."

"How in the world would Haley know anything about Lucas being here?"

"She went for a walk while we were out on our adventure today and strayed onto a new road being built not far from here. She came upon a chain gang-breaking rock where she saw and recognized Lucas Durano. She had known him since she first came to Black Rock Cove when she was barely ten years old. Besides, they are also engaged to be married to one another."

"Is it not possible she may be mistaken about his identity?"

"Quite possible, dear. But Edmund, would you please go and check at the prison and go to the chain gang tomorrow? See if there is a convict there that might resemble Lucas Durano. Then, find out what name he goes by and what is his crime?"

"Very well. I will do this for you, Amala. And for the interest of that poor fella. But I don't think it's even possible that this felon seen on the chain gang can be Lucas Durano. It is difficult to imagine such an easy-going vagabond like him would be in prison for any crime." With that said, he excused himself from the supper table and went to the back patio to smoke a cigar.

Amala was tired from her full day of adventure and soon retired to bed. Before going to bed, however, she dropped by Haley's room and told her she spoke to Edmund, and he promised immediate attention to this matter.

With this beautiful gleam of hope, the poor girl, the faithful betrothed of Lucas Durano, retired to her bedroom.

Lieutenant Richter was on duty at the barracks until noon the following day. Then, in the afternoon, he did as he promised Amala and began his errand of mercy. Finally, after almost four hours, he returned home with the result of his quest.

Amala met him at the door and took him into the sitting room, sat down with him on the couch, and implored Edmund to tell her everything at once!

Amala rushed him to his discussion, "First, Edmund, was the man in question Lucas Durano?"

"First of all, the man in question wasn't Lucas Durano," laughed Edmund.

"I thought so. Well?"

"But he was enough like the Lucas Durano to have deceived his own mother... if he ever had one."

"Tell me about it, Edmund. Start at the beginning."

"Very well, dear. After I got off duty, I went out looking for someone whose name, offense, and term of servitude I was completely ignorant of. The only clue I had was that he resembled the Lucas Durano of Demon Gorge. So, I went up and down the road you talked about, looking at all the faces of the convicts as they broke rocks with their pickaxes. Their ankles were fettered. A chain connected each one where there was no escape for any of them. Only a half dozen guards were looking after them."

Amala had a sad expression on her face while she shuddered.

Edmund continued, "I walked up and down the line. I still had my military uniform on, and they took me for an inspector sent by the prison's warden. Then, that is when it happened. I came upon a man whose presence made me start."

"The man that Haley Dawn saw?"

"He must have been, Amala. Despite his disfiguring cropped hair and prison clothes on, he was such a counterpart to Lucas Durano that I was for a moment convinced that our poor vagabond was standing right there in front of me."

"Oh, Edmund!" interjected Amala.

"I went up to the guard and asked him if I could speak to that man. He quickly answered and said it was okay with him. So then, I went up to the fellow, and... I assure you, Amala, addressing the real Lucas Durano with as much reserve as I could have felt."

"And?"

"Well, I asked him what his name was. He looked at me and said, 'What is that to you?' he growled, turning up to me a face deformed by rage out of likeness to Lucas and into that of a frowning demon. I was very startled but composed myself and said, "I took you for a man I once knew back in Black Rock Cove in Oregon in the States... a man by the name of Mister Durano."

"Mister——!" roared the scowling ruffian as he slammed down his pick ax.

While sitting on his horse, the guard looked down at me and said, "Best let the brute alone, sir. He is one of the worst prisoners we have in all of them."

"What's the fellow's name?" I asked the guard.

"He is Number 6666 and about the hardest case in our prison camp, sir."

"What is his real name and crime?"

"Number 6666 and a bad one, sir. That's all I know of him. If you wish to know more, you can check in with the warden back at the prison."

"Amala, I thanked the guard, turned my steps towards the prison, and went to the warden at the prison. The prison is just next to the barracks. I found out that Number 6666 was not Lucas Durano."

"Well, said Amala, with a great sigh of relief. "I am glad that he was not Lucas Durano. I will go and tell Haley Dawn."

Amala departed the room and went to visit Haley. On entering, she said, "Haley, you can set your heart at rest. The convict you saw was not Lucas Durano."

"Oh, Ma'am, pardon me for differing with you, but indeed, he was," said the girl, mournfully shaking her head.

"Haley! Edmund went to where the convicts were breaking the stones and spoke directly to him. He bears another name.... Jack Dannells," patiently said Amala.

"He might have said that name, ma'am, maybe to hide from the other charge of murder back home, but he is Lucas Durano all the same!"

"Haley, do you want that convict to be Lucas Durano?"

"Oh, ma'am!" replied Haley in an involuntary voice of reproach.

"He is NOT Lucas Durano, however strongly he might resemble him. He is an old convict, though a young man. Listen, Haley, to what I am saying!"

"I am, ma'am. Is there any way Mister Richter would take me with him and let me speak with this man everyone calls Jack Dannells? It seems to me that is the only way we're going to resolve this entire matter, Amala."

"Okay. Here is what we will do since nothing else will satisfy you, Haley. The Chaplain visits the prison on Sundays between his morning and evening service. The convicts will be in their cells at this time. I will ask him to take you with him to see this man on Sunday."

"Oh, thank you, Amala, thank you," said the girl raising and kissing the hand of Amala.

"Enough, Haley Dawn. I am tired. Go and say your prayers and go to bed.

"Goodnight, ma'am," Haley ended her conversation and retired for the evening.

The following day was Saturday.

Amala, with an apology coupled with a laugh for troubling her husband with the love affairs of Haley Dawn, asked if there was any way she could be allowed to go to the prison and see who she calls Lucas.

Edmund agreed to contact the Chaplain, who calls on the prison every Sunday after morning services. But he said, "That woman is such a dummy. She can't be brought to reason, Amala," he concluded impatiently.

"Please, sweetheart, don't be so harsh with her. She needs to see for herself. Once she sees what you said is true, she will be contented, and we shall not hear another peep out of her," pleaded Amala.

"I hope so, honey," said Edmund while shrugging his shoulders.

Edmund went to see the Chaplain and agreed to take Haley Dawn with him on his call on the prisoners at the prison Sunday after he finished his morning services.

Edmund, Amala, and Haley Dawn attended Sunday morning services at the barracks, where the Chaplain finished his message. After the service was completed, Haley walked with the chaplain to the prison. They were conducted through the gates, past the various guards, and over to a long narrow building that housed many of the prisoners. They walked along and stopped in front of the ground floor cell occupied by Number 6666. They had both walked so quietly in the hallway that the prisoner, seated on the side of his small cot behind the steel bar door, didn't perceive their presence.

Haley Dawn gazed upon him as he sat quietly on the edge of his bed, with his arms folded across his chest.

"Dannells!" cried the chaplain.

Wow! What an instantaneous and awful change!

The man jumped up and began walking up to the bars. His face transformed into that of a wild beast! "What in the Hell do you want?" he demanded. "Speak now, you son-of-a-bitch!" he added while also saying a volley of other swears that made Haley Dawn throw up her hands to her ears in self-defense.

"This young woman here has come to see you, thinking you are one who once lived in Black Rock Cove back in the States," said the Chaplain as soon as the man's torrent of profanity had expended.

The man was mad! He stared at Haley and the chaplain as if he would have loved to tear them apart with his bare hands!

"You and this here young woman can go straight to Hell. Do not pass go and do not collect a penny of any money!" roared the demoniac, followed by another volley of blasphemy and obscenities that made even the chaplain's hair rise on end. It also sent Haley shuddering and running down the corridor.

The chaplain followed quickly behind her and caught up at the outer door, where he found her trembling. "He's not the man you had hoped to find?" asked the chaplain.

"Oh, no, sir! The likeness to the man I was searching for was very striking when he sat on the side of the bed. But as soon as he got up and began cursing at us with an ugly and cruel expression on his face, the man I was searching for disappeared. I saw him on the chain gang earlier and thought he was my old friend and neighbor who lived nearby. I thought it was Lucas Durano, but now that I've seen this man closely, face-to-face, and heard all those terrible curse words from his mouth, I'm completely satisfied that he's not my dear friend from back home," Haley explained to the chaplain while walking next to the preacher while leaving the prison yard.

"I'm glad you say so, Miss Haley. Now, go home. The streets are not safe places for a beautiful young woman like yourself walking all alone," the chaplain said while splitting ways with Haley and returning to the barracks.

No sooner did Haley reach home and walk in the door than Amala said, "Well, what did you find, my dear?"

"He was not the man I sought. Moreover, I am fully convinced that Jack Dannells was not my Lucas."

"You must try and find some patience, Haley. You told me you thought you might find him here. A forlorn hope at best, dear. I think Lucas is hiding somewhere, probably under an assumed name, and he must remain in hiding until the real murderer of Samuel Knight is discovered and he is freed from the blame of that crime."

"But... never to hear from him, ma'am," sighed the young girl.

"I know it is hard. But you must hope. Lucas will probably write to his friends in Demon Gorge. You can write to them and inquire of news of him."

"Yes, ma'am, I know I can do that. But Mrs. Meret, nor Claudia, either, ever go to the post office. So, my letter would just lie there and go unanswered."

"Then, enclose it with a letter to Doctor Cantu, with a request that he will have it sent to the Lighthouse. It would be sure to reach Victoria Meret then."

"I will write a letter and send it on the ship departing tomorrow afternoon for the west coast of the States."

The next day, Monday, Edmund, and Amala were engaged to lunch with the Ambassador and Bernice. They went early and found the two of them alone. Amala's mother had not recovered her spirits. She was obviously having difficulty getting over the memory of her wrongful doings and the humiliation of their discovery.

As the four visited together, the accidental meeting between Jack Dannells, the convict, and Haley Dawn was discussed. In the middle of their conversation, Bernice said, "This man, Dannells, who is a splitting image of Lucas Durano, seems to have been in Black Rock Cove at the very time of the mysterious assassination of Samuel

Knight. Then, Lucas Durano was charged with committing the awful crime. Warrants were issued along with large rewards. There were three distinct accounts of his whereabouts, one that he had crossed over to Lourenco Marques in Mozambique via a ship that left Seattle, another that he still lurks in the neighborhood in Black Rock Cove, and another that he went to Australia."

"Yes, we remember that. What deduction do you draw from that, Bernice?" asked Edmund, while Amala looked on very interested.

"What inference do I draw, you ask? Why, this one... that the man named Dannells was in the neighborhood of Black Rock Cove, in particular, the mansion of Samuel Knight outside of town, and that he might have been the assassin of Samuel. And that he was mistaken for Lucas Durano by one of the persons who professed to have seen the latter," said Bernice.

Since the statement given by Alyssa Nicole in regards to what she saw in the hallway that night of the murder was made public, few, if any, believed in Lucas Durano's guilt, although the warrant for his arrest and rewards offered hadn't been withdrawn.

Edmund broke the silence after Bernice had her say. "This theory had not occurred to me. But, Bernice, I think you have certainly found a clue to the mystery of that murder. I will lose no time in writing to the Black Rock Cove police department to have this clue followed up on. If we can associate this crime back home to this man called Dannells, he will be sent back to Black Rock Cove for trial. We can kill two birds with one stone and get rid of a bad dude, and an innocent man will be freed from guilt."

Bernice changed the subject. "Say, Edmund, now that you have come into so great of wealth, I wonder why you don't go ahead and resign from the army?"

"Because I just changed over to the Army and got my commission. Besides, it is a point of honor right now for me not to resign."

Lunch was announced.

The four sat down to an oak round table adorned with an elegant service of Wedgwood China and supplied with a tasteful meal.

As soon as lunch was over, Edmund and Amala made their adieux and departed. As they drove downtown on the way back to their home for officers at the barracks, a large commotion of people was seen near the front gates of the barracks.

As the taxi pulled up, Edmund rolled down the window. "What's up, gentlemen?"

"They say a prisoner has escaped, sir," replied the gate guard.

Edmund didn't think much of it and signaled the taxi cab driver to continue.

As soon as they got to their quarters on the base, the lieutenant went to his office and began writing a letter to the chief of police at the Black Rock Cove police department. He asked them to follow up on the clue suggested by Mrs. Jessup Austin.

When he came out to put the letter in the mail bin, he was faced with the fact that it was no ordinary malefactor who had broken free from his chains and escaped the prison. Instead, it was a ferocious evil man, Dannells, whose name was a terror to all who had heard of him.

The prisoner's escape spread panic over the entire female population in Lourenco Marques.

Not one single woman would go out and have a pleasant walk or drive beyond the city limits of Lourenco Marques until the fugitive monster was recaptured!

Chapter EIGHT
The Ruined Lighthouse of Demon Gorge

W e have left the beautiful Alyssa Nicole Courbis, only halfway reconciled with her husband, Oliver Courbis, a few chapters back. We have also left Victoria Meret, the old crone, hoarding her ill-gotten gold coins and quarreling with her daughter Claudia at the ruined lighthouse at Demon Gorge. So, now, we must leave Bernice mentally and spiritually atoning for her offenses in the presence of the noble-minded ambassador who loved her enough to make her his wife.

We also leave Edmund and Amala enjoying their long-drawn-out honeymoon at the barracks in a faraway land with Haley Dawn Johnson bewailing her lost lover.

We must now return and go after Lucas Durano, the omnipresent, who was seen and sworn to be in three different places when he could have only been in one.

Three fishermen swore they took him to the docks in Seattle, where he boarded a ship overseas the same morning as the murder. Then, the preacher man saw him off to Denver that same day. But finally, he couldn't have been heading to the mentioned places as he was having his head repaired by Claudia and Mrs. Victoria Meret in the hidden basement of the ruined lighthouse at Demon Gorge.

Lucas Durano, the constitutional tramp, or vagabond, who could never rest very long in one place and was never happy unless he was on the go, was most tired of his seclusion in the hidden cave below the lighthouse.

Lucas longed for his freedom. But, now that the opportunity had come, it was decided to escape, and he concluded it would be a great idea to use his wit and make good his escape from Black Rock Cove and the ruined lighthouse.

He didn't confide in either of the two women... the old or young ones. First, he knew to do so would surely provoke a storm of opposition, and second, never-ending arguments. So, Lucas decided to avoid all the fuss by quietly stealing away from the hidden cave and the ruined lighthouse.

Let us recall our memory. On the first night after the detectives left the lighthouse, Claudia came down from the upper part of the house through the secret passageway to the cave, where Lucas was still sequestered. She did so to relieve the old crone and her mother.

Victoria offered the exchange of assistance and went back up to the upper floor to the more comparative comforts and luxuries of the lighthouse with lots of fresh air. Young Claudia remained down below.

The two younger people talked over the incidents of the tragedy at Samuel Knight's mansion, and Lucas displayed a lightness of feeling over the killing that surprised and displeased her.

Lucas told her that he couldn't regard the murder seriously because he didn't believe that Samuel had ever been murdered in the first place. That he had only been half-murdered. And, the man came to while sleeping on the table with a sheet over him and not liking lying flat on his back got up and walked off on his own two legs... he stole his own body! The conversation he had with Claudia left her spellbound. She had no power for anything other than total amazement at Lucas's words.

She never made one word of response to Lucas and just sat staring at him with her eyes wide open. Let's continue with their conversation now.

"Well, Claudia, if Samuel Knight didn't come back to life and walk away with his own body, where is it now?"

Claudia found her ability to talk. "Lucas, you are such a fool! I don't think I can trust you to leave the country without me. You will get into another scrape and come to harm because you are such a fool!"

Lucas laughed and said, "It's my bedtime. Since I am much better now, I will leave you, Claudia, with the mattress and the pillows. I will take a blanket and cuddle up at the end of the cave next to that big rock down there. Give me a goodnight kiss, Claudia," he said as he turned to walk away.

"Goodnight, Lucas! God forgive us our many sins, and God save you!" said Claudia with tears in her eyes.

"You too, Claudia. Amen," said the vagabond as he turned and walked away.

One could hear him snoring away within five minutes of leaving Claudia's side. They could be heard all over the vast open cavern.

Lucas slept soundly until almost four o'clock in the morning. Then, he suddenly sat up and said, "Jesus Christ, if I hadn't almost overslept," he yawned deeply. Then, "If Claudia had woken up before me, I would never have gotten out of here without her stopping me," he stood up and stretched.

After washing his face with the water from the underground spring, he dried off with the small hand towel that was brought down to help clean his wounds. Then he walked over to where Claudia was sound asleep. "Heaven save her! She is a wonderful woman, the best of all of us. I am so glad she gave me her blessing before we both went to sleep last night," murmured the tramp under his breath.

He stood above her, staring down. After a long hesitation, he whispered very lightly, "I wonder if I dare kiss her goodbye again?" he asked while looking regretfully down at the sleeping face. "Most likely, I shall never see her again. To heck with it... I will risk it." He knelt beside Claudia's mattress and softly touched her forehead with his lips.

Claudia slightly stirred and whispered while in her dreams, "Poor, dear Lucas," and fell back into slumber again.

Lucas stared at her deeply and then arose to his upright stance. He reached down and dusted off his knees.

He made his way to the opening at the end of the cave that took him up to the cellar of the lighthouse. He reached it, walked across, pushed the stone away that concealed the opening, and went up some stairs to a large iron door that was actually the back of an old Dutch oven in the rock wall of the chimney.

He was at the top. He tiptoed across the room and saw Victoria sound asleep on her bed. He then walked gently across the floor up to her bed. Looking down, he whispered, "I owe you my life, old woman. Take my many thanks and my assurance that I will repay you a hundred times over if we both live to meet one day again." He stooped and gave the old woman a kiss on the forehead without, in the least, disposing of her stillness.

Lucas gathered some needed things in a blanket and tied them up. He then walked over to the wall, pulled out a loose rock, took a handful of dollars from his hidden stash, and put them in his pocket. He then started out the door, stopped, took the ballcap that Hugh Jackson left on the hall tree, and put it on his head.

He headed out the door just in time. After the blackness of a long night, the Earth's star rose on the horizon, spreading its gold in every direction. She came in the way that natural forces do, needing no invitation yet feeling her welcome.

Lucas turned his back to the rising sun and headed westward towards Shaw's Bend, not taking the beaten track but cutting across fields, breaking through thickets, and always keeping himself out of the eyesight of anyone seeking a big reward for his capture.

After a few hours of walking, he came upon the barren old castle building at Shaw's Bend. He prowled along under its gray garden walls, waiting to get a sight of the woman he loved. Victoria and Claudia were right when they said that he would risk his neck to not leave the country without first saying farewell to the woman he loved... Haley Dawn.

He didn't have to wait long. Haley came out of the side door and into the backyard to draw water from the well. He looked in all directions, and seeing no one near, he said softly, "Haley! Haley, my love."

She heard Lucas and dropped her bucket and looked in every direction.

"Here! Here I am, sweetheart."

She stopped and saw him and stared in terror. Then, she ran towards him, eagerly saying under her breath, "Oh, Lucas! Is that you? What in the world have you been doing to yourself? You look so thin and pale. You've lost your long black hair and beard! Where have you been, Lucas? Some people have said you went to Seattle and shipped away overseas. Others said you went to Denver. Then some said you went to Australia!"

"Do you honestly believe I would have left the country or gone somewhere without first bidding you goodbye, my love," he answered. "Haley, come through the gate in the wall. I can't come in there, or I will be seen."

"Oh, Lucas, it is so dangerous for you to be in the open around here. Surely someone is going to see you. Don't you know there are warrants for your arrest?" said the trembling young girl.

"Yes, my love. I know all about those arrest warrants. I also know about the big reward for my capture. But, Haley, you don't think I'm capable of committing the crime I am accused of, do you?" gravely asked the vagabond.

"No, not me, Lucas!" exclaimed Haley Dawn.

"Haley, sweetheart, I never did murder Samuel Knight and never could have done it. Yet, I am running from justice as if I were a guilty man!" exclaimed Lucas bitterly.

"You are definitely running from injustice," replied Haley Dawn.

"You are so right, love. They say in the eye of the law, running and hiding is a confession of guilt! I am one hundred percent innocent of the crime and running because I can't prove my innocence. Circumstantial evidence proves me guilty in the face of the truth, Haley. Therefore, I must disgracefully flee to save myself or remain here to be innocently sent to the electric chair. A fine alternative for an honest man!" Lucas laughed.

"Oh, Lucas... please go! Much as I love to have you remain, I feel what the risk is to you. Please go, Lucas!" pleaded Haley Dawn while trembling.

"Haley, tell me the truth! Have I changed enough in appearance from what I once was? Would a person passing by who knew me recognize me at a glance? Please, tell me the truth, sweetheart."

There was a brief silence. Then, Haley looked at Lucas steadily for several long seconds and said, "No, Lucas, I don't think anyone would recognize you. At first, I didn't recognize you with your hair cut so close and your entire beard shaved off. In addition, your once long and shaggy eyebrows are cut short. To tell you the truth, my love, you look a whole lot like Samuel Knight, to be honest... more so than you look like you."

"Reward posters are hanging all over the county. They even hung one on this wall that I went and tore down but kept. I can show it to you if you want to see it?" asked Haley eagerly.

"Yes, very much so," replied Lucas.

Haley rushed away through the garden gate, across the garden, and into the house. In a few minutes, she was running back with the poster in her hand.

"Is no one moving around in the house, Haley?"

"No, it's just my stepmother and me right now. I do most of the morning work, and she gets up later and does the daytime work."

"Okay. Well... Haley Dawn, I am in love with you. I suppose you knew that already. I will travel to Mozambique and make my fortune there, where diamonds are everywhere, or at least I have been told. As soon as I discover my fortune, I will send for you and marry you and make you a fine lady with no care in the world," said the vagabond.

"Wait, Lucas, listen while I read this description," said the girl. She sat down on a pile of rocks by the gate with the poster between her two hands and read it aloud to Lucas.

"Two Hundred and Fifty Thousand Dollar Reward

By order of Oliver Courbis of this county, the above reward is hereby offered and will be given for the arrest and apprehension of Lucas Durano and Johnny McLean, charged with the murder of the late Samuel Knight of said county. Said Johnny McLean——. Oh, never mind this part. Let me skip to you, Lucas. Ahh, here we are. The same Lucas Durano is of medium height and size. He has long black hair," she stopped reading and looked up. "Your hair is cut so close that it looks rather small." She paused after patting Lucas on the head. "He has a sunburned complexion and large brown eyes and a very full and long black beard," she again looked up at Lucas. "But you are as pale as a ghost, Lucas, not much eyebrows to speak of and no beard at all." She stopped.

"Lucas, I don't see anything that resembles you from this description," said Haley as she rolled up the poster.

"Neither do I!" exclaimed the vagabond. "I think I will be plenty safe once I get out of the neighborhood."

"Lucas, one question, where did you get that nice set of clothes you are wearing?"

"They were loaned to me by Hugh Jackson, the night watchman."

"Hush, dear! Someone is calling!"

"Haley! Haley Dawn, where are you," Haley's stepmother shouted. "Where are you, my girl?"

"Oh, my goodness, I must hurry back," she moved closer and wrapped her arms around the man she loved. After backing away, she said, "You must hurry and go, Lucas or she will find you! Goodbye, my love! I will think of you and love you always, dear Lucas! I will pray for you every night."

"Goodbye, my love Haley. I love you, but I must go! Goodbye. I seem to leave my life in leaving you! But I will find a boatload of diamonds, bring you out to me, and marry you, Haley Dawn! I will make a lady of you. I promise with all my heart! Goodbye!"

The lovers were locked in each other's arms for a long moment and broke suddenly apart. Haley turned and ran into the gate to meet and stop her stepmother from continuing past the garden.

Lucas was off rapidly with his small sack of needed things and ambled along a narrow path towards the main road to Black Rock Cove. He wasn't gone long around the street when he saw Doctor Cantu driving down the road, who stopped. Now, if a man would ever recognize him under his present transformation, that would be the good doctor. Doctor Cantu had tended to the boy as a child and again when he was a beardless youth through more than one spell of broken arms and legs. So, this pale and black-bearded tramp was not one unfamiliar to Doctor Cantu.

He recognized Lucas Durano at once! The vagabond saw that he did. "Lucas! Stop! You are wanted by the police. Stop! You must give yourself up," said the doctor while jumping out of his car and shouting at the young man.

Lucas stopped suddenly and looked at the doctor for a moment with an expression of quizzical mirth. Then, he burst into a thunderous laugh and said derisively, "How long have you been a cop, Doctor Cantu, and where is your warrant for my arrest?"

The doctor reached out to grab Lucas, but the young man laughed, sprung to the side, and dashed off into the thick wooden thicket.

The doctor wasted no time and drove into Black Rock Cove to police headquarters and reported his encounter.

In the meantime, Lucas came out of the woods near the Portland Highway and continued on his way to Black Rock Cove. Nobody bothered him. All the people after the large reward were looking for a sunburned and black-bearded man, not the pale-skinned and smooth shavin' neatly dressed young man... one who looked more like a poor student from the University than the notorious murderer, Lucas Durano.

The vagabond continued his trek toward Black Rock Cove in peace and safety. The further he got away from the Knight or the Courbis Estate, the more secure he felt.

The more secure he felt every step of his way further away from the sight of the murder. Along the road, nailed to telephone poles and other small outbuildings, posters were pasted up offering an excellent reward for his arrest. But, since his appearance had changed so much and he wasn't anything like himself, he only laughed at them, repeating Haley Dawn's words, 'they are as good as a free pass for me.'

He continued his trek for several hours until he came to a large hayfield. As the sun was almost down, he elected to grab a place to the side of a large haystack for the night. The next day he began to get closer to the Portland Highway, and before heading into Black Rock Cove the next day, he found a dilapidated old barn and slept under the overhang of the building. Then, finally, on the third day, he made his way into the outskirts of Black Rock Cove. At dusk, he found himself near a lonely roadside inn. Since he would not turn a head from the description on the reward posters, he marched boldly into the inn. It had a swinging board in front bearing the sign, "The Bird House."

The topic of the grand reward being offered for the arrest of Lucas Durano was on everyone's lips.

A man sitting at a table near the jukebox took his stiff forefinger, stirred up, and poked down the cherry tobacco in his pipe. He replaced it to his lips and smoked vigorously. "You know, gentlemen, the $250,000 ain't to be picked up by any of us, that's for sure."

Another gentleman added, "It would be something if he would just walk in like a man, and we could take him straight to the police headquarters and get our money and split it amongst us."

"Ummm, how much would that be for each of us," asked a man in a cacky blue shirt and brown pants."

After looking around the room, one man replied, "At least thirty to forty thousand each."

"Don't trouble your minds, friends. That rascal won't be coming in here to give himself up. Take my word for it," he concluded.

The six men immediately stood up, with one seeing the traveler come in the door, and said, "Sorry sir, we were just talking of that killer, Lucas Durano, who killed Samuel Knight at the Knight Estate.

We were just wishing we had him here with us right now," explained the old man.

Lucas sat at a bar stool, called for a pint of beer, and leisurely sucked it down before speaking. "What about it?" He asked.

"What about what, Mister?" asked the old man.

"This murder that you and your friends are talking about. I'm a stranger to this neck of the woods, having been absent for many years and of which I just returned recently."

"Oh, then, young fella, you don't know about the big reward offered to anyone successful at retaining this man, Lucas Durano."

"Big-time reward! Sorry, but I know nothing about that. What is it for? The biggest pumpkin or the largest sheep... what?" demanded the vagabond.

"Oh, goodness no, Mister. It is for the apprehension of the villain, Lucas Durano!"

"Lucas Durano? Who is he?"

"You don't know anything, do you mister? He's the man that assassinated Samuel Knight at midnight while he slept in his bed. He then cut off his head and cut him up into pieces and stole his body and sold it to doctors for research," said the old man as he dumped the ashes from his pipe and refilled it again with cherry tobacco.

"My God! What an atrocious villain he is indeed!" the real Lucas exclaimed.

"There he is up there!"

"Where?" demanded the vagabond, affecting to start.

"There!" said the old gray-haired man while waving his pipe in the direction of the reward poster hanging on the wall in the pool room. "There he is with his bushy black beard and long black hair. Ahhh, the man that grabs him, sir, will definitely come into a fortune!"

"Ahhh," said the tramp, looking as if he wanted to be himself who would fall upon a piece of good luck.

With those words, Lucas went to his room for the night in the inn and washed, and went to bed on fresh white sheets. But he no sooner laid down in the bed than fell asleep... an unbroken sleep for almost ten hours.

As Lucas woke from his long and restful sleep, he saw the sun shining through the quaint little window of his room.

After another refreshing wash, he got dressed and went downstairs to order his breakfast. While sitting there, a man walked into the dining room and said, "They have got that rascal, sir!"

"Whom do you mean? The person who murdered Samuel Knight?" inquired the tramp.

"Yes, sir... they got him!"

"Ahhh, they finally got him!"

"Yes, sir. They found him among a bunch of homeless camped out under the bridge outside Black Rock Cove. He is a horrid-looking lout as ever you set eyes on, sir. Those that captured him came by here on the way to police headquarters. That's how I was able to see him."

"Are they sure they got the right man?" asked Lucas as he took a bite of scrambled eggs.

"Oh, yes, sir. He looks just like the wanted poster hanging on the wall in the pool room. No mistake about him."

"Glad to hear it," said Lucas as he drained his coffee cup and stood up from the table.

"You should have heard them when they came by this morning hooting and hollering."

"Actually, no. I was tired, and I slept soundly."

"I wished you were awake, sir. You should have seen him. He looked like a wild savage beast."

"No doubt he did. Can I have my bill, please?"

"Certainly, sir."

Lucas paid his bill and was on his way toward town. Whenever he stopped at places alongside the roadways, he was greeted with talk of how the murderer of Samuel Knight was caught and brought to justice.

Sometimes Lucas listened to the conversation in silence, and sometimes he joined in on them.

His thoughts began to catch up with him. At his last stop, he sat by a window looking out and said, *"I wonder if there is a good enough likeness of the brute? I wonder if circumstantial evidence is enough to hand that poor rascal in the absence of him being able to prove an alibi. Maybe I should go forward and give myself up to save a man who is just as not guilty of that crime as I am myself. Maybe I should take the risk?"*

These thoughts troubled the vagabond. The words ran through his head as he got back on the road and troubled him. But, then, he passed through the main street of a small community and met a newsboy standing by a shoeshine stand and gave him a quarter for the newspaper's morning edition.

He folded it up and put it in his back pocket until his noontime rest and lunch gave him the leisure to look it over.

He was now not far from Black Rock Cove. A U-toT-em gas station and convenience store were on his way at noon, where he went inside, sat down, and ate a hotdog with a coke. After taking his first bite, he stared out the large plate glass window as cars filled up and thought, *"They will surely hang that man if I don't go forward. They are saying that he can't prove an alibi. Everyone swears that he is Lucas Durano and was at Samuel Knight's house on the night of the murder. As Lucas Durano, he will be sent to the electric chair for the murder of Samuel Knight... unless I go in and give myself up to save him! The big question is, should I go in and give myself up and save the man from the chair even if I am as innocent as he? No, that doesn't make any sense. Nope! I can't let that man die. I will go to the Black Rock Cove police department as soon as I get into town and report to the police. This will surely turn free the man they have locked up now. But... honor is an honor, and I must not let another man swing for Lucas Durano... guilty or innocent!"*

He pulled out the paper and leaned back on his chair to read the news. "Hello!" he exclaimed aloud. "What is it we have here?" He looked at the second-page heading.

"Not Lucas Durano.

The man who was arrested yesterday, for the notorious Lucas Durano, turns out to be another man, one Jack Dannells, a convict recently returned from Mozambique, where he was serving out his term of ten years for burglary and who, since his arrival here in Black Rock Cove, has been up to his old tricks. Therefore, Jack Dannells is freed from the charge of murder of Samuel Knight. However, he is held for robbing convenience stores up and down the Portland Highway. The criminal, Lucas Durano, is still very much at large!"

Lucas read this paragraph very carefully from start to finish and then threw his head back and began laughing long and loud.

No sooner did he walk outside the U-Totem to resume his journey, he muttered to himself, "Now, then, Lucas Durano, instead of going straight down to police headquarters and giving ourselves up to go to prison or to the electric chair, let's go to the docks in Seattle where we can grab a ship to Mozambique and get rich in the diamond fields. His steps bounced away, for a significant burden was lifted from his mind.

The day ends, and Lucas finds himself in Black Rock Cove at an obscure inn where he took supper and was very tired from a long day and retired to bed.

The next day, after a long walk across the fishing village, he came to the docks where the river was crowded with all the chaos associated with ships landing and clearing their freight. Then, finally, he came up to a man who looked like he knew what was happening at the docks.

"Sir, I wish to work my way overseas to Lourenco Marques. Can I speak with someone about getting a job helping onboard the vessel?"

A man walked up. "What is it, man, you need?" asked a man who overheard Lucas's request.

"I wish to work for my passage to Mozambique, sir," replied Lucas, touching the brim of his ball cap.

"The ship's officer looked him up and down and saw that he was an able-bodied young man. "What is your name, fella?" demanded the ship's officer.

Lucas hesitated for just a moment. The question from the officer caught him a little by surprise. He answered, "Duplicate Knight, sir."

"Dupe... what?" questioned the man, bending his eyebrows.

"I was a twin, sir. My first brother was called by a Christian name, Valentino because he came into this world on Valentine's Day. Then, there's me. Since I was a duplicate of my brother, my parents called me 'Dupe' for short. It just stuck with me."

The officer looked at him and said, "Well, don't just stand there. Go ahead and start helping, and we will sign the papers later."

Ay, ay, sir!" promptly responded 'Dupe,' touching his ballcap.

Once there, he was able to get a job on a ship sailing for Lourenco Marques in Mozambique. He would make his riches from the lucrative diamond mining fields in a few months.

So, Lucas Durano... ooops, Dupe sailed for Mozambique.

Dupe sailed on a ship that first went north to Seattle, where he departed and got on another ship that set sail for Mozambique. It was the fifteenth day of January, six weeks later, when his ship arrived at the wharves in the big city of Lourenco Marques.

The city was thickly crowded in the beautiful valley where it had been first laid out and thinly scattered up the sides of the lovely wooded hills that formed its suburbs.

As soon as Dupe got his pay, he made his way into the big city of Lourenco Marques to find out what was happening and how he should work to gain some income.

In addition to its regular great activity of a growing city, Lourenco Marques was now undergoing those sporadic attacks of mental fervor to which she was subject whenever the exciting news of gold was discovered in the foothills outside the great city. That's right! Gold... not diamonds.

Dupe wondered if all the houses in the city weren't emptied out by all the adult men and left to only the women and children.

He waited almost an hour at the local bank to get his paycheck cashed. From there, he went to a barber shop, thinking, *"I don't dare let my hair or beard grow, even out here in this faraway place. And, I must not abuse my skin and keep it a smooth chin and well-trimmed head. Then, no one will ever recognize me."*

He reached the barber shop and found it not to be crowded. Dupe sat down and said, "I wish to have my hair trimmed short and to give me a slick as a baby's butt shave."

The barber began cutting. As it does in a woman's beauty salon, the scuttlebutt began. "I suppose you heard the news, young fella," he said as a crisp black curl fell under his scissors.

"Not really. I just got off the boat at the wharf and came straight here," replied Dupe.

"Ahhh, indeed. I heard a large crowd came over by her today. Are you going to the diggings?"

"Never have I been lucky to be there when the diggings were first started. What is your news?" asked Dupe.

"Why, the richest gold field as has ever been discovered in the world. At least that is what they say, although it is always the biggest found when it is first discovered," cautiously added the barber.

"Where is it?" eagerly demanded the vagabond, his interest rising.

"At Dead Damsel's Creek, about fifty miles from here."

"When was it found?"

"One week ago. There's not a handful of people up there now, but they are beginning to rush upon it."

"Who found it?" Dupe asked.

"A fella up in the mountains hunting and fell after tripping over something. He looked down and found a yellow knob as big as a door handle sticking out of the ground. He stared at it momentarily, realizing it was gold, and began digging. Lo and behold, when they finished their excavation, it was found to be a gold nugget that weighed almost two hundred pounds."

"This place called Dead Damsel's Creek... why do they call it that?"

"Because a young girl went lost one day, and they found her body near the site of this gold dig. Ever since her body was found there, it has been called that," he stopped and put his scissors down and finished, "well, sir, there you are!" concluded the barber. He removed the white sheet from around Dupe.

Dupe decided to go to the new gold fields instead of seeking the diamond fields he came for. Everyone was hot on finding the gold and not the diamonds.

He went to the neighborhood stores and got all his needed supplies. From there, he took them to an inn where he engaged a small room for one day and prepared for his trip. That evening he had a good supper and slept for the night.

So, the following day, Dupe Knight set out to seek his fortune.

He didn't have to ask for directions. Instead, he had only to follow a group of men dressed like him who were leaving the city and headed north.

He walked all day. The sun sunk below the western horizon, and nighttime shades fell fast.

Just as he was ready to sit down and rest, he came upon a group of men who had stopped to rest. "Hello, friends! Headed for the diggings?" asked Dupe as he sat down.

"You guys look like me and prefer to travel by night," said Dupe while pulling out a cigar and passing a few around to his new friends.

The men helped themselves without returning any thanks... but would not have expected any thanks had they treated others to a smoke.

"Yes, we walk by night because, in weather like this, it is far easier and the quickest way, too."

"And we make better time in the cool of the nights than we could in the hot days," added another man as he struck a match and lit his cigar.

Another man added, "You will see that as we go along, we will overtake and pass those who walk by daytime only."

The first man continued, "We usually begin our walk up the mountain at around six in the afternoon and walk until eight o'clock or so the next morning. We then eat and sleep during the hot part of the day. What do you think? Do you wish to join us?"

"Yes, sir, I think it is a good one."

"Very well," said the older man. "Shall we make it up to the peak ahead of us and stop for the day."

Dupe rose to his feet, shouldered his belongings, and began to march up the mountainside with the men.

The giant of a man, the red-bearded one, the party's spokesman, walked beside Dupe and led the way.

Dupe continued his conversation with the red-headed gentleman. "Are you really okay with me joining your group?"

"Why shouldn't we be, friend? The more of us, the merrier, you know."

"Ahhh, but there is a sequel to that old proverb. The fewer, the better cheer," laughed Dupe.

"Oh, I know there are narrow-minded and short-sighted people digging for gold when a new field is discovered somewhere in this world. But, to me, a rush is the best thing to happen to a new discovery. So come on, Dupe, and welcome! You have as much a right to the gold as anyone else."

As they continued and listened to the men talk, he realized they were all from back in the States who left there and came to find their riches in Mozambique.

"By the way, young fella," said the leader, "what is your name? You don't need to mention it if you don't wish to."

"My name is Dupe Knight," gravely replied our adventurer.

"Dupe... what?" demanded the red-bearded man between a frown and a smile.

"Yes, sir. Duplicate Knight, to be exact," solemnly continued the adventurer. "I was the second born of twins on Valentine's Day. My oldest brother, the firstborn, was given the name Valentino in honor of the saint. But, on the other hand, I was called "Duplicate," or Dupe for short, because I was exactly that... a duplicate of the first. Do you see?"

"I've never heard anything like that happening to anyone all the days of my life."

"People just call me Dupe for short. I have also been a duplicate on several occasions, the last like to have cost me my life! It left me with this scar," he lifted his hair on his forehead, "that I shall carry to the grave with me," said the explorer.

"Ahhh, that sounds like a good story, my friend. Do you wanna tell me to pass the time by?"

"Not now, but sometimes perhaps. But, my friend, let me ask. What is your name, please?"

"I was only waiting to see if you took enough interest in me to ask. My name is George Simmons. Most of my family comes from the west coast of the US. I have an uncle there now who is a butler on the Knight Estate in Oregon. I also have a brother, the Reverend Paul Simmons, a minister in Black Rock Cove. Bless his soul. He is gone now, but he gave my brother and me a good education. It took every dollar he ever made to do that. My brother Paul got his own church, and I came out here to search for my riches in the gold-digging."

"I hope you made it, George," said Dupe, speaking sincerely. He was filled with surprise at the discovery he had just made.

"Not yet, young man, but I will get lucky one day," said the gold digger with a smile.

"You say you have an uncle back in the States. Have you ever visited him there?" asked Dupe in somewhat of a panic. He wanted to know how little or how much he knew about the murder at the Knight Estate.

"I've never set foot in that part of the country. I also never laid eyes on my uncle in my entire life. I have never corresponded with him, either. My father left the place as a young boy and never looked back. He didn't leave with any ill will. The brothers just drifted apart and became estranged from one another. Paul got his first church there. But, Dupe, you talk like you know all about this place. Were you reared near there?"

"You might say so... yes, I am from outside Black Rock Cove."

"What area?"

"Demon Gorge," replied the adventurer after a bit of reflection.

"Ahhh, never heard of the place."

"The place has a foolish legend associated with it. They say that it was made by demons in only one night!"

"Oh," is all the red-headed man said.

They continued to walk over a rough trail up and down the foothills under the nighttime sky. The dark purple transparent sky was studded with great, splendid stars.

The hours passed.

The morning sun rose above the horizon when the men emerged from the thick woods onto a plateau, where the trees were stunted and far apart. In front of them was a large family scene. There were two wagons with canvas covers and four strong oxen pulling each. Men, women, and children were talking and laughing. The fragrance of bacon cooking at their campsite was wonderful and appetizing.

The group of people was obviously one who preferred to travel by day and sleep at night.

It was an incredible scene to come upon after a long night's weary trek up the mountainside. Mind and heart were gratified by the presence of human affections for one another and interests found suddenly in barren places.

Chapter NINE
A Domestic Circle is Found

The men coming from the woods on foot and the camping party perceived each other simultaneously. A simultaneous shout of greetings came from both.

"Throw down your stuff and take a load off your feet. Then, come have some breakfast with us... Then, mother, put another pot of coffee on for our friends!" cried a blonde-headed man of about forty years of age who appeared to be the leader of the bunch.

"Thank you, sir, so very kindly. But there are eight of us. Maybe too many," replied George Simmons with a glance back at his seven friends and then one back at the fragrant coffee kettle over the campfire.

"Nonsense, find a place to sit. You are all welcome here. We entertain strangers every now and then, according to what the Bible scriptures say... don't we, Nita?"

"Yes," replied the reticent woman in a straw hat.

George replied, "But, of course, you will permit us to pay you since we are a large group of guys?"

"Oh, my goodness, no. Your grub here won't cost us a penny more. We get it on the trail as we travel. If it concerns your conscience, then how 'bout a dollar each. If not, then don't worry about it. You are still most welcome either way."

"Great offer, sir. We have just cold meat and bread in our packs, and a square breakfast and a good hot cup of coffee will be a godsend to us."

"Okay, then. These all are my brothers, sisters, brothers-in-law, my sons, and daughters, and my wife who doesn't look like she is a mother of fourteen children... does she now?" said the leader of the bunch while jerking his thumb over his shoulder as the wife was still slicing some bacon.

"I wouldn't have taken your wife to be more than a day over thirty-five, sir," said Dupe, who had kept silent in the background longer than he usually does.

The leader laughed. "Add ten more years to that, and you will be all right. She's forty-five. And, there are our twin girls, Mattie and Cassidy, each seventeen years of age."

"Wow, you definitely have a bunch of the kiddoes," said George.

"Ahhh, yes, my blessed wife has blessed me with a baby every year of our marriage! The house of Smiths is not likely to run out anytime soon."

"Well, mine might be John Smith or anything you please... but it is Duplicate Knight," replied the latter with a smile.

"Dupe... what?" inquired the leader Smith in the selfsame words and tone in which the question had been asked twice before.

"Duplicate Knight," answered the weary traveler.

"Well, as I mentioned earlier, our first two children were twin girls. I named one Cassidy and the other Mattie. I would like to see their mother's face if I had named the second one *Duplicata*," he said with a gentle laugh. "Ahhh, the wife is calling us all to breakfast, gentlemen. Let's go," said Mister Smith leading the way to the tablecloth.

After a long silence, all the men, women, and children ate up a storm, and each was abundantly satisfied and refreshed.

No sooner were all the wagons packed and ready to travel than a group of horsemen rode into camp. "Hello!" was the first greeting exchanged between the new arrivals and occupants of the campsite.

The horsemen were rude and rode straight through while saying unspeakable curse words.

No one answered or said a word to the men and put the wagons into motion with the men walking beside them. The wagons traveled over a stony, undulating ground covered by coarse grass and occasionally dotted by scrub oaks in spread-out locations.

As the sun continued to climb higher and higher, the temperatures began to increase. By nine o'clock, it was still and hot. This is where the eight men took leave of the Smiths and let them go on before them.

"We will see ya later at the gold dig, Mister Smith," said Dupe kindly to the head of the household.

Dupe and the others sought the shady side of a large clump of trees off the beaten track. They unrolled and spread out their blankets and used their backpacks as a pillow.

The sun was setting when the first one of the party woke up. He was the oldest man and obviously the lightest sleeper. He rubbed his eyes and awakened the others.

After eating their cold meat and drinking water, they continued their trek through the foothills and skirting smaller mountains. Their road grew worse and led further into the wilderness. Dangerous canyons had to be passed, and perilous streams forded.

The day was destined to bring them into more savage, desolate and repulsive regions. All the ravines, streams, and rivers became difficult to cross with any safety. The entire country turned into a formidable, terrible ordeal to cross.

In the meantime, the men plodded on, ignorant of what was straight ahead.

Then, in the dead of night, in the most challenging stretch of their journey, a feeble wail of a young infant was heard. Just a moment later, they saw a campfire's red gleam. One man was on the watch to keep the fire burning all night. Seeing a large party of men walking into the campsite, he said, "Who goes there?" He stood with his rifle in his hand.

"Friends," answered Simmons. "Gold diggers like yourselves, on our way to the new gold fields." Then, he paused and continued, "we walk by night and rest in the heat of the day."

"A good plan where it is practicable," assented the stranger.

In the meantime, the baby had stopped wailing, and the woman and child retired to one of the wagons.

Our traveling group bid goodnight to the camping party and continued on their way. They had to walk slowly because of the uncertain light and the perilous road ahead. They passed other small campfires and people and were challenged at times by the camp's watchmen but always allowed to pass in peace.

For several hours they saw looming ahead of them through the semi-darkness a large mass of thick black that appeared to stretch all the way from the east to the west and up from the earth high into the heavens.

As the morning dawned, the men began to see a lofty mountain range whose largeness bristled with stunted evergreens and boulders all up and down the side.

"We shall have to stop here, men, until sunrise. It would be useless to find the pass of the huge mountain range in this low light," announced George Simmons. "But we will need a fire here. This terrain looks rugged, and we probably need the protection of a good campfire.

The men began looking for some dry firewood to burn. But unfortunately, there was none to be found.

"Give me a little while," Dupe said. "I am accustomed to rough walks and will look a little further from here and find some dry brush and gather it."

As he was looking away from the camp, he came up close to a fire burning they had seen at a distance earlier. He saw a single man who sat on the ground beside it. No single person, a wagon, oxen, or horses were nearby.

As Dupe got closer to the fire, the lone man jumped up and was holding his revolver in his hand. "Who goes there?"

"A friend... a gold digger bound for the new gold fields. I am just looking for some kindling wood for our fire a way back."

The man suddenly dropped his revolver, caught up a burning branch from the fire, and held it close to the stranger's face, exclaiming excitedly, "Who are you? Your voice is so familiar... your face... Great Scott! Lucas Durano!"

"Hushhhh! Samuel! Jesus Christ, way out here. It's you! Shush, don't call me by that name, or you will surely place a noose around my neck," demanded the vagabond, lost in total amazement at the unexpected encounter.

"Very well. Ahhh, yes, I am Christian Lucas, at your service," said the lone man.

"Oh, beg your pardon, sir! I mistook you for someone I had once the honor to serve in the states. I am happy to make your acquaintance, Mister Christian Lucas. Allow me to introduce myself... Dupe Knight is my name."

"Dupe... what?" demanded the lone man.

"Duplicate Knight. There was another Knight who had a Christian name. I am his duplicate."

"Oh, I see! I see," laughed Christian, "but how can I find you here when I left you in the lap of luxury rolling in the dough as the servants would say? Or, did you bolt?"

"I did bolt, sir... I mean, Mister Christian Lucas. But I didn't bolt because I was tired of grandeur or anxious to resume my roaming the world over. Instead, I bolted because I had to in order to save my neck."

"How is that?"

"I had to get out of there for my life... Christian. I was charged with your... with the murder of Samuel Knight."

"Ahhh, now I see what happened. You couldn't play your part. I went missing; naturally enough, you were suspected of having made away with me. I had no idea whatsoever that I had left you exposed to such peril... though I ought to have thought of it, my poor Lucas—-"

"Dupe, sir."

"Why didn't you explain?"

"I couldn't, sir. 'Samuel' was found dead in his bed."

"What!" exclaimed Mister Christian, with his eyes open to their widest extent.

"It's a fact, sir. Murder charges were brought against me and your valet, Johnny McLean."

"Whoa! What craziness are you telling me?"

"Yes, a crazy tale sure enough, but a true one, all the same... Mister Christian. Samuel Knight is dead. There is a headstone with his name at the cemetery, and Oliver Courbis is the new heir of the entire estate."

Mister Christian Lucas was not one for profanity. He had been brought up proper by Doctor Quentin Clair, a good man of the cloth, but on this occasion, he let out every bad word in the book! "Where in the ever-living fuck did those son-of-a-bitches find a body to sit upon?"

Before Dupe could reply, a shrill shout came from the bushes, "Coooo-eee!"

"It's one of my friends looking for some firewood. I will run and meet him and give him this kindling and be right back in a second!" answered Dupe as he turned and ran away.

"Coooo-eee!" called the voice in the bushes again.

"Coooo-eee!" replied dupe, running toward it.

Dupe ran into George Simmons about a hundred yards away, hurrying towards him. "Thought you went and got lost, lad!" exclaimed Simmons.

"No. I met a friend from the states. He is all alone. I am going to return and have a chat with him and keep a watch on his fire. I'll be back in an hour or so. Here's your firewood... plenty of it," said Dupe hurriedly.

He left George and returned to where Samuel eagerly awaited his return with uncontrollable impatience.

When Dupe returned to where Christian Lucas sat by his fading fire, the sun began to peak above the horizon.

Dupe began laughing as he approached.

"Jesus Christ, man, what is the matter with you?" testily demanded Mister Lucas.

"I beg your pardon, sir—-"

"To Hell with that. Tell me what you were laughing at."

"To see you, sir, looking so jolly like me in all particulars that we might be taken for twin brothers!" replied Duplicate.

"We are that... Dupe. We have the same body shape, features, sunburned face, and three months growth of a black beard... and look at our clothes, they are almost the same buckskin shirt and pants," assented Christian Lucas.

"I say, sir... Mister Christian Lucas, when I first fell in with the men down below, they naturally wanted to know my name. At the time, I borrowed the name of another and told them my name was Duplicate Knight because I was the last born of a set of twins on Valentine's Day. I told them my twin brother was named Valentino, and I was named simply the Duplicate of the first. Dupe for short. I think I should introduce you to my friends as my older twin brother."

"Ha Ha Ha! Well thought of, Lucas!"

"Dupe, if you please, sir!"

"Dupe it is. But we must think before either of us speak, or we will surely betray each other."

"Yes, sir, quite right."

"Tell me, now that we got all that straightened out, what happened after we parted ways at my home on my estate back in the states?"

"Well, sir, I should tell you, in the very first place, that if I had been sober that night, I would never have consented to play a part that I must have known I couldn't carry out successfully."

"Were you not sober that night?"

"By no means, sir."

"I think we best finish our discussion before we join your friends."

"Very well. I said that I wasn't in my right senses when I agreed to play the part I did, sir... else I should never have ventured on acting out a plan that nearly cost me my life in more ways than one."

"I still don't understand. Why do you say that you weren't in your sober senses?"

"Because I know I wasn't. Your butler put me to work in the kitchen and employed me to wash dishes. And when washing them, there were dozens of wine glasses half full of wonderful wine. More so than I had ever seen. So, instead of pouring out the glasses, I commenced to drink the wine... or should I say a mixture of all sorts of wine. It truly made me a little crazy and reckless."

"I didn't perceive that you had gotten drunk that night," said Christian.

"Well, let's just say I wasn't myself."

"Very well. Now, proceed with your story. Tell me what happened after I left you."

"Well, when you and Johnny McLean had left the room, and the sound of your footsteps died out in the hallway, and I knew you had gone and wouldn't turn back and detect me in my bedroom, I crept out of bed and turned on my flashlight. I looked at myself... all clean-shaven, with a mustache and not a beard and nice clothes, and thought what white linen brought to a man. I bowed to myself in the mirror and thought it was good to be Samuel Knight."

"Okay. Go on."

"Well, at first, I wondered how I could have ever been talked into playing out this plan of ours. Why I ever agreed to it? But then, the wonderful fragrance of the sheets in your bed and all the splendid surroundings were so delightful to my mind and body that I became determined to enjoy them. Moreover, I just wanted to put off the day of being found out as long as possible.

I knew well that although I was transformed into a perfect duplicate of Samuel Knight and could make my voice sound like yours, I hoped I would not betray myself too soon."

"Gosh, I never thought for one second of anything but playing a practical joke on my tiresome old guardian Doctor Clair and getting away from him," laughed Christian Lucas.

"Well, sir," resumed Dupe.

"I suppose for the time being it is of no use to ask you to drop the sir?" interrupted Christian.

"Not in the least... sir. I can't help it. It is a force of habit, and it is strong. But I will drop it of necessity when I get among my friends not far down the hill from here."

"Okay. Go ahead."

"Well, I gave it a lot of thought. I laid there thinking how I might be able to enjoy the delights of my new position, if possible, without any discovery, and I made up my mind how to do it."

"And that was?"

"I decided to stay in my bed the next day and not allow the light to fall fully on my face for fear that I might be discovered. I would keep to my bed as long as possible and let the staff wait on me in my room... bring all my meals and books and lots of wine."

"Well, you had plenty of room. You had the bedroom, a large dressing room, and a sitting room. So, you weren't cramped for space, that's for sure," Christian said with a gentle laugh.

"So, I thought. I also thought that after all the company left, I might go downstairs and walk around like I owned the place in all its splendor and pass myself off for you, who, by the way, wasn't very familiarly known, even in the Black Rock Cove area.

"No. You are right. I was not."

"With my complete transformation, I must admit that it was so overwhelmingly great, even down to the smallest detail, I would make my detection by most persons impossible."

"You were a splitting image of me. But I agree with you."

"With this prospect of enjoyment before me and knowing with conviction that I might impersonate you for a long time yet to come and perhaps long enough for you to go and see the world carefree and then return. But I fell into a long sleep."

"What do you mean?" Christian asked.

"I don't know exactly how long I slept when I was awakened by a noise in my room of something falling as if accidentally knocked over. First, I remember shouting, who was there? Then, I remembered that I didn't lock the door after you departed. At that moment, I saw a dark shadow rush up to my bed, raise a club of some type, and hit me over the head. It happened so fast! A crashing sound came through my entire head... a flashing light that made the room spin in an array of colored lights and then... total darkness."

"Wait one sec! There was an attempt to murder you?" asked Christian.

"Yes. An almost successful attempt. I was out for several hours, and when I came to, I was in a room with a white sheet covering me with large casement windows."

"That was the parlor."

"I was so weak when I recovered my consciousness that I could hardly move. I didn't move an inch and listened as there was a stir at the other end of the room. Then, a voice I heard that I had heard before. It was the Coroner from Black Rock Cove. I heard him ask if everyone in the room had come to their verdict. There was a consensus that Samuel Knight died on the morning of the second of September from a sharp blow to the head by a blunt weapon of some sort. There was a consensus that the blow was delivered by Lucas Durano, a tramp... a vagabond and assisted by one Johnny McLean, your valet, Sam—-."

Christian Lucas began laughing. "I really can't help but enjoy all of this, Lucas! Seeing you here, now, in perfect safety, you know!"

"Well, I didn't enjoy it... not at the time. I was weak and still dizzy in my head, especially listening to the verdict of the witnesses in that room. I had an idea that I was about to be hauled off to jail and die in the electric chair."

"It didn't occur to you... Dupe that you had impersonated me, and as the murdered man, they had been holding an inquest on your body, supposing the entire time it was mine?"

"I passed out again as my head began to spin from so much blood loss."

"Okay, this is too good. What happened next?"

"Well, I suppose they left me there for the undertaker the next morning. When I did regain consciousness, the entire room was dark. The only glow was from a full moon that night shining through the windows. My memory began to come back to me. I remembered the blow I received that knocked me out for hours. I also remember the coroner's report. I had the impression that I was being held in custody for your murder. I became anxious to escape. I rolled over and fell to the floor. It shocked me, but I found I was all alone. I struggled across the room to a window. I was able to raise it and looked on the nightstand by me and saw a bottle of Remy Martin Louis the XIII. I threw it up and took a good swig. I climbed out of the window, made my way to the Lighthouse, and managed to reach it by sunrise. I remember walking inside and the two women saying something, and then I fainted. I suppose it was from my loss of so much blood."

"You must have startled them a little," Christian said.

"Actually, that's an understatement. When I finally regained consciousness, they had hidden me away and were nursing me back to health. They had already seen the posters and rewards for my arrest."

"It's kinda strange to me that the Lighthouse was not one of the first places the authorities searched," said Christian.

"Oh, it was! Not only searched, but they put two detectives around the clock on guard there until—-." He started laughing.

"What's so funny?"

"I beg your indulgence, sir! I can't help laughing to think of it."

"You remember those three fishermen from town, Dylan James, Rusty Simms, and Thomas Davison. They went to police headquarters and told them that Lucas Durano rode on their fishing vessel to Seattle and hitched a ride over to Mozambique. They left him there, ready to catch the big ship overseas."

"You see, sir, it was not you the authorities were after. They sent word about your capture or about my capture at the other end of the ship's travel in Lourenco Marques."

"Well, that's funny that you say that. I never went with those guys to Seattle."

"No?"

"Certainly not. I went an entirely different direction!"

"Then who was it that looked so much like you that they said they took?"

"That I don't know, but it wasn't me. Now, go on with your story, good friend."

"Well, just as soon as the detectives were lifted away from the Lighthouse, I left it and made my way into Black Rock Cove without any difficulty. Sickness and loss of so much blood had bleached my complexion, and with my beard smoothly shaved and my hair trimmed, I passed safely to the wharves. The description on the wanted posters posted everywhere was my ticket to freedom. I looked nothing like the description they were giving."

"What did you do in Black Rock Cove?"

"I knew I needed to hightail it out of town. Everyone was talking about the diamond mines outside Lourenco Marques, and I worked as a seaman for my passage here to strike mine diamonds, but I found out about this gold strike and came in this direction instead. What did you do?"

"Well, I kinda did what you did. I heard about the gold-digging from everyone in the village talking and took the next ship out and came here and arrived about two weeks ago. I loitered about the town for several days and then started on foot into the mountains on the way to the new gold fields. The talk was that the diamond fields had played out, so I was like going on an adventure."

"Yes, of course. But, sir, I hope in your own interests that you succeeded in bringing over a large amount of money and jewelry that," he started laughing, "I am charged with robbing you after I killed you!"

"Oh, yes, all but about one hundred thousand dollars lodged safely in the Bank of Lourenco Marques to the credit of Christian Lucas."

"Nice! So, what happened to your valet... to Johnny McLean? He never showed back up at your home in the county there. Thank goodness because there was a price on his head, too."

"The good Mister McLean walked with me on my road from the estate to downtown Black Rock Cove. We went to the ferry landing, and I put ten one-hundred-dollar bills in his hand, and he crossed the ferry to the island. I think he had the hots for some French maid the Reynold's family employed there."

"Very interesting. The French Maid disappeared without a trace that same day," said Dupe.

"Ahhh, that explains it. I have never seen nor heard of my worthy valet since that notable morning."

"No, doubt the two of them are off to bigger and better things in life. I am happy for them."

"But, Lucas, one more thing. You said that my cousin, Oliver, had succeeded to the title of my estate?"

"He certainly has. After the inquest and I was wanted for your murder, the heir presumptive succeeded to the title and estate."

"Yes, but my good Mister Duplicate Knight, Samuel Knight's body has disappeared, or I should say your body up and walked out of the parlor.... From the Room of Death!"

Dupe began laughing. "They thought that your body had been snatched. Large rewards were offered for its recovery or any information that would lead to its recovery. The talk was that several medical universities had already cut it up and used it for medical research."

"So, no doubt now that Oliver Courbis reigns over the entire estate. Well! Let him reign for a year longer until I have my frolic and reach my fruition of being wide and free. Then, my friend, I will return with you, Johnny, and my indelible birthmark to claim my rights and eject the interlopers!"

"Of course, sir. I will return with you. But how will you be able to put your hands on Johnny if you don't know where he went?"

"I have his solemn pledge to meet me at my estate on my twenty-first birthday. I know if he lives, he will keep his word! But, Dupe, what movement is that I see among your friends below?" asked Christian while looking at the burning fire below his camp.

Chapter TEN
It's a Small, Small World

"**B**y the way, I can smell breakfast cooking. I think it might be quail,** as one of the men was successful yesterday morning before we began walking alongside the mountain. Oh, by the way, I know this is a small world, but it gets even smaller. George Simmons is a brother of your pastor, Reverend Paul Simmons. But the man has never been in the state of Oregon in his life. He doesn't know any of his relatives. "

"Wow, how small and crowded this earth is, after all! It seems like people can't even go halfway across the world and not meet other people they have known or heard of," said Christian Lucas.

"That's so true. But these are good men. They are very kind and considerate. Shall we go down the hill and join them for breakfast?"

"If you like."

"Also, since I've told my yarn about my twin brother and you do me the honor to resemble me, shall I introduce you as that esteemed older brother?"

"Yes, of course. But... Dupe, stow the 'sir' business, okay?"

"Indeed, I will, sir! This is the last time I will use the word sir in my conversations until you and I return to Black Rock Cove when you shall enjoy your twenty-first birthday and be back in control of your estate and send Oliver Courbis packing back home," said Duplicate Knight as he stood up and led the way through the bushes and the campsite where breakfast awaited them."

George said, "Oh, good, Dupe... you're back! We thought you might have deserted us."

"Oh, no, not at all. I have brought with me a valuable recruit! The fella I met was no other than my honored twin brother, of whom I boasted to you all earlier and the one that I am only a duplicate of. But see," he stopped and stood beside 'Samuel' and continued, "you see what an honest copy I am when you look at him. So, my friends, let me introduce you to my oldest brother, although by only four minutes, the son and heir to a large estate in Oregon of our distinguished family... Mister Valentino Knight."

Valentino lifted his hand to George Simmons, who welcomed him to the party of men around the morning campfire.

The party of men, now increased to nine by Valentino's addition, sat down to regal themselves with a good hot cup of coffee, some toasted bread and butter, and a tasty quail or two.

All the men were silent as they ate their breakfast, especially Dupe's newfound brother. None ate their food with keener relish than the daintily nourished Valentino Knight.

Dupe watched his friend with admiring delight and surprised him by suddenly saying, "You enjoy this sort of life, Brother!"

"Yes, greatly," replied Valentino.

"Ahhh," the red-headed giant of a man interjected. "Tramping all day and camping all night gives one a big appetite, eh? But Valentino, we reverse the rule by tramping all night and camping during the day. Of course, that has been true until today. I fear we must tackle that mountainous barrier that stands before us by daylight instead of by darkness. There's no way we could ever get past it during the nighttime. It would be too dangerous."

After breakfast, the men began their trek up the mountain.

Their perilous path took them through an almost impenetrable thicket up the front of the mountain. After that, their path diverged to the right sometimes and then back to the left along the sides of a bottomless abyss. Then down they went into a deep ravine and across a roaring riverbed torrent of water hurrying over the rocks.

It is amazing what men will encounter and endure in pursuing gold?

Valentino spoke very little. He wanted to see the world and be free for a year, and he was definitely getting an adventure by coming to Mozambique and exploring the gold fields.

At the end of the day, darkness put a stop to their progress. Finally, the nine men sat down to rest near the top of the giant mountain. The spot for their overnight camping was the most savage wilderness the eye would ever see.

Tremendous precipices towered high above their heads. Gorges like the Demon Gorge back home opened at their feet. Thorny thickets were all around them.

Some of the men went right to sleep. However, the party members were too weary to sleep and sat around the fire talking.

Valentino said, "I wonder how in the world a horse, oxen, much less wagons, could get over this barrier. I can only imagine!"

"By a different route, of course," said Dupe.

"I would think such a giant of a mountain as this would present an impassable barrier."

"Not a bit! Wherever man can go, the oxen can go, as well."

"Yes, I can understand what you are saying, but in going down the mountain, it seems to be difficult to impossible... dangerous enough to the extent of certain destruction?" said Valentino. "I think I am going to sleep," he added as he turned over in his blanket and went to sleep.

This day, their first on the giant mountain, was only given as an example of what the men went through in their trek towards the gold-digging. The second mountain was just like it... only a little worse.

Two days passed.

The third day brought the nine men to the foot of the great mountain, but—-.

Having passed the mountain barrier, they fell into cavalcades of horsemen, wagons pulled by oxen, and many men on foot... all bound for the same place, the new gold fields.

This was, by far, the most incredible rush that had ever been seen since the Alaska Gold Rush a hundred years earlier, and it was happening halfway across the world!

Among the many adventurers was a woman who looked completely out of place. She was in her sixties with solid gray hair, was riding on a mule, and appeared to be by her lonesome.

"Hello, ma'am. Are you going to stake a claim and dig for gold?" asked Dupe with jocular good humor as he found himself walking beside the woman.

"Oh, my goodness, no, boy," she answered earnestly. "I do, however, travel to the gold fields to make ten times what I made back home."

"What can you do?"

She lightly laughed. "Have you looked around you? There are at least a hundred single men to every married man who brought his wife."

"I agree."

"Well, I come to cook, wash, iron, and sew their clothes for them. I will make more money than most of them will make in digging for gold."

"I agree. I have never made anything by digging. I have, however, seen fortunes dug up all around me. It's just my luck, I suppose."

"Look over yonder. Do you see that fellow with the buckskin horse he is walking holding onto the reigns?"

"Yes."

"Like me, he takes after all the new rushes for discovering riches in the hills."

"What does he do?"

"He's an entertainer. The man can sing, and the gold diggers like to sit back and drink their whiskey and listen to him sing,' she answered and kicked her mule a bit to indicate their discussion was over.

Dupe fell back with the group of men he was traveling with.

After the fifth day of travel, George, Valentino, and Dupe declared they were less than a day away from the new fields. With this prospect in view, they made their last fire, cooked some supper, and after eating, stretched themselves out in their blankets and slept.

"Tomorrow evening, then, we might expect to be at the end of all of our work getting there," muttered Valentino as he turned and rolled over on his side.

"Yes," said Dupe, "of this sort of work, at least," as he dozed off to sleep.

An early start kicked off the next morning. By the dawn of the day, the entire encampment was stirring around the campfire. By the time the sun started climbing above the horizon, the men were on their way and would reach the new gold fields before sunset.

About eleven o'clock in the morning, Valentino and Dupe, walking ahead of the pack by fifty yards or so, ascended a quartz ridge. They looked down from its highest point and were absolutely struck with amazement!

Below them, in a large valley, a panorama of life like nothing ever seen before in the world except right here in Mozambique. The men had come unaware of the marvelous new gold field!

Below them, almost as far as the eye could see, were thousands of people of all nationalities, ages, colors, and sexes. It was an amazing sight to behold.

Down in the depths of the gully on each side of a stream that ran forever were men with tin pans engaged in washing for gold.

"What does all of this look like to you, Dupe?" asked Valentino.

"Well, actually, I have seen a lot of gold fields, and this is unlike any of them I ever saw," answered Duplicate. They continued to walk into what appeared was the downtown district with bars and hotels. "Well, what do you think of this free-as-a-bird sort of life, Valentino?" asked Dupe.

"It is absolutely amazing! But I think a week of it will be enough for me. I actually came to only satisfy my curiosity. Then, I shall leave your side, Dupe. I must see the rest of this amazing country in all its wonderful stages. I must experience everything."

A bartender overheard Val talking and said, "To do that, you must go to Van Diesel's Land, where you will experience everything this great country has to offer."

Five minutes later, the rest of the crew showed up at the saloon, wasted no time, and set out to investigate the fields.

One of the first parties they encountered was the Smiths, who gathered around their wagons and tethered bullocks. Greetings between the two groups were exchanged, and they continued on their way.

George Simmons and Duplicate Knight entered into a partnership and staked out a claim and secured it by a deed which was no more than striking a pickax stuck into the middle of the ground, and that was it!

The other men did the same, except for Valentino. He remained and experienced the gold rush for two weeks and then left to return to the big city of Lourenco Marques. As he departed, he put five hundred dollars into the hands of Dupe and forced him to take it. "You have a right to this much and much more for all the damage you have suffered because of my whim to see the world. Please write to me if you ever need any help or money," he said as he wrote a note with his bank in Lourenco Marques. Your mail to this address will find me wherever I may be. Oh, and yes, Dupe, please address your correspondence to Christian Lucas." He shook Dupe's hand, rushed over, jumped in a wagon, and headed back to Lourenco Marques.

So, Valentino left the gold fields to travel to places in the country that he had not seen before. The next time we meet him will be in the wilds of Van Diesel's Land and under startling circumstances.

All the excitement back in Lourenco Marques over the escape of the most devilish desperados in all the maximum-security prisons had not abated in the least amount, even when an entire month had passed since the event.

No woman or child dared to venture out of their home into the country for fear of coming across this unchained demon!

It was almost five weeks since the escape of Jack Dannells.

This somewhat eccentric young man passed his time since we saw him last traveling the countryside enjoying the sights of this remarkable country. He saw all various walks of life in the eastern region of Africa. He had been guests of every type of people who were part of the life of Mozambique. He had roughed it among the gold diggers. He had gotten lost in the bush, as they called it, and he had lost his money and almost his life among the evil men of the backwoods. In essence, he passed through enough adventures to fill a large volume. However, none of these adventures have much to do with our story, so we only allude to them a little in this narrative.

And now, he came upon Van Diesel's Land, to which he wanted to become acquainted with the life of convicts in a penal colony. So, at length, he made his way back to the wharves in Lourenco Marques, where he would take a voyage back to Black Rock Cove in Oregon.

He was barely a day out from Lourenco Marques when the sun began to sink below the horizon. However, he didn't actually see it go out of sight as the thickness of the foliage surrounding him kept its view out of his sight.

He stopped his horse for a few moments while he took a map and a compass out of his coat pocket. Then, he began to look over the map to see how far he was from Lourenco Marques and rather or not, if he kept going, he would reach it before nightfall. Then, he heard, "Help! Help! Help!" echo from the woods. Then again, "Help me! Father!"

Christian jumped down from his horse, pulled his revolver from his belt and cocked it, and rushed into the thicket from which the woman's voice came. Breaking through the underbrush, he came out from where the cries were coming. Within only a few more steps forward, Christian came upon a shocking scene.

A young and most beautiful young woman was struggling with all her strength to try and escape from the arms of a hideous monster who held one arm around her and his other hand covering her mouth.

Christian didn't hesitate. The sight of the damsel in distress filled his soul with rage and horror. He fired his revolver impulsively and brought the evil man down before the wretch could cry for mercy.

Christian rushed over to the girl's side and watched the evil ruffian lay rolling and screaming with pain and rage.

He looked to see if the young woman was harmed. She sat with a disordered dress and disheveled hair, bewildered and trembling, scarcely comprehending the nature of her danger or the man who had saved her.

Even at that moment in time and with all the intense excitement, Christian Lucas perceived the woman he had rescued as one of the most beautiful beings his eyes had ever beheld. He bent over the girl and said, "Do not be frightened. The danger is over. You are safe, my dear.!"

"Oh, thank you! How in the world can I thank you enough, sir?" asked the woman in a very faint voice.

The terrible screaming of the evil wounded fiend was so loud next to them it almost prevented their conversation.

"Please, my dear, let me escort you home or back to your friends. Are you able to walk?"

"Yes, I am better now. I do thank you very much. And my father will thank you, too," she said, looking at the evil man rolling around on the ground. "Do you think that man is suffering, sir? Is there anything we can do to help him?" asked the woman in a voice softened with compassion.

"What? Are you crazy? Do angels pity the demons in all their rage. The wretch you see there suffers deservedly."

"Yes, sir. I have a home on the mountain there," she pointed. "I will show you the path and thank you for taking me there. So will my father, too."

"Lead the way."

"But wait. Is there nothing we can do to help that poor man before we go?"

"No. Let us be on our way," Christian said.

"But wait! What harm can come of my going to him? He is suffering and is disabled. He might be dying. The man would not hurt a fly now," she answered in a tone of pity.

"Let us go. Neither you nor I can do any good for the man. I will guard you safely home," Christian said.

"Very well. I will get my father to send someone to help this wounded man when I get home," replied the young woman leading the way out of the thicket.

"Do you know this man? Is that why you are so set on helping him?"

"No. But I know he is a poor soul suffering terribly in his mind and body. But, please, sir, do not think I am ungrateful for what you did for me and for saving me from that brute. I know you had to shoot that man to save me, and I thank you deeply for doing so. But I can't help not feeling sorry for that awful man," she added, looking over her shoulder at the fallen ruffian still hollering and rolling on the ground.

"Let me ask you again. Do you know this man?" asked Christian Lucas.

"Of course not," she replied.

"He is an escaped convict. The outfit he has on and the number 6666 stamped on his back, he is no good."

"I'm sorry, sir. I can't blame them for trying to regain their liberty," she replied.

They began their walk through the woods and up the mountain. Then, it opened into the most fantastic homestead Christian had ever seen. "What an eerie plateau for such a magnificent home... in the middle of nowhere."

"It was my father's fancy. I like it."

"Your father built that?"

"Yes. He first bought the land, and before he could have his house built, he had a road made by which to haul what building materials he needed to build the house. All the labor was supplied from the government in which he paid."

"Has your father many convicts in his employment?"

The young woman hesitated before answering. She then replied, "One."

"Do you usually extend your walks as far from your home as you have done this evening... at your peril?"

"Actually, yes. Every day if the weather permits. I enjoy walking. It's one of the things that I really like doing."

"Isn't this some wild country out and away from your home?"

"In all the years that I have lived here and wandered in the woods below, I've never met a human being until today when I met my assailant... and, of course, my rescuer. It would almost seem as if my guardian angel saw that awful man in my path and sent you here to save me!"

"Well, I hope you will not venture down in that wilderness again without company or protection," Christian said very seriously.

"You are right. Although I think there is only a one-in-a-million chance of ever happening again, I still would not risk that one," the young woman solemnly answered.

The sun had set, but the glorious afterglow of the western sunset skies still illumined the heavens and the earth.

Christian Lucas and the young woman came in sight of the large and spacious white mansion built all by itself on a large plateau jetting out from the side of the mountain halfway up.

A long flight of steps was cut in the solid rock that led them up to the lowest terrace, beautifully landscaped with green grass and well-trimmed shade trees. On both sides of the flagstone walks were long lines of roses with an occasional arbor with rustic seats.

There were three terraces, all beautifully aligned with all sorts of blooming plants until they came to a final flight of steps to where the mansion was built. This terrace was by far the crowning pride of the grounds. It was stair-stepped grass plots bordered with low hedges of flowers and bushes of the most exquisite beauty Christian had ever seen in all his life. There was nothing as beautiful as what he saw back home at his estate. In the middle of the courtyard was a giant fountain whose bright waters sang a tune as they rose and fell, splashing in the wide-open marble reservoir below.

"My God, I have never seen such beauty. This is a most charming place... an oasis in the middle of nowhere... in the middle of a forest. One might even say a mansion paradise in the middle of purgatory!

The only way I could put it is that the work on this place had to be by fairies!" explained the young woman's protector and knight in shining armor.

"Actually, sir, it was the work of convicts," said the woman as she led the way up to the palace. Although, after all, it wasn't a big house, it was definitely magnificent enough to call a palace.

The lady led her protector up a flight of broad, marble steps to a long open space extending from end to end of every palace story up to the lofty roof.

As they walked up the steps, they passed marble pillars covered with running roses up to two large front doors, more significant than any Christian had ever seen, with four French windows on each side.

The woman opened this door and admitted her newfound friend into a spacious hall whose floor was inlaid in octagons of all sorts of rare woods, those which came from the surrounding forest. The walls were covered with artistic paintings in incredible murals for as far as the eye could see.

At the end of the hallway was a magnificent carved spiral staircase that led up to the stories above.

Numerous walnut wood doors opened on all sides of the many suites of rooms.

If one looked to the very top of the domed palace, one would see that the area was lighted by a stained-glass window that poured a rosy radiance over the entire area.

Christian glanced in all directions, and for one who was accustomed to having numerous servants in his home back outside Black Rock Cove, he found none whatsoever in the hallway or anywhere he looked.

The young woman opened the door to their right and motioned Christian to enter.

He obeyed her gesture and walked in. There he found a room decorated as though it was from China. The walls were covered with

Japanese silk. The floor was covered with matting. All the furniture was made from bamboo, and the tables were carved and inlaid with wood.

Christian looked near the bay window. The sole inmate was a noble-looking elderly man with a smooth fair face and a smooth chin. He had long gray hair, which a part ran down the middle. It fell in long waves past his shoulders.

His eyes were closed as he reclined back in his rocking chair, fast asleep.

"Ahhh, my father is taking his afternoon nap! Please, sir, sit. I will go and wake him. It is late in the afternoon, and he won't sleep tonight if he sleeps all day," said the young lady.

Christian Lucas did as the woman instructed and gently sat down across from the old man.

The lady walked over and gently kissed the old man on his forehead. This gentle salute awakened him. "Ahh, my angel child! Is it you? Have you returned already? He looked at his wristwatch, "You are later than usual, my darling.

"Yes, Father. But I have had an adventure," she answered, looking into his kind blue eyes with a smile.

"An adventure, Aurora! What adventure do you speak of my child?" demanded the widely awakened old man whose uneasiness could have been anxiety but for the reassuring smile of his daughter.

"Yes, father. I met an escaped convict, and he -—oh, he was rude to me and—-."

"Aurora!" exclaimed the old man, growing paler than average.

"He didn't hurt me, Father. He only frightened me, and... then, opportunity showed itself when a gentleman traveler came up and brought me safely home. Will you please see him and thank him for me, Father?"

"Aurora, this is a strange story that you are telling me. How was this convict rude to you?"

"He frightened me with his speech, his cursing, and how he acted."

"Who is this gentleman who brought you home?"

"I don't know, Father. He is a very kind and brave man. He is here now. Will you see him and thank him for me?"

"Yes, my dear. And learn more of this adventure that you seem to not be telling me. Bring the gentleman here, Aurora."

Aurora looked over her shoulder. "Will you come and see my father, sir?" said Aurora smiling upon the stranger who heard every word of the conversation.

Christian Lucas walked up and stood before the old man and gave a gentle nod of his head.

"Father, this gentleman brought me home safely," she said while turning and looking at Christian. "Sir, this is my father, Mister Viktor Serafin," said the young lady, presenting the stranger.

Christian again bowed deeply.

"I am happy to see you, my dear sir, and to have this opportunity of telling you just how much I appreciate you stepping in to stop this convict's behavior toward my daughter. Tell me, who should I mention in my prayers this evening for what you did to help my daughter?" Serafin said with much emotion.

"My name is Lucas. Christian Lucas. But indeed, sir, you vastly overestimate the small service I was more than happy to offer Miss Serafin—-."

"Enough, sir. The fact remains the same. You have saved my daughter from death or a fate worse than death. We keep to ourselves and don't venture out much here. But, I hope, as you are a traveling man, I presume, will honor us with your company here as long as you can endure our dullness."

"Very well, sir. Tonight, I will take you up on your kind offer," Christian replied with a gentle nod of his head.

"It is settled, then. We will not let you depart in the morning, next week, or the week after without an effort to detain you. "Smitty! Smitty!" The old man shouted. It wasn't long, and a servant answered the old man's call.

"Tell me, young man, where I can send for your luggage," said Serafin.

Christian began laughing. "My luggage Mister Serafin consists of a pair of saddlebags across the back of my buckskin steed. But where he is now, I have no idea. I threw myself out of my saddle and rushed into the forest at the cry I heard from your daughter."

Aurora's father turned his gaze immediately on his daughter.

"Come now, Father. I told you the man frightened me, but he didn't hurt me... really," said Aurora with a smile.

"Aurora, where did this mishap occur?"

"Down near the Fairy's Spring," answered the young woman.

"Okay, everyone. Smitty, grab some of the others and go looking for this man's horse and belongings," he said while turning his head in the stranger's direction. "And you, sir, my home is your home. I have plenty of changes of clothes, and we all are most heartily at your service," said the old gray-haired man.

"Oh, and father, my love... while you are sending some men to find this man's horse, will you send a stretcher down to bring that poor soul up to the house so that he might be properly attended to," said the young lady.

"What poor soul, Aurora? What are you talking about, my child?" asked the old man.

"That poor man who frightened me, Father. He is wounded and lying out on the bare ground, alone and no more there to help him. He might die and needs help. He needs to be brought here as fast as possible."

Mister Serafin glanced from his daughter to Christian Lucas in alarm!

"Sir, I was obliged to shoot the lout. There was no time for a discussion," said the adventurer.

"Father! I am not in the least hurt. There's not a bruise or a scratch on me," said Aurora, with a smile.

"I realize you are not hurt, my dear. However, the fact of my living to say so should prove that I know you are safe. If harm were to come to you now, my Aurora, death would surely come to me."

"And since I am unhurt, you will send for that poor, wounded man to be brought here and helped?"

"Yes, I will send for him."

"Yes, I will. And afterward, I will inform the authorities at the prison camp. I have no doubt that this evil man is no other than Jack Dannells from the chain gang. We got word from the town of his escape."

"Sir," said Smitty. "What are your orders?"

"Take a few men with you, Smitty. Go down to the Fairy Springs and search for the buckskin horse our visitor left. He should be carrying a pair of saddlebags and bring them here. Also, carry a stretcher with you and find a wounded man in the same area. If he is still alive, you should hear him moaning. He has been shot. Bring him here, also."

"Yes, sir."

Aurora said, "And be sure to bear him slowly and carefully because he is in great pain," added the young lady.

"Yes, Miss Aurora."

"Anything else, sir," Smitty asked.

"Come, Mister Lucas, let me show you to your room." He immediately led his guest to a bedroom over the parlor where they were sitting. The two large casement windows overlooked the front terraces and the grand fountain below.

After the first good bath he had enjoyed for many days, Christian encased himself in a full suit of his host's clothes, which, if they were not a perfect fit in all respects, did very well in an emergency.

He left and went down to the library, where he was asked to wait until a suppertime call was made. He walked over to a book table and picked up "Seeing the Power of God" by Sidney St. James, bound in crimson and gold and beautifully illustrated. While he looked over some of the first lines in the novel, he raised his head as the door opened. It was she... Aurora entered the room in the form of his young hostess.

He stepped forward to meet her, and as he took her hand to lead her to a chair, he thought how he never had seen so fair a beauty. She wore a trained dress of white silk, embroidered down the front and around the border and on the edges of her short sleeves and low-cut neckline. A string of pearls adorned her lovely bosom. She also wore a pair of white gloves like they do back in Black Rock Cove at his last nineteenth birthday party.

"I hope you will not find it dull here, Mister Lucas," she said.

Before he could say a word, the chef came to the door and said, "Come, sir, it is time for supper."

After supper, they all went and were seated on the front piazza, enjoying the coolness and fragrance of a moonlit summer night. They could look out over the giant mountainside's magnificent face and the valley below's dip. Then, a man came up to the steps, stood, and gently bowed.

In his tall form, Christian recognized Smitty.

"Well?" asked Mister Serafin.

"Well, sir, I've got the ruffian, saddlebags, and a chase I had. The animal tired himself out and was willing enough to let me bring him home. The saddlebags and the beast are in the stables, sir."

"Very good. Be sure to bring the saddlebags up to the house."

"Yes, sir."

"And what about the wounded man, Smitty?" inquired Aurora.

"The other men found him right next to the Fairy Spring. They are still bringing him up along the road."

"He is still living, then?"

"Yes, but I have never heard so many cuss words come from someone in my life. His language ain't fit for no lady to hear, Miss Aurora," added Smitty.

"Enough, Smitty. Go and bring the saddlebags up here."

"Yes, sir. Anything else?"

'No."

"Are you sure, sir?"

"Yes, I am quite sure."

Smitty went away and was not on this occasion called back by Mister Serafin.

No sooner did Smitty disappear than a procession appeared coming up the front entrance. A man was stretched out on a cot as if he were dead.

Aurora began to race away to meet the procession.

"Wait, Aurora. Go into the house. This is no place for you," said her father.

The girl didn't argue and went inside.

"Go with her, Mister Lucas. I will attend to this matter," continued the old man.

"I hope you will call on me, sir, if I can be of the least service."

"Certainly, I will call if I need you."

Christian followed Aurora inside and found her at the main windows in the parlor, looking out.

"Aurora," Christian said.

"Is that miserable man dead? Do you think——-" He was still stretched out on that cot.

"I really don't know. But what I don't understand is what if he should be dead. Why does it concern you so much, Aurora," asked Christian with a shade of annoyance in his voice.

"I don't know. I hope that man gets well so he can live a better life before he leaves this world."

"Take him to one of the vacant servant's quarters," shouted Mister Serafin.

"Oh, Mister Lucas, he is not dead, then. I'm so glad!"

"To what purpose do you say that, Miss Aurora?" gravely inquired Christian.

"To redeem his pats... to live a better life," replied the young woman.

"To break into more stores, cut a few throats, and to finally die in the electric chair instead of on a cot stretched out," amended Lucas.

What further might have been said between the two was prevented by Mister Serafin walking into the room. He looked over at Christian. "Sir, please come with me and see him?"

The two men passed into the hallway to the back of the house where the servants' quarters were located. They turned into a room where a cot with the stretched dying man was in the middle, his head on a clean pillow and his body covered with a blanket. The man's face had been washed, and his hair combed. His convict suit was exchanged for a clean set of clothes. He was lying very still. His eyes were closed. His bloodless face looked pale in contrast to his jet-black hair and short beard from four or five weeks of growth.

The two men stood at the door looking at him.

Then, Christian followed the old man's lead and walked closer to the body. Christian had not seen the face of the man distinctly at the time he shot him in the forest. He suddenly gazed upon him with changing color to his skin and a sickening heart.

It wasn't because the convict was dying of a wound inflicted by his own hand, though that circumstance affected him more deeply than he would like to confess.

Christian looked down as the man opened his eyelids and fixed his dark eyes entirely upon the face of the younger man, who jerked and jumped back suddenly, exclaiming, "Oh, my God! Lucas! Lucas Durano, my dear friend. Heaven of Heavens!"

Chapter ELEVEN
A Deathbed Confession

"**Y**ou know this man, Christian?" asked Mister Serafin in some surprise.

Christian didn't reply. He looked down at his friend and said, "Lucas! Lucas! Is it possible that I find you in this condition?" demanded Christian in a tone of great mental distress. He bent down closer to his friend, who only stared stupidly for an instant and then, with a sigh, closed his eyes.

"Christian, what is going on, son? You know this man...."

"Yes! I know this man and have known him since childhood back in the states. I've also known him here for a few weeks before I left to see the sights," he gravely and most sadly replied.

Silence passed between Mister Serafin and Christian. His heart was broken! He bled an ocean through his eyes. His soul felt wafer-thin, and his body trembled and chilled.

"I judge from your words and manner that you just now recognized him and that you didn't know him when you put a bullet in him?"

"No, I did not. And now... I feel deeply saddened to have found him in this manner."

While Christian bent over close to his friend's face, Mister Serafin looked intently at both faces. "My God, boy, you and he are brothers, are you not," he said.

"The likeness has been often noticed back in the states," Christian replied.

"I beg your pardon, sir, but there are brothers, and then there are brothers," he added. "Your face, the hair, eyes, you each could pass for the other... it's incredible."

"Is he going to die?"

"I don't know. The doctor has been summoned and should be out in the morning," said Viktor.

"Is it necessary that he should be watched tonight?" asked Christian.

"Yes."

"Then I will stay with him through the night."

"You are off a long journey yourself and need some rest."

"I'm sorry, sir. But I can't sleep. I can't go to bed. I will not leave this room tonight. Lying there on that cot is my best friend since childhood, slain by my own hand, dying before my very eyes. Say what you may. But he is my childhood friend who was fallen by my hand, and I must not and will not desert his deathbed. I will remain in this Room of Death."

"Very well, young man. I understand."

"Understand? Mister Serafin, I don't regret shooting this man under the circumstances. I only regret the existence of the circumstances that compelled me to do so, that's all."

"Well, I will leave you here with your friend. Goodnight to you, sir," said the gentleman as he stood to leave the room.

"Goodnight to you, sir." The door closed, and Christian pulled a chair beside the bedside.

Lucas Durano slept quietly.

For a moment, Christian thought about how he didn't say goodnight to the beautiful Aurora. Instead, he left her side to go with her father to see the wounded man and left her staring out the window.

He certainly expected to return to her side and finish the evening properly, but instead, he was sitting in a quiet room with his dear,

dear friend dying on the cot in front of him. But, with all said, he knew that he would see her in the morning and that she would warmly approve his action in taking care of the 'wounded' man during the night... his best friend!

After almost two hours, Lucas's breathing became long sighs, and Christian stood up occasionally and examined his features by the light from the Gone with the Wind Lamp on the nightstand.

Then, Lucas's eyes opened. His eyes and Christian's met.

"Hello, Lucas. How do you feel?" inquired Christian.

"What in the Hell, you bastard do you mean by calling me Lucas?" demanded the wounded convict with a savage scowl.

"Mister Duplicate Knight, then! How do you feel, my friend?" Christian again asked.

"You are one crazy son-of-a-bitch!" His screaming curse words came from deep within him and forced their way from his mouth as if his terrified soul had unleashed a demon.

The wounded man watched as Christian poured half a shot glass full of brandy and handed it to the man. "Drink this. It will help relieve you, Lucas."

He smelled the contents and then swallowed it eagerly. He sighed with satisfaction. "Ahhh, now that is some good medicine!"

"Lie still now, Lucas. You need your rest," said Christian.

"Jesus Christ! There you go again, you bastard! Who in the Hell is this Lucas fella?" he growled.

"Oh, I'm so sorry. Mister Duplicate Knight," said Christian.

"And who is the bloody Hell is Mister Doubletake? You are one big idiot, Mister."

"Come, now, Lucas—-"

"Lucas Durano! You are the third person who has called me that name in the last month and a half. What in the fuck do you mean by——? Ohhhh!" The wounded man broke off his words and groaned with pain.

"Try not to talk. To do so causes you to suffer. Lie still. The brandy will help you go back to sleep."

"I'd like to get my damn hands on that bastard who emptied his fucking revolver into my insides!" snarled the brute, grinding his teeth.

Although Christian was a very truthful man, he didn't think it wise to let Lucas know any different on this one occasion.

Lucas then calmed down and laid still. Then, while staring at the ceiling, he said, "I wonder what makes people call me Lucas... what is it?"

"Lucas Durano. They call you that because you at one time went by that name, whatever you might call yourself now," replied Christian.

"See here, crazy fella, you, and everybody else is way wide of the mark. I must, for some reason, resemble this man," he said while pointing at the brandy glass. "Give me another shot of that good stuff. I feel as weak as a mouse."

Christian remained silent. He wanted his patient to relax and get some rest.

But, on the other hand, the convict was strengthened by an extra shot of brandy and felt more inclined to talk.

"You think I am Lucas Durano?"

"Yes, I do!"

"You really do?" asked the wounded man.

"Absolutely. I still sit here and wonder why you should play this deception trick on me... a man who has known you since you were seven years old and onward," said Christian.

"I don't remember ever to have seen you before in all the days of my life. Yet, you sit there talking to me and swear that you've known me since I was almost a baby."

"If you are not Lucas Durano, then who on earth are you?" He asked, knowing the question might throw his dear friend into a fever!

"Someone who looks a whole lot like the person you have known all your life. Maybe that's because I have been confused with someone in the States and here in this country, too."

"You have?"

"Yep. The first time I had to leave a small village on the west coast, Black Rock Cove, in a hurry. I got onboard a fishing vessel and offered the skipper a hundred bucks to forego his fishing trip and get me up to a ship departing Seattle for the gold mines here in Mozambique. The man took my money and called me Lucas Durano the entire trip. I never said a word. I didn't care what he called me."

"Ohhh," replied Christian, and a light bulb went off in his head.

"Then, there was a time when I came back to the states a month later and was nabbed by the police and put in prison again. This time they said I killed someone named Samuel Knight. First, I never killed anyone, and second, I never even heard of that man. Then, they decided to send me to the prison camp here in Mozambique. I don't know why they sent me here, but they did."

"Ahhh," said Christian.

"Now, wait, there is a third time. Six weeks ago, I was working on the chain gang here when up came a beautiful woman who looked me in the face and screamed, 'Lucas Durano!'

"Wow, you have been confused a bunch of times," Christian added.

"Oh, Mister, there was another time, a fourth and last time. It is you, whom I have never seen in all the days of my life, telling me that I am crazy and that I am Lucas Durano. You sit there and tell me you have known me since I was a knee-high to a grasshopper!"

"If you are not Lucas Durano, who are you?"

"Well, that's none of your damn business. Give me some more brandy. I am starting to feel faint again."

"I'm scared to give you more. It might not be good for you."

"Come now, fella. You shot me! At least give a dying man another drink. I'm as cold as an icicle and as weak as plain water. Feel my head! Feel my pulse! Now, give me some damn brandy!" He said faintly but vehemently.

Christian poured a half glass of brandy and gave it to the dying man. "I'm glad you're not the man I mistook you for! I was shocked to think that I had—-"

"Whoa! I might be a bad son-of-a-bitch, but don't go off on a tangent on me, fella. I never meant to harm one hair on that beautiful girl's head. I might be rough around the edges, but I ain't that rough. I only wanted the gold chain off her neck and the diamond earrings she was wearing. She became so scared and began screaming loudly. I tried to cover her mouth to quiet her down. I swear to you, I wouldn't have hurt her willingly. I am happy that she isn't hurt and—-." He stopped his words and groaned. "Mister, I am feeling very fatigued. Feel my pulse? Am I dying?" he asked weakly.

"You are making yourself tired. You must stop talking and get some rest."

Christian sat back down in his chair.

The sound of three bells from the German grandfather clock came from the hallway.

"Thank goodness it is near morning. The sun will come up soon," he whispered as his chin hit his chest and fell into a light doze.

The sun finally crept up above the horizon for another day. The household began to stir. Christian stood up and leaned over the wounded man, who was sleeping and breathing regularly. He reached over and put the palm of his hand on the man's forehead. "Oh, God, I fear I might have given him too much brandy. What else was I to do? Oh... how I wish the doctor would hurry up and get here."

The doctor didn't answer his mental request. But someone else came.

The door opened, and Mister Serafin, still in his sleeping pajamas, entered the room and walked up to the bedside. "How's our patient, Christian?"

"He's sleeping, but he has a high temperature."

"How did he pass the night?"

"Restlessly until I gave him a third glass of brandy. That seemed to have done the trick."

"Well, why don't you go to your room, have a hot bath, and change your clothes? By the time you finish, breakfast will be ready," suggested the old man.

"You know, Mister Serafin, I think I will take you up on your offer," he replied, getting up and turning his chair over to the elderly man.

Christian returned to his room, took a bath, changed his clothes, brushed his jet-black hair and beard, and went down to breakfast, where Aurora awaited him at the breakfast table.

She was a magnificent portrait sitting at the table, her fair, golden-hued hair bound back by a pale-red ribbon flowing down over her shoulders.

As he approached the table, she said, "Thank you, Mister Lucas. My father said you were so kind as to sit up with the wounded man last night. How is he doing this morning?"

"He was sleeping when I left him forty-five minutes ago. However, he has a high fever this morning," Christian replied.

Mister Serafin entered the room and pulled up a chair to the table. While there, Smitty came in and said, "Mister Serafin, the doctor is here, and two detectives from the police department in Lourenco Marques are with him."

"Detectives?"

"Yes, sir. They wanted to see if the man was in convict clothes and bring him back to jail."

"Put them in the parlor. I will be there shortly," he said while looking at Christian. "Will you join me, Christian," inquired the old man, standing up.

"Certainly, sir," replied Christian, following his example.

When they got to the room, they found Doctor Jeffery Sanders, the red-faced and round-bodied physician, and two tall detectives.

"Hello Viktor, sorry for my delay. We would like to see the wounded man at once, not only for me to examine, but these two officers wish to identify him, if possible. They suspect him to be no other than the escaped convict Jack Dannells, who broke out of prison six weeks ago. He has been on the loose ever since," said Doctor Sanders.

"Yes, of course. Let's go to his bedside now," replied Viktor, turning to lead the way to the servants' quarters.

When they arrived, Viktor's housekeeper was in the chair pulled up to the bedside. Her patient was moaning in a restless sleep.

The housekeeper rose up and nodded her head, and left the room.

Doctor Sanders bent over the sleeping patient. "Yep, gentlemen, this is the fugitive convict, Jack Dannells."

Christian quickly interjected, "How long has he been in Lourenco Marques, and what crime has this man been convicted?" he anxiously inquired and was still profoundly affected by the perfect resemblance of Jack Dannells, the convict, to his old lifelong friend, Lucas Durano.

One of the detectives answered, "He has been in lockup here for about eight years. But since the last conviction, only about a year. Somehow, he had returned to the States on an outbound ship and committed a robbery there. He was tried and convicted and sent back here to prison with a sentence of ten years. He is a tough case, sir."

Doctor Sanders began to examine the condition of the wounded man.

Christian couldn't help but stare at the man during the examination. He could only wonder at the unaccountable resemblance that rendered the two men, in form and features, voice and... well, everything as they were exact counterparts of each other and himself.

When Samuel or Christian first met Lucas Durano in the mad rush to the gold fields, he learned from the vagabond all about the perplexity occasioned in the neighborhood of Black Rock Cove, which seemed to be the miraculous ubiquity of the one Lucas Durano or his equally miraculous multiplication of three Lucas Duranos.

Now, Samuel understood the mystery. But we should be careful and continue to remind ourselves that he went by the name of Christian Lucas.

The vagabond was the first and only real Lucas Durano... he who had foregathered with the doctor in the neighborhood of Shaw's Bend on the morning of his flight from Samuel's home northwest of Black Rock Cove.

The second Lucas Durano had ridden on the train with the pastor on the day of his departure from Black Rock Cove.

And now, this felon lying on the table dying was the third Lucas Durano, the man who escaped to Seattle on the fishing boat of Dylan James and friends on the morning of the homicide of me at my home.

All was clear now!

"Sir," the doctor said to Christian, "will you please sit with the patient for a few minutes? I wish to go and speak with Viktor and the detectives in private?"

"Yes, sir. Certainly," assented the young man.

"When the four men returned to the parlor, Doctor Sanders said, "Dannells is dangerously close to dying. I fear he is fatally wounded, but I can't be sure. The bullet passed through his body, and missing a vital organ is almost impossible. My diagnosis is unfavorable. I'm afraid a few more hours will decide his case for life or death."

"What can we do in the meantime, Doctor?" asked Viktor.

"Nothing can be done to help him avert death if his injuries are what I think. Much, however, can be done to alleviate pain."

Viktor quickly asked, "He mustn't be moved?"

"Of course not. To move him would be certain death. I will ask one of the detectives to remain and the other to remain back to town with me to report our findings here."

Viktor returned to the convict's bedside. Christian Lucas watched him, who had just laid a cold, wet cloth over his forehead. "How are you feeling, Mister Dannells?" the old man kindly inquired.

"Feel as if I was in Hell! But how I feel, it should be only hours, and I will be there," snarled the convict.

"No, sir. Doctor Sanders is giving you a slight chance of pulling through this. We will do all we can to help you get over the rough spots and ensure your survival."

"No! I don't wish to recover. I wish to die and be done with this life of mine," groaned the man, clenching his fists together in pain.

"Few of us are prepared to die," Christian said. "Are you?"

"As well as ever I shall be," the man moaned in pain.

"Go, Christian, and get some fresh air out in the gardens. I think Aurora is out there to keep you company. I will watch our patient for a while."

No sooner did he walk into the garden; he saw Aurora sitting on an arbor with her hat lying at her feet. Her long golden hair was flowing over her graceful shoulders, glistening in the morning sunshine like that of a mantle of golden fleece.

"How is the poor fella, Christian?" she asked while motioning for him to come and sit next to her by patting her hand on the bench.

"He is in terrible pain, Aurora," he answered while taking a seat.

"Is he in danger of dying?"

"I'm afraid so, but no one can tell for sure. The bullet appears to have passed through his body, but rather or not it any of the vital organs is a different story."

They were both silent. Christian looked out over the countryside for miles upon miles with his elevated view. "Ahhh, what a wonderful country! An absolute paradise!" murmured Christian as he looked.

"Yes, it is Switzerland, but with a tropical sky and all the tropical vegetation," answered Aurora.

"Really? You have been to Switzerland?" asked Christian.

"Oh, yes... many times," she replied.

"I find myself wondering that a man of such great wealth and position with such a beautiful daughter should choose to live out here in the boonies, cut off from all civilization?"

His young friend suddenly grew pale as death, even to her lips, which assumed an ashes-of-roses hue.

Christian remained silent. He felt this deathly emotion had been caused by his words earlier. Yet he thought that he must not seem to notice this agitation and to do so would add insult to injury. He knew he best change the subject quickly.

"I find this place a magnificent place to live. It is so lovely as this might attract any man fond of solitude. Everything I see is simply magnificent!"

"Shall I show you more of the place... Christian?" she asked with a low and hesitating voice.

"Yes, by all means... lead the way, Aurora."

The young stranger was attended by such a lovely young woman whose angelic beauty seemed in perfect harmony with all the beautiful surroundings.

Christian had so many unanswered questions. Had Aurora been banished from Heaven? What had she left behind? What had she lost? And, what has she suffered?

Christian couldn't tell, and he dared not ask a question or even hint at a question like he had asked earlier. No more being stupid and sticking his foot in his mouth... that's for sure.

The two go into the home to join Aurora's father for lunch. They sat at the table, and Viktor said, "Our friend still has an elevated fever. He is insistent that he will not survive this shooting. The man believes he's going to die! He asked me to send for a minister," he said as he passed the mashed potatoes down to Christian.

"What! That convict who doesn't fear God and has no regard for man! That man asked for a pastor?" Christian exclaimed in surprise.

"Yes, he did, my young friend," sighed Viktor. "I sent Smitty to town to fetch the minister two hours ago. I hope he gets here by nightfall."

"Father, who is sitting with that man now?" asked Aurora.

"The housekeeper, my dear. It is usually either her or Christian that sits with him."

"May I go and take the housekeeper's place after supper, Father?"

"Sweetheart, you make a strange request. This man is a ruffian. He already tried to rip your heart out once, darling."

"Yes, I agree. He is a ruffian by birth, I suspect, Father. He can't help being a brute, poor soul! Besides, he is a seriously wounded ruffian and will probably die. He can't hurt anyone now," pleaded Aurora.

"Well, I must say, the man did ask to see you."

"There!" exclaimed Aurora. "What were his exact words?"

"He said he wished to see and talk to the young lady he frightened, but whom he never intended to injure beyond taking her jewelry."

"You see, Father, he is human after all. You will let me go to him immediately, will you not?"

Before Viktor could answer, the door opened. It was Smitty. "The minister is here, sir."

"Indeed. I thought it would be a few more hours. Where is he?"

"In the parlor, sir."

Viktor looked at his daughter. "Aurora, my dear, you must defer your visit to the dying man until after the pastor has seen him. You do, I hope, understand the necessity of that?"

"Yes, perfectly, Father," replied Aurora.

"Christian, will you join me? You have such a connection with this man. It would be good to have you with us."

They reached the parlor and found Reverend Triem sitting in a wingback chair, admiring the gardens out the window.

"Ahhh, Reverend, sir. I am glad you came," exclaimed Viktor with an outstretched hand. "The Reverend Edward Triem, I presume?"

"Yes, sir, at your service."

"Yes. My name is Viktor Serafin. And this gentleman here is Christian Lucas."

"Nice to meet you, young man," the pastor said while outstretching his hand.

"Come, Pastor, let me take you to the dying man's room. He has asked for you."

"Thank you. Lead the way, Mister Serafin."

The three men proceeded to the servant's room where Jack Dannells lay dying.

Reverend Triem looked down at the prostrated sufferer. He forgot all his violent and habitual insolence to him when he was in prison. Today, right then and there, he looked down on the agonizing and dying sinner... needing his ministrations.

"You wish to see me, Mister Dannells?" he asked gently as he bent over the agonized brute.

"I wanted to see your reverence... yes. But, ohhhh, if I were a Catholic, I would wish to make a confession. As it is, I wish to tell you a story, pastor... Ohhh, the pain. It hurts! Pastor Triem, there is no doubt that I am a brute... a convict... a desperado. But I am also the son of a wealthy nobleman with large land holdings in Oregon!"

The three men went silent for a moment. Then, finally, they looked at each other.

"You gentlemen may stare, but I repeat myself... a thief and a convict as I am called. I am also the son of a very wealthy estate outside of Black Rock Cove. You will all believe me when I tell you my dying story," said the dying convict in a faint voice.

Viktor leaned over, "Pastor should Christian, and I leave the room for you to listen to this man's last confession?"

"Why?" demanded the convict in a whisper.

"Because you might wish to tell your story to your minister alone," explained the old man.

"Not true. But what is true is that I would like to have some more brandy," murmured the ruffian.

A half-glass of brandy was fixed and handed to the man.

The three men grabbed a chair and pulled it up to the bedside.

"Thank you, gentlemen. I wish you, Christian, would grab that notebook off the table and write down my words as I speak them. I ask this because a man is being pursued with a warrant for his arrest for a crime I committed. The one crime weighs the heaviest on my soul at this exact time. This is also why I wish to have all three of you men here by my bedside so that what I say is duly witnessed."

The convict started telling his story.

No one knew, but probably the most interested listener was the gentleman who called himself Christian Lucas.

The man spoke in a less faint voice, somewhat strengthened by the half a glass of brandy he had just consumed.

"I told you that I was the son of a very wealthy aristocrat, known as an Earl in England and part of a family who pulled up roots and has lived in Oregon for over two hundred years. I am the son of the late Johnathan Knight, the fifteenth Earl of the Knight Estate in America.

He wasn't the earl but was the heir to the Knight Estate. He was Captain Knight of Her Majesty's Secret Service and called upon when needed. Well, aside from that grand title, I wasn't born yet. He met and married a gypsy girl who became my mother."

"Married!" repeated all three men at the same time.

"Yes, married. Captain Johnathan Knight, the fifteenth Earl of the Knight Estate, did really marry Rose Lucas, who became my mother."

The expression of amazement, dashed with incredulity, on the faces of three gentlemen was too much for the convict that he burst into a soft laugh. He said, "Oh, my friends, don't be alarmed! I am not here claiming anything to do with the entire estate of the Knight succession. I couldn't do it even if I were to live. Listen carefully, and I will explain.

Trust me when I say that it was not the usual infatuation of a poor girl for a fine and wealthy gentleman who made love to her that caused my mother to become Captain Johnathan Knight's wife. The captain was almost sixty years old. She was only sixteen, with no more dreams of love or marriage than if she had been six years old.

You see, gentlemen, she was a splendid redhead who got her name Rose Lucas from the radiance of her hair. She had a complexion like roses on snow, hair like sunshine, and eyes like stars. Such was my mother.

She was part of a large group of gypsies but was adopted and not cared for very much. Captain Knight bought her from them with a promise to make her his bride.

The gullible child of only sixteen years was sold and later married to Captain Johnathan Knight, a sixty-year-old veteran soldier under the laws of the gypsy tribe.

However, one thing never happened as per the marital contract. She was not married in a Christian wedding. She didn't know any better. She believed herself a wife and a lady and went away with the captain, more as a child than a woman.

After a while, my father went to Seattle, where his regiment was stationed. He procured lodgings for my mother in a retired part of the city. But again, gentlemen, I must emphasize that the last condition in the contract between the gypsy tribe and my father was never fulfilled. So, my mother, a gypsy maiden, was never married under the eyes of God by Christian rites.

My mother was very young. She didn't know there was any difference and went along with the marriage as usual.

They lived in Seattle when my father, Captain Knight, was placed in the reserves and his pay reduced to half. So, he took my mother, his gypsy wife, away to the slums of Seattle, where everything was cheap, and he could live comfortably on his half pay.

We lived in these conditions, during which time I had two sisters who were born but did not live long and one brother who was three years younger than myself. When I turned five, and my baby brother was not more than two years old, something happened that left an indelible impression on my memory.

The first was a total catastrophe. My poor, beautiful mother was very fond of the ocean and used to take us down on the beach every fine afternoon. My mother had a friend that loaned her the use of his rowboat. We all got in the boat and rowed out past the breakers. It was actually a smooth and beautiful day. Unfortunately, we hadn't rowed out very far and the rowboat overturned with all of us.

Oh, God, I still remember my mother's piercing scream. She had only time for one... the plunge, the shock, and the awful struggle... the flashing of light and my body feeling like it was floating in space. I became unconscious."

Dannell's voice demonstrated signs of weakness that Mister Serafin prepared another half-glass of brandy and gave it to the wounded man.

"I've always heard that drowning is an easy death," said the old man as he took the empty glass back from Dannells and placed it on the nightstand.

"Don't you believe it, sir? Never leave this world by water unless to keep you from going out by fire. Trust me. The prelude of terror and strangulation... the anguish of mind and body's agony is not very enjoyable." He paused and reached for the empty glass. Viktor poured another shot and handed it to the man.

"Well, the next thing I remember was that I tried to cry, but it hurt terribly to try and breathe, much less cry for help. I saw people surrounding me when I opened my eyes and saw that I was in bed." He looked up at Viktor and said, "If you ever go out of this world by water, don't come back again. Drowning is bad enough, but bringing you back is a great deal worse."

"After I returned to consciousness, I found that only one person in the boat was saved, and that was me. My mother, baby brother, and the man who rowed the boat drowned. The body of the man rowing the boat and my mother were found. The body of my baby brother had not yet been found, and, in fact, it never was found. I was saved by another man in a boat who seized me by my clothes and drug me into his boat.

After my mother's funeral, another event was just as startling as the first but differently. One day, my father received a letter that caused him a lot of excitement and caused him to make a trip to Black Rock Cove, leaving me in the care of a girl named Suzanne, who had been in service to my mother and in her confidence as long as I can possibly remember. She came with my mother from this traveling gypsy tribe, having been like her, an adopted child of the wandering vagrants. I learned all I've told you today from Suzanne about my mother's early history."

The man reached for another shot of brandy. Viktor saw it gave the man strength and did not refuse to fill it halfway and hand it to him.

"My father returned after a week's absence, and I noticed that no one called him Captain Knight any longer. Everyone just called him 'Sir.' He became the heir to the great Knight Estate outside of Black Rock Cove. Some even called him the Earl of Knightwood. I was too young and stupid. I suppose to appreciate this elevation in society.

But, at that time, to my sorrow, I was broken up from my father and Suzanne and placed among strangers in a boarding school for young boys. I was the smallest and youngest out of all of them.

In only thirty days, you can imagine my life. It totally changed. I had been bereft of a father, a mother, a brother, a nurse, and, just as important, a home.

I only saw my father once a year when he would come by the school, pay the bills, and give me some pocket money. That particular time, one year later, was the last time I saw my father for the last time.

Suzanne, my mother's maid, married a gold digger and went with him on a ship and worked as a stewardess between the newly discovered gold fields, and whenever the ship was in port in Seattle, she would come onshore and watch for an opportunity of seeing me when I walked out of the school.

She was a most beautiful woman and was known to have been a trusted servant to my father. She was always allowed to speak with me. Each time, she would hug me and remind me that I was the eldest son of Johnathan Knight and the heir of the entire estate outside of Black Rock Cove.

Well, I must try and wrap my story up before the brandy kills me or the bullet. Time went on. I was now ten years old and had received a good education. I hadn't heard of my father for many years. I can only suppose the bills were being paid for me by somebody, or I would not have been allowed to remain in school.

It was when I was ten years old that I lost Suzanne, who one day met me when I was out walking in the schoolyard. She told me she was going back to England. She gave me twenty dollars and many kisses and told me goodbye.

My heart was dearly broken. Suzanne was the only person on earth who loved me or... whom I loved. As one can imagine, I lost my spirit and my appetite. I couldn't sleep. I just sat in the classroom staring out the window and brooded about my lonely life.

The other boys in the school had visits and gifts from friends and relatives. They went home for the holidays. I had no visitors and no vacations. This lonely life didn't change year after year after that.

So, after a few years of living a very lonely life, I started thinking about running away from school. I found out what ship Suzanne was a stewardess on and went to the wharves and took a boat to Mozambique, where the word was that she went. Unfortunately, she was not on the ship I found, but someone that knew her said she had departed two weeks prior.

I had hoped to see her. She was my only friend, the only person that I dearly loved. She was a mother to me. I have had many disappointments in my life, gentlemen, but I think that was the bitterest I ever experienced! I was a ten-year-old boy lost in the world.

Here I stood all alone. There wasn't another ship setting sail for Mozambique for three or four weeks later. My next impulse was to seek after my father. I knew from what Suzanne told me that my father was the Earl of Knightwood, a giant estate and home just outside Black Rock Cove.

So, I traveled by foot, working my way back to Black Rock Cove. I spent all my money and had to go on foot and live off the countryside for several weeks. When I got to Black Rock Cove, I made some inquiries, and everyone knew who Johnathan Knight was. They would say it was a wealthy Englishman the entire community loved living only ten miles from the Cove. I set out on foot to the grand estate of Johnathan Knight.

Chapter TWELVE
The Queen's Anteroom

It was in the middle of August, a sweltering day that I remember when I reached the gates of Knightwood. No sooner did I arrive, I discovered my father had just died and was buried a few days earlier. The new heir to the estate was a boy of only five years of age, living under the care of a pastor and guardian.

This was another disappointment in my life, but not so bitter as the first. I understood them when I heard that there was a young heir to the entire estate and a boy of five years of age. This meant my father must have married again, and I had a younger brother. Oh, gentlemen, how my young heart yearned toward that younger brother!

As soon as I reached the grand estate, I asked one of the gardeners raking leaves if I could see the pastor taking care of my brother. The man only stared at me and, without saying a word, pointed toward the servants' entrance. I went to the door and rang the bell. I then asked the man who opened it if I could speak to the parson caring for my little brother.

This man did the same thing. He didn't say a word at first, then he asked me if my brother was in school. I told him I didn't know if my brother was in school or not. I just wished to see the person who was taking care of him.

In a short while, an older gentleman came to the door. He wanted to know what I wanted, and I told him I was the eldest son of Johnathan Knight, who had just passed away and that I was the young boy's older brother, and that my mother and other brother were drowned just before my father gained his title to the entire estate. I also told the Guardian that I only came to see my father and found out he was dead and buried. I told him I wished to see my younger brother.

It wasn't long after that Doctor Quentin Clair escorted me to a vehicle and, without a word, sent me off. He didn't believe a word one of my story. He didn't even take the time to check into it, which was wrong.

The car drove all day until I was left in a boarding school without anyone saying a word to me. Oh, God, what can I say? I hated the place. I watched for every opportunity to run away from those who seemed to be my enemies.

Gentlemen, why should I prolong this sad story? My life got worse at every turn when I ran away from school. I fell into a group of thieves. Our first need in life was food. I had to eat. I was too young and couldn't get work. It wasn't until I had my fifteenth birthday and skin and bones that I became a tool for a bunch of burglars. They knew I could get in hard to get to places and used me to do their bidding.

One night we all got caught, tried, and convicted. Things went really bad, and a man was killed. Two of the men were executed in the electric chair. Three were sent to prison. I was sent to jail for seven years.

Gentlemen, that brings me to why I am here. There was a prison in a faraway country, Mozambique, the very country that I was sent to. I was placed on a prison ship out of Seattle. Trust me when I say that the horror of such a ship is a reproach to Christianity! The voyage lasted almost six weeks. We finally reached Lourenco Marques, and our penal servitude commenced.

I was put immediately to work on a chain gang clearing the public roads. I wasn't an evil criminal, and many were released who were far more violent than myself. Most of those nasty criminals were released, and I still served my time for a lesser crime.

Put all I have told you today in your pipe and smoke it, Reverend. Please understand why Jack Dannells, with some bit of instinct of manliness left in him, preferred to be called a ruffian and a desperado rather than to know himself to be a hypocrite!" exclaimed the convict looking at the chaplain rather roughly.

"Give me some more of that brandy. I'm afraid I shall not last much longer and wish to finish my story."

Mister Serafin filled the convict's glass once more.

He sighed and resumed his story with great satisfaction when he drank it all in one large swallow.

"Gentlemen, the outdoor life and working in the open air each day and a round course of meals daily continued for almost eight years. It helps develop the muscle into what I was two months ago.

At the end of my prison term, I returned to my home in Black Rock Cove. I left a pale young lad and returned a real man, muscular and robust as possible. I couldn't help it. It was just me, I suppose. I fell into the wrong crowd really quick and robbed a bank. Everyone except me was caught, but those guys turned on me, and a warrant for my arrest was made. I left the city and headed to the Knight estate to find out what had happened to my baby brother. By this time, I found out enough about the law that told me that my poor mother's gypsy marriage, though it did vindicate her from reproach, did not whatsoever entitle me to the succession of such incredible wealth and the title and deed to the grand estate.

Maybe I just wanted to see the face of my brother. I don't know. But I went there to find out whatever became of my brother, who inherited my father's large estate. He was so much more fortunate than me, but whose face I wanted to see one time before the law caught up with me."

Almost fifteen years had passed since my last visit to Knightwood. Back then, I was only ten, and my half-brother was but a child of five years. After all the years, I was now a man of twenty-five and my brother, if still living, a young man of nineteen or twenty.

You know what's funny. It seems like I always arrive at an eventful time in my brother's life. The last time I was there, my father had just died and had just been buried in the cemetery. Then, on this occasion, it was just before a big birthday party that I reached the grand estate. My brother was preparing to celebrate his nineteenth birthday.

I didn't join them at the time. I wouldn't dare show my face during the daytime. Someone would surely recognize me, and they would serve their arrest warrant on me. I stuck around until after the sun went down. There was a giant fireworks display, and inside the home was a big dance and lots of wine and women.

I know I have sat here and told you my life story, gentlemen, but I really do feel weaker by the minute. I must finish. Now Reverend, sir, I come to the one act of my life that really does trouble me. It was the crime of Cain, and it cursed my soul beyond redemption!" exclaimed Dannells as an expression of mental anguish for a split second displaced the smile of contempt that was too often on his face.

The preacher man gazed at him with the eyes of tenderness and compassion as he murmured gently, "Don't say that your soul is lost beyond redemption, my brother. On the contrary, the mercy of Jesus Christ is infinite."

Jack Dannell's mocking smile displaced the look of anguish as he said, "If the infinite mercy of an all-powerful God should restore the dead to life and wipe off the guilt of fratricide from my very soul. But I can't be quiet any longer. I better tell you how I came to commit the great crime I never intended to commit.

Opportunity makes the thief! Fate made the fratricide. It was such a beautiful display of fireworks. The crowd was cheering outside, and the men and women inside were out on the balconies enjoying festivities. People were coming and going from the mansion. This was when I thought, for a skilled burglar like me, how easy it would be to steal my way inside the house. I thought to myself how easy it would be to rip off a small portion of all that wealth which should have been mine anyhow, but I was born into an illegal marriage.

So, I went inside the house unobserved. I hid in a dark closet of one of the upstairs bedrooms. There was a key on the outside of the door. I took it out and locked myself from the inside.

I knew I had to wait a long time, so I sat on the floor, had patience, and fell asleep. Then, I was awakened by voices. I couldn't distinguish their words as they were muffled. I know they spoke in almost a whisper, and they would break out in a peal of low laughter every once in a while. Although I could hear them talking but not understand what they were saying, I knew something was afoot between the speakers.

I knew it was early morning because no more noise was heard through the house. I slipped out of the closet quietly. There was a full moon that night. The entire room was aglow. I looked around, and the place had been ransacked. Boxes were open. Dressing tables were all opened, and all the contents were scattered on the floor. I stopped and stared all around. There was snoring from the bed, so I knew the occupant was sound asleep.

I was quiet and began searching the drawers and boxes to see if there was any gold and jewelry my predecessor left before me. But I hit the jackpot. I found a billfold full of one-hundred-dollar bills. I took them out and stuffed them in my shirt. Over on the nightstand was a gold watch which I stuffed in my pocket. I also found a gun cabinet full of pistols when... Someone said, 'Who is that?' It came from the bed.

I rushed over and took one of the pistols from the cabinet and hit him over the head. I meant to make him quiet... not kill him! He fell to the floor. I went about looking around the room for more gold and jewelry. I didn't find anything else, and just before I left the room, however, I saw on the floor a blue wool scarf that was certainly no part of a man's wardrobe. I knew then it was dropped by my predecessor. I picked it up, wrapped it around my neck, and hightailed it out of there.

From there, I got out of the house with no problem being seen. I headed back to the wharf in Black Rock Cove, hopped on a fishing vessel, and convinced the men to drop me off in Seattle. I no sooner got on the boat, and the fishermen called me Lucas Durano. I didn't say anything. They wanted me to be this Lucas Durano, and I was. After three days, I dropped the blue scarf, and one of the men picked it up and looked at it. He looked at me and said the scarf was some of the handy work of Victoria Meret, the old crone who lived in a lighthouse somewhere outside of Black Rock Cove. He went ahead and said that he was sure because he watched her knitting it one day. He showed me the initials sewn in the material, 'L.D.'

He left me in Seattle to take the next vessel to Mozambique. He was jealous of my making a fortune in the gold fields overseas from the way that I threw money around.

No sooner did I land back here, there were already wanted posters for the apprehension of Lucas Durano and Johnny McLean, charged with the murder of Samuel Knight, the Earl of Knightwood, on the morning of September first, 1965.

This was the first time I had any idea that I killed a man, who I had only intended to stun... and that the man I murdered was my own brother! I was a fratricide. The curse of Cain was upon me!"

The dying convict, overwhelmed by such an awful memory of his killing his brother, unintentionally though it had been, covered his haggard face with the palms of his hands. He relapsed into a silence that continued for almost a minute. The three gentlemen remained silent, waiting to see if he would continue.

Then, with a deep sigh, he said, "Yes, gentlemen, I felt that the curse of Cain was definitely upon me. I had killed my baby brother, the one I had never seen, but in my heart, I had loved and longed to look upon him from the first hours I had heard of his existence. Then, finally, I fell into a state of despair!

I didn't give a damn what became of me. I wandered listlessly toward Black Rock Cove, stopping at roadside cafes to eat. Finally, I came upon an encampment of gypsies, one that I think was the tribe that my mother belonged to. I asked everyone there if anyone remembered Rose Durano, an adopted child. Some said they remembered her. I told them I was her son. I also sat around a campfire and told the same story to them as I am telling you. They then said to me that I could stay with them and that they would defend me from anyone who wished to take me away.

But two days later, I was arrested. It wasn't for murder, but for the bank robbery I pulled off with others. I was arrested, however, as Lucas Durano, the man accused of the murder of Samuel Knight, my brother, and for whom the reward was offered.

I was carried into police headquarters, and several detectives assured the chief that I was Jack Dannells and not this Lucas Durano they were looking for. Or, for this Johnny McLean, I think Samuel Knight's driver.

I was put back on a prison ship and sent back to the penal colony outside Lourenco Marques in Mozambique. My sentence was for fourteen years, of which I had served a year on the chain gang before escaping.

I am telling my story today to get off my chest this heavy burden that I did, in fact, kill my brother. And secondly, to vindicate an innocent man, my double, Lucas Durano, who might otherwise suffer for what I did wrong. I don't expect to be saved. I don't expect to be pardoned by the Lord Almighty. I look to pass through a lot of suffering in the next stage of my existence... before my soul can be redeemed, if that is even possible." Dannells stopped talking and turned his head to look out the bedroom window on a glorious sunshine day.

The Reverend looked at the weakened man and said, "I thought you said you were not a Christian man."

"I am not. I am nothing!" replied the injured man.

"My poor friend, let me pray with you," pleaded the pastor.

"No! Not now. It's no use. I am not fit for heaven. If I hadn't killed my brother, I might pray. But, as I have killed him, I dare not pray! There!"

"Oh, my dear friend, don't say that. Please. To give up hope of the Lord's mercy is the most fatal of sins," said Pastor Triem.

"I am not lying here and despairing of the Lord's mercy. On the contrary, I give up hope for myself. Reverend Triem! You never killed your own brother! What in the world do you know about how it feels?"

"Jack Dannells, let me pray with you."

"I can't, I tell you!"

"Never say you can't pray," pleaded the reverend.

"Fine, Pastor. I won't, then! Will that suit you better?" demanded Dannells.

"Ahhh, what can we do with this poor soul?" asked the chaplain in a low voice.

Mister Serafin sorrowfully shook his head back and forth without saying a word.

But here, the stranger-guest, Christian Lucas, who had been silent the entire time of Jack Dannell's confession, surprised everyone by saying, "Gentlemen, if you please, if you will leave me alone with this man for just a short while, I think I can bring him to a better state of belief."

Mister Serafin and the pastor looked at each other and returned to Christian.

Christian again said, "If you will permit me to try something?" he asked with a grave smile.

The two gentlemen didn't reply and rose from their chairs and left the room. They closed the door behind them.

Christian Lucas found himself sitting right next to Jack Dannells, all alone.

Undoubtedly, the young stranger had been the most interested of the three men in this convict's story. Thus, as he chose to call himself, Christian Lucas was compelled against his will to believe the dying convict's story. So now, Christian found himself alone with this miserable felon, whose face was turned sulkily to the windows looking out over the courtyard. He bent over him and gently asked, "Is it your brother's death that weighs heaviest on your mind?"

"You know something, if you weren't born such a damn idiot, you wouldn't ask such a stupid ass question. But, how should you know, right? No one can feel the weight of sin except for the person who feels it lying in his heart. You never killed your brother!"

"How can you lay there and say that? You don't know me. You don't know what kind of life I've led. If I have not killed my brother, I have come as near as possible in doing exactly that," said the stranger with a voice of sorrow.

"What are you saying?" asked the convict.

"I am saying that I must have killed my brother! But, listen, Mister Dannells, as sure as there is a Heaven up high, you never killed your brother!" said Lucas solemnly.

"There! Mister, I no longer think, but I know you are an idiot! I know it! Give me some more of that brandy. It's helping with the pain."

Christian filled his glass and handed it to him.

"What did you mean by calling Heaven to witness that I hadn't made an end of my own brother?"

"I was saying that you didn't kill your brother because your brother is very much alive," replied Christian as he set the empty brandy glass on the nightstand.

"You don't know a damn thing of what you are talking about. Samuel Knight was my brother. He was found dead in his bed. It was my hand and that pistol that caused the death blow over his head," said the convict in a tone of despair.

"Nope! You are mistaken," he said calmly.

"You're mad as Hell!"

The young Earl of Knightwood or Samuel Knight is alive and well," said Lucas.

"I know the present one. The one that is the heir to the estate."

"Oliver Courbis is not the earl because Samuel Knight, the Earl of Knightwood, still lives," quietly persisted the stranger Christian.

"I will prove it to you. I tell you, Jack Dannells, that nobody killed Samuel Knight. You never even struck him with that revolver. As a matter of fact, you never had a chance to strike him. He was far away from Knightwood on the morning after his nineteenth birthday party," said the young gentleman.

"Look here, friend!" he murmured under his breath. "Do your friends allow you to go out without a keeper? It is, so dab blasted wrong if they do. You are gone, man! Out of it! You should know that there was an investigation into his murder, and the entire countryside was ringing with the news of Samuel Knight's death."

"Of course. I know that!"

"How can you sit by my bed and say then that Samuel Knight is still alive and well?"

"Because it's true."

"True? I think you are missing a screw in that head of yours. That's what I think."

"If you will just give me the benefit of the doubt. Just listen. A body that closely resembled that of Samuel Knight was found in his bed, in a state of what looked to be death. A physician did a quick examination and said he was dead. The wound left on the top of his head was bleeding profusely, so they wrote off the death from a blow of a blunt instrument of some sort. You cleared that up... the blunt end of a revolver."

"What are you getting at?" demanded Dannells in a tone of hostility.

"Just listen to me for a second. Your story you told bears the truth to what I am about to show convinced me."

"Go ahead. I will listen," said the dying man in a faint voice, "and I will lay here and rest while listening to you."

"First, you saw Doctor Quentin Clair when you first went to the Knight Estate, did you not? Don't answer. You should have been overwhelmed with the severe sternness of the old man."

"Yes," assented Dannells with a long, drawn-out moan.

"Think about it. Think what must have been the condition of a young boy, Samuel, without a father or mother, sister, brother, or anyone left to the sole guardianship of such a grim disciplinarian... to be under his watchful eye day and night when he was eating and drinking, studying without a break for many years.

"Ahhh, I see. Poor brother!" Dannells moaned.

"This treatment made a maniac out of the boy. Then one day, he found going to school with him another young boy three years older than he, whom he grew fond of as a dear, dear friend. The name of this schoolboy was Lucas Durano."

Jack Dannells' eyes grew wide. He turned his head and showed sudden access of interest.

"He is the grandson of an old crone named Victoria Meret, who lived in a dilapidated old lighthouse near Demon's Gorge on the coast, not far from the Knight Estate. The old woman made her living by telling fortunes and other things that weren't quite legal."

"Go ahead," whispered Dannells.

"Samuel used to sneak out of the house to meet and play with the only companion he had while his guardian, Doctor Clair, was taking his nap in the afternoons. This young boy, Lucas Durano, bore such a remarkable resemblance to Samuel that they must have been perfect counterparts. Lucas was a vagabond, poor and his clothes showed it, while Samuel always dressed the nicest. But so striking was the likeness that the people in the surrounding area began to say they had to be brothers. But I must continue. Enough to say that all the enjoyment that fell on Samuel Knight came from his companionship with Lucas Durano. He envied the young boy's freedom and went and did as he pleased.

A warm closeness was formed between the two boys. This continued for years as they grew up."

"Okay, Mister, I am getting weaker. Can we speed up to the murder?" growled the convict.

"So, Samuel Knight had no more freedom than the child had. As a matter of fact, he had less. Not a day nor an hour passed where he wasn't supervised and looked over. This grew more oppressive and intolerable as the years went by. That brings us to the night of this so-called murder at the Knight Estate."

"Great, finally. Tell me," said Durano, alias Jack Dannells.

"Samuel Knight returned from the university in Portland to the estate. He was to spend his summer vacation there under the watchful eyes of Doctor Clair. Under his supervision and on his nineteenth birthday, it was decided to throw Samuel a big birthday party and a ball inside the house.

During the party, Samuel was free to roam among all the villagers that came to celebrate. But, then, a sight to behold when he saw once again his good friend who had been traveling the countryside free as a bird... Lucas Durano had just returned from the gold mines in Mozambique. Oh, Samuel was so jealous. How he would like to have a breath of freedom.

The two young men were now more alike in personal appearance; the only difference was in the kind of clothes that they wore. They were the same height and had the same features and complexion. Samuel envied his dear lost friend. However, Samuel had to be careful and not spend too much time with his friend and made an appointment with the vagabond to come to his bedroom later that night. He also arranged that his driver, Johnny McLean, should be on the watch to admit Lucas Durano and conduct him to his room.

"Ahhh... finally. Here it comes!" said the convict.

"Lucas was escorted to Samuel's room."

"That was the conversation I heard from the closet that night."

"Yes. Lucas washed up in my bathroom, was cleanly shaven except for a mustache just like Samuel's, his hair trimmed and put into the finest of pajamas and put to bed to impersonate Samuel."

"How did Samuel grow a beard so fast?"

"He didn't. He put on a black wig and false black beard from a masquerading costume Johnny McLean found. Samuel walked out with Johnny McLean to begin his new life as free as a bird to be a vagabond and have a joyous life. Now, Mister Dannells, do you see the light?"

"Oh, yes, it was Lucas Durano that I killed and not my brother! Thank God!" breathed the convict.

"Wait a sec, my friend. You killed nobody, thank Heaven! Your hands and your conscience are free from the crime of murder, so far as that night's doings are concerned. And you didn't intend to kill Samuel or anyone, right?"

"No, I didn't. I only meant to knock him out and get out of there without the man hollering and waking the house up."

"You did exactly that. You only stunned the man. You didn't kill him."

"How do you know all of this?"

"From Lucas Durano himself. When the vagabond found himself alone under the white sheet in the room, he began questioning why he was there. He remembered exchanging places with Samuel. He was scared they would surely bury him alive if he passed out again. He then came to fully after everyone left to get up and run away."

The convict said, "go on."

"Well, he rolled over and fell off the table on the floor. The shock of the fall got his blood pumping. Then, by the dim light from the moon shining in the window, he crawled over to the night table by the window and drank straight from a bottle of brandy."

"Ahhh, I agree with the man. A good drink of brandy will get anyone working again."

"Yes, it did, which reminds me, you should be sitting up a little," he said while pouring another brandy. Instead, the convict drank it all down.

"The vagabond struggled to his feet, went out the window, and walked across the empty grounds. He made his way to the lighthouse where his grandmother, Victoria Meret, took him in and doctored his cut on his forehead."

"Good for him!" said the convict.

"His grandmother almost didn't recognize him under the disguise of Samuel Knight. Then, finally, a man arrived and said that Samuel Knight was killed and Lucas Durano was charged with murder, and they had better hurry and hide him. They did just that."

"How did they hide him?"

"Victoria and Claudia, the two women there, took Lucas to a secret hiding place under the lighthouse, where they nursed him back to health. Then the news the next day was that someone stole Samuel Knight's body, and a huge reward was offered by friends of Doctor Clair's."

A gentle laugh from Dannells stopped the narrator for just a moment.

"In the meantime, Lucas Durano recovered. The reward posters described him as one with long black hair and a beard.

Lucas then headed towards the wharves to get a ship back to Mozambique. He heard as he was trying to escape that another man, who closely resembled the description of himself, had been arrested in his place. He was prompted to give himself up and run the risk of going to the electric chair for a man alive and well... but one he could not prove to be alive. But just before he turned himself in, the man that was arrested was identified as Jack Dannells, the convict that returned from overseas."

"That was me."

"Yes, I know. Lucas Durano made good his escape. He headed to Mozambique to finish making his fortune in the gold fields. I parted from him almost a year ago, from where I got news of him scarcely a few weeks since."

"Yes, but that rich Samuel Knight, where is he?" asked Dannells, fixing his deep, burning brown eyes on the speaker.

"Samuel Knight is also out here in the gold fields."

"How do you know that, Mister?"

"I came on the same ship with him and traveled all over Mozambique. I was with him when I ran into Lucas Durano in the gold fields."

"So that must mean you are the driver, Johnny McLean?"

"No, sir, not quite. But I assure you I am a very dear friend of Samuel Knight."

"He is a good man, is he?" asked Dannells.

"Oh, very nice and admirable," replied Christian.

"Wait. If you are not the driver, then who are you?"

"I told you. A good friend of Samuel Knight."

"But your name, sir."

"Christian Lucas, at your service!"

"Well, if that is your name, you have given me a new lease on life. I did not kill my brother or anyone, for that matter. So, as the Lord knows, I never intended to be. But, your words, Mister Lucas, have done my aching body better than all the brandy I have drunk tonight. And, it has done my soul better than all the reverend's preaching will ever do!"

"I am so happy to hear that! You don't fear now that you are going to die?"

"Nope. Not at all."

"And you will listen to the pastor and let him pray with you when he returns?"

"Yes, I will, Christian."

"Good. So now, you must get some rest. I will leave you and send the housekeeper back in to sit with you. Her presence will not bother you," Lucas said as he got up and left the room.

Chapter THIRTEEN
Confiding a Secret

Christian Lucas told the wretched convict enough information to ease the guilty conscience of killing his half-brother. But he had not given the man his complete confidence. He reserved that for the present. If Dannells were to survive his gunshot, he would never tell him more than he had already spoken. But, if the convict was going to die, he would confide in a particular secret.

With these thoughts in his mind, he walked down the hallway and joined Mister Serafin and the pastor in the parlor.

The two gentlemen knew it was going well as they could hear them talking from time to time. "I'm happy to hear of the man's improved mind and curious to know by what means you were able to keep in such a lengthy conversation. I will go to him now," said Pastor Triem, rising.

"I think I would wait. Part of my success was due to extinguishing the brandy bottle, and Mister Dannells has been more excited and fatigued than I am sure is good for a man dying from a gunshot wound. I left him trying to sleep," said Christian.

"Very well," he said, turning and looking at Mister Serafin. "If it is okay with you, I would like to delay my return until he gathers his strength to speak with him once more."

Supper was announced.

The three gentlemen and Aurora, joined by Victor Serafin and Pastor Triem, sat at the dining table.

"Father, how is the wounded man?"

"I think his symptoms are much more favorable."

"Have you any medical experience, young man?" asked Pastor Triem.

Christian smiled widely and said, "As a matter of fact, I have had more than a year roughing it across the countryside that has brought me to experience many men with wounds like Mister Dannells. If the bullet hit any of his vital organs, he wouldn't have had a lengthy conversation with me, and his fate would have been decided before this. No, sir, the bullet that hit him passed through his body without piercing a vital organ. He will recover."

"Oh, thank God, Mister Lucas!" fervently breathed Viktor.

"Amen!" answered back Christian.

Pastor Triem turned his attention to the beautiful daughter of Viktor Serafin. In all the years he had been a chaplain at the prison, he had never seen anyone show such compassion for any of the outcasts working on the prison gang. This heavy pity that moved the minister's admiration won Christian Lucas's love.

After supper, the chaplain relieved the housekeeper, keeping watch on the convict. He walked into the room, and as the housekeeper left, he closed the door and locked it behind them. He then walked over and seated himself beside the bed.

The two young people left the evening meal and walked out onto the garden smothered by the moonlight. Then, after an hour, they went back inside, where they assembled in the parlor.

"Well, Pastor, how is the wounded man doing now?"

"I would like to report Dannell's spiritual condition. As my friend here stated earlier, his symptoms are now more favorable."

"Thank goodness, Pastor," again replied Viktor.

After some light chit-chat, they retired to their bedrooms.

The doctor arrived in the middle of the following day, ready to perform a miracle surgery to save the man's life. But instead, he found him alive and well and eating a bowl of cereal.

He walked back out to the parlor where Viktor, the pastor, and Christian waited for his report.

"Gentlemen, when a bullet passes straight through a man from the middle of his chest through his back, the chances are a thousand to one some vital organ is damaged. I must report that our patient has been favored by 1 in a thousand. He will recover!"

The convict must have said some words that swayed the minister in their last time together. The doctor went to the minister and said, "Pastor Triem, because this fellow is so atrocious a criminal that he can't even feign repentance, you, therefore, wish to have some favor shown him," said the surgeon.

"No, not so. You are unjust to the man, Doctor. He is not an atrocious criminal, as you say. He has never committed an atrocious crime. He is only a desperate criminal... rendered desperate by circumstances that I wish to ameliorate. I wish to try an experiment with the man, and I want you, doctor, to help me."

"What is it that you want me to do, Pastor?"

"First, I wish you to let the man regain his strength here as long as possible. But, don't report him fit for duty back on the chain gangs until he shall have got, not only well, but strong again."

"I can do that. What next."

"Help me prevent him from being sent back to hard labor. Join me in recommending he provide service to an outstanding citizen as a laborer or something."

"Who could you get to take such a desperate man like him into his service?" inquired the doctor incredulously.

"Our host, sir, Mister Viktor Serafin," answered Pastor Triem.

"What are you saying, Ed? Have you asked him?" questioned the doctor.

"Yes."

"Even after the brutal assault on his daughter?"

"Yes, well, kind of. I will ask him more formally, but even if he hesitated, his daughter would be the first to not press charges against the wretch."

"Well... very well, Ed. I will go and recommend as you ask on behalf of Jack Dannells."

The discussion ended.

The men were preparing to depart and leave the ruffian in the care of Viktor Serafin.

The pastor asked, "Viktor, it is our belief that once the convict is better, you take him into your service."

"What! Take that man into my service," quickly replied Serafin.

"I think if you should be disposed of, you may do it with perfect safety," said Pastor Triem.

The doctor added, "I agree with these two gentlemen, Viktor. From my observation of the man, I see that though he has been brutal enough under exasperation, he is not terribly treacherous. He will not steal from you."

"Or hurt the hand that feeds him," added Christian.

"Oh, father, give this poor man a chance to save himself! Why are you hesitating?" pleaded Aurora.

"I do so for only your sake, my dear," he answered.

"Then, for my sake, hesitate no longer. Take Mister Dannells as your servant. You have always said you need more help in the gardens. Let him do that work. I'm not in the least afraid of him. He won't hurt me," pleaded the beautiful young woman.

He turned to the doctor and the pastor as they prepared to return to Lourenco Marques. "If you gentlemen think there's a chance the authorities will agree to my taking on his services here, then I agree."

"Oh, thank you, Father. You have made me so very happy!" She exclaimed with a blank look of expression on her face. No smile. No tears.

Christian Lucas watched her closely and wondered why she showed no expression of appreciation, but the words said so.

Young and as beautiful as this girl was, she impressed Lucas as one who had gone through some terrible ordeal. The more he studied her, the deeper his impression of her became.

The men departed, and Christian and Aurora walked out onto the upper gardens and watched the men go out of sight. Christian watched the girl's fair and colorless face and her tender blue eyes staring. Then, finally, he said, "Aurora, how is it that you have so much pity for and so little fear of a man who assaulted you in the woods?"

"I don't quite know, Christian. I never thought about it," she answered in slow words. Then she restarted, "But isn't he to be pitied... is he not?"

"But, when he recovers and gets strong again, he will be on these grounds where you would reencounter him in your daily walks?" inquired the young man.

"This man will never hurt me."

"How can you be so sure, Aurora?"

"Because we have shown him compassion. We have taken him in and made him well. As a result, I can see in the man's eyes that he is not a brute. On the contrary, he is easily influenced by kind treatment."

"Aurora, I agree with you one hundred percent. Jack Dannells will never harm you."

"No, he will not."

"I have also just learned that Dannells will not be the first convict taken in by your father. The pastor informed me that you have a young girl from the prison in Lourenco Marques who was convicted of murder and sentenced to death but whose sentence was commuted to private service for life." No sooner did Christian say these words, he jumped back. "Good Heaven! Aurora!" he exclaimed, reaching out and catching the young lady in his arms before falling to the concrete piazza. He took and gently placed her on the settee.

"Help! Help Doctor Sanders!" He shouted and looked out at the doctor getting into the car to go down the road back to Lourenco Marques. "Oh, Doctor, for Heaven's sake, come quickly!" The young man cried in terror. He had never in his life seen a woman faint.

Doctor Sanders raced back up the steps shouting, "What is all of this? What happened?" He reached down and took the poor girl's hand in his. "What caused her to faint?"

"I don't know. We were talking about Dannells when she suddenly fainted or something!" exclaimed Christian.

Aurora began to open her eyes.

"Best lie quietly, my dear."

Viktor rushed up. "What is the matter, sweetheart?"

"Nothing, Father."

"She fainted," Doctor Sanders added.

"Oh, father, quick bothering yourself. I am quite well," said Aurora, rising to a sitting position.

"Gentlemen, who was with my daughter? Can you give me more light on this matter?" asked Viktor looking at each of the three men.

Christian answered, "I was with her. One moment she was happy, and the next, she fainted."

"She will be fine, Viktor. We must be on our way now."

"Thank you, doctor."

Everyone departed. Aurora and Christian remained on the piazza. She was sitting on the settee while he stood in front of her.

Christian wasn't born yesterday. Nevertheless, he could tell that Aurora wanted the subject matter dropped. After a moment of silence, Aurora lightly smiled and looked up at Christian. "Mister Lucas, please sit back down beside me. I have something to say to you."

After Christian sat next to her, she was silent once more and said very quietly, "Mister Lucas, just before I fainted, you were speaking of these wretched convicts—-."

"Yes, Jack Dannells?"

"Yes, you were speaking of him, but you also spoke of another young girl who was a convicted murderer and assigned to my father as his servant. You were speaking of her, were you not Mister Lucas."

"Yes, Miss Aurora, I was."

"Do you know who she is?" She said in an almost inaudible tone.

"No, I do not. The minister mentioned that Mister Serafin already had one assigned servant, which would help when requesting another to be sent here. He did say the girl was tried and found guilty of murder, but it was changed from the death penalty to lifetime service for your father."

"You never heard the young girl's name?"

"No, I didn't."

"Her name was—-" Aurora paused and caught her breath. Her heart began to race. Then, she added, "Her name was Elise Austin."

"Elise Austin!" exclaimed the young man. "Oh, my God, I remember that trial now. She was the girl convicted of killing her infant cousin so that she could inherit his property, of which she was the next heir. Did your father know these facts before he agreed to take her own as a servant here on your place?"

"Yes, he did," she said with a faint voice.

"Oh, my goodness. That trial was in all the papers. I can't understand how your father could endure the presence of such a mad killer under the same roof as you. I don't know how your father could even subject you to such danger. No wonder you never smile.

"Oh, you have it wrong. My father believes that though she was convicted of the crime, she was not guilty," said the young woman in a faint voice.

"You say this, Aurora, that your father believes this. From everything I read in the papers, the evidence that proved her guilt was overwhelming. There wasn't a loophole in the trial whatsoever."

"That's so true. But you sit there agreeing to have Jack Dannells provide private service for my father and then turn around and find that poor girl who was only fourteen years old guilty of a crime which she could not think up, much less plan. We know that Elise Austin is no felon," said Aurora.

"I don't know, Aurora. You and your father seem to have a boundless charity to the criminals."

Aurora sat up tall on the bench. She said, "It's not charity. It is justice, sir. Mister Lucas, I see how challenging it is for you to understand how my father and I should hold our opinions in the face of such stubborn facts as those seen in the trial. But facts aren't always truths. There are mental and spiritual convictions that can't be proven. Such are the convictions of my father and myself regarding Elise Austin," she ended in a faint voice.

"Very well. I will forget I brought the subject up, Miss Aurora."

"Thank you, sir. But I must say that the name of the unhappy girl we have been talking about is never mentioned in my father's presence. Therefore, I ask you to never allude to her existence. Now, I agree with you. Let's drop the subject at once and forever more."

Christian stood up, gave his arm to the young woman, strolled her daily path to the fountains, and returned.

No more was said about the convict, Elise Austin.

Christian Lucas, our alias for Samuel Knight, don't forget, recalled all the circumstances of the trial when he was back in Black Rock Cove. He followed it in the daily papers, from the first time the murder happened to the end of the entire affair when her death sentence was commuted, and she was put on a prison ship and sent to Lourenco Marques to serve a life sentence in the penal colony.

He recalled his last summer vacation at his estate when it did nothing but rain the entire month of June. He was unable to go outdoors and stayed inside and awaited the delivery of the Black Rock Cove newspaper. He remembered that the thunder was just as heavy as the weather. His thoughts turned back to one morning when he read on the first page,

'STRANGE DISAPPEARANCE OF A CHILD

The neighborhood of Rock Island has been thrown into considerable excitement by the sudden disappearance of Anthony Thompkins Austin, one-year-old, only son and heir of the late George William Austin estate. It seems that on Tuesday morning, the nanny in charge of looking in on the young boy went to the crib and found him gone and the bed clothing in disorder.

At first, the nurse was not alarmed as she thought the mother might have come and taken the baby back to her room with her. However, when she went to check, she found the boy was taken, and it wasn't by the mother or anyone else in the household.

A thorough home examination was conducted, and the child wasn't found. After detectives swarmed the place, no clues were found about the child's disappearance. So large rewards have been placed for any knowledge of the baby's whereabouts.'

This was the first news report in the paper of the incident, destined to develop into a heartrending tragedy ever to hit home in recent years. It shocked a civilized community.

At the end of the week, in the Friday news, another update on the case was written on the first page,

'BOY OF ANTHONY THOMPKINS AUSTIN FOUND AT BOTTOM OF WELL

The discovery of the mutilated remains of the child at the bottom of a dry well less than a mile from the Austin estate was found. No clue has

been found as to who the murderer is. An inquest is being performed today.'

Ten days passed. Finally, at the end of the following week, the front page said,

'THE ROCK ISLAND MYSTERY

Startling developments in the murder of Anthony Thompkins Austin have been found.

Elise Austin, a young girl of fourteen years and a cousin of the deceased, was arrested on the charge of murdering tiny Anthony Austin. Public opinion has the young girl to right. 'She's insane' were words shouted at the courthouse. Everyone has reported that the doctors think it was nothing but the insanity that could have driven such a young girl to such an atrocious crime.

After much investigation, it was concluded that Elise murdered the young boy as she was next in line to the wealthy estate.

No one here at the newspaper or anyone we have talked to has one bit of pity for the young girl. People rushed as witnesses, and the District Attorney, Johnny Adams, summed up his case, "This depraved creature who was old enough in evil to conceive, plan and pull off this atrocious murder is quite old enough to suffer the maximum penalties of the law. We seek the electric chair."'

For people following this case, we have the following story of its development.

Stephanie Elise Austin, known her life of fourteen years as Elise, was the orphan niece and the adopted daughter of George William Austin of Rock Island. She was the legal heiress presumptive of his entire estate worth millions. She was the darling daughter of her aunt and uncle, who were old and childless.

Elise lost her aunt. Her father remarried a woman with several children and brought her to his Rock Island estate home. It was told that Elise was full of jealous rage. The new aunt didn't wish to have her in the family and sent her away to a boarding school in Portland, forty-five miles away.

During her two years there, a child was born... a son and a new heir to the estate who arrived ten months after their marriage. After that, his health started to go downhill fast, and he sent for his niece from the boarding school, whom he never ceased loving.

Elise Austin returned to Rock Island to receive her uncle's dying blessing, attend his funeral and hear his last will and testament.

George William Austin left Elise ten thousand dollars and a home at the estate with her aunt and baby cousin. However, the bulk of his wealth was left to the infant child to have when he came of age.

Elise Austin did not get along with her aunt or step-sisters from her prior marriage. She refused to have anything to do with them. All the servants from the house testified to this account during the trial.

One of the detectives on the case demonstrated how the key to Elise Austin's bedroom also fit the bedroom of the young infant. And how she used her key to push out the other key that fell onto the carpeted floor noiselessly. She then unlocked the door, went inside the room during the dead of the night, and stole the child from his crib. She then ran outside in the gardens, and when far from the house, she strangled the child and then dropped its body into the depths of a dry well only a few hundred yards away.

To this story was a witness attached to each piece of the evidence.

Josephine Johnson, the eldest daughter of Mrs. Austin and who shared the bedroom with the accused, swore and testified that Elise got up and left the room, taking the key to the door with her.

The nursemaid for the child testified that she slept next to the baby but got up that night to tend to her toothache and saw Elise bending over the baby's crib. She remembered the grandfather clock in the hallway striking three bells. She didn't think much of it, took her pain medicine for her tooth, and returned to bed.

Another eyewitness, the gardener, heard a noise outside his cottage and went out to see what it was. Elise Austin was leaning over the dry well. It was in the early hours, and he only watched as she crossed the gardens and returned to the house by the front door.

After a short consultation, the jury deliberated the case and delivered a guilty verdict fully endorsed by the entire country to the west coast and the small fishing village of Black Rock Cove.

Everyone has this young girl sitting in the electric chair. No mercy!

Elise Austin appeared to be abandoned by all except her deceased mother's family, who had plenty of money and power. They petitioned the court to not execute the girl but instead commute her sentence to life. The courts finally agreed but voted to send her to hard time at the penal colony for the worse offenders of the law across the waters to Lourenco Marques in Mozambique, a far, far way from home.

So, Elise Austin was sent to Van Diesel's Land Penal Colony onboard a prison ship. The heiress presumptive of an old and grand estate, the fourteen-year-old died that social death far worse than physical death.

Christian Lucas continued walking side-by-side with the beautiful girl going over the case in his head, remembering how the details of this shocking tragedy were written up in all the papers daily when he was on summer vacation. This happened four or five years earlier when he was almost the same age as Elise. This is how he passed the dismal, drizzling holidays in June at his home.

Now that he had forgotten all about Elise Austin and her terrible crime of murder, to think for one second, he would be in the wilds of Mozambique, a long way from home, and find himself under the same roof with the young murderess, where she served out her penal servitude as a private servant for Viktor Serafin.

He thought, *"Maybe Mister Serafin was one of the relatives on the side of her mother who was wealthy and powerful? Maybe he paid for her defense and petitioned the courts successfully to change her sentence from death by the electric chair to a life sentence? If he did, he obviously came out here to take his unfortunate young niece, whom he thought innocent, into his private service as a servant. In doing so, he would soften her fate!*

This all makes sense to me. It would account for everything that seemed strange in his way of life. But, then, had he not done this at an immense sacrifice to his own innocent and beautiful daughter?

Christian longed to know the truth but knew not to hint the subject to Aurora or her father. He had been warned that the matter was painful to the old man.

It was getting closer to suppertime, and the two began their walk back to the house, touching on all the beauty of the gardens and flowering plants he had never seen back in the states.

When the family gathered around the dining table, Christian Lucas couldn't help watching Mister Serafin and his daughter with a new interest. He didn't let them know his thoughts, but *"why in the world would a wealthy and kind gentleman and a beautiful daughter come to this mountain wilderness, close to a penal colony halfway across the world, to make their home for life? Why did they build way out away from all the people in the city of Lourenco Marques? And, why did they take so very deep of interest in the fate of the convicted murderer, Elise Austin."*

They talked very little during supper. This allowed Christian's thoughts to continue to flash in his head. *"Where in the house is this convict servant employed? Surely, I have seen all the female servants by now?"*

What is Elise Austin to the Serafins? All the evidence from the trial makes it impossible for me to even think this murderer is someone the

Serafins wish to care for. The only answer is that this young girl is a
relative, a niece to Mister Serafin, and a cousin to Aurora.

While Christian was flashing back to that month of the trial and
turning all that he had learned over in his head, he became caught
up, so in his questions to himself, he drew the attention of Mister
Serafin.

"I fear you find our Mountain Estate somewhat dull, my new
friend?"

"Oh, no, sir, quite the contrary. I was only thinking that I have
trespassed on your hospitality too long and that I should be leaving
soon," he replied.

"Is that so," he said in a voice of sincerity, one that couldn't be
doubted.

"Yes, sir. I thought I might leave tomorrow."

"I beg you, Mister Lucas, to reconsider. Remain with us for a few
weeks," he pleaded while Aurora looked on, silent but interested.

"You are kind, sir. Nothing could give me greater pleasure than
to prolong my stay here. I'm just a tourist in this country and not
needed back home for a few months yet on my twenty-first
birthday."

"Then pray to consider yourself as a son to our household and
endure us a bit longer," said Viktor cordially while a smile that he
hadn't seen on Aurora's face beamed in her eyes.

Obviously, the spirits of both the father and the daughter were
raised by the prospect of keeping their guest with them a bit longer.

After supper, the two men went to the servant's quarters where
Jack Dannells was resting comfortably. He no longer required the
attendance of the housekeeper.

Viktor Serafin sat by the head of the bed, and Christian sat at
the foot. Viktor said, "How do you find yourself this evening, Mister
Dannells?"

"Better than I expected to be... sir," answered the convict.

"You are going to get well, you know?"

"Yes, I heard."

"I sometimes wish the pastor had given me my ticket into paradise or Hell. It would have been better for me to die than to return to that infernal chain gang," he said.

"You are not being sent back to the chain gang."

"What!" incredulously exclaimed Dannells.

"That's right. The pastor and the doctor have taken my application with them to have you assigned to my employ and serve your sentence working for me."

Jack couldn't help but break out in laughter. "That's a good one! Although the doctor and the parson are kind, who in the world would dare take me on as a private servant of some kind?"

"I will do so if you choose to serve me, Mister Dannells," replied Viktor gently.

The ruffian raised himself up on his elbow. He stared at Viktor for several seconds in total amazement. Then, "Please, Mister Serafin, say that over again... slowly."

The old man replied, "I will gladly take you into my home as my gardener if you would be willing to remain with me in that job function."

Jack Dannells looked at Mister Serafin a moment, then closed his eyes and fell back on the pillow. He turned away from both men. It looked as though he met this offer with ingratitude. But, after a few moments, the covers over the man began to tremble. The convict underneath them was sobbing with increased violence that shook the entire bed.

Neither of the men said a word and remained silent while the convict's storm of emotions subsided.

While under the covers, Dannells stuck his hand out, and Viktor grabbed it in a handshake. The man drew the old man's hand under the covers and held it to his heart and then to his tearful eyes before finally releasing it.

He turned over and brought his head out partly. "Pardon me, sir, for not thank——" He broke off his words with his out-of-control emotions.

"Say nothing more, Mister Dannells. Your strong emotions speak far stronger than words," said the old man kindly.

"You will have me as your gardener?"

"Yes, if you agree."

"I am the worst criminal in the penal colony... and you want me?"

"Yes. We will give you a chance here."

"I don't understand. I assaulted your daughter and nearly killed her from fright. I swear by all I hold sacred... I swear by my mother's grave that I never intended to do her injury! I only meant to take her gold chain because I was starving."

"Well, Mister Dannells, you will never be tempted to such violence again."

"You forgive me for all that? You are going to take me out of those chain gangs and put me in Heaven out in your gardens?" asked the man who was inspired by the goodness of his benefactor.

"But your daughter, who I assaulted and terrified so terribly? She will no longer venture out into the gardens by the sight of me."

"Not true, Mister Dannells. My daughter is courageous and very sensible. She understands. She has already told me she is willing to forget that entire episode in the woods by the fountain."

The housekeeper came into the room with a tray.

"Ahhh, your supper is served, sir. We will leave you to enjoy it. And then, sleep well and heal," Viktor said while stranding.

"Sir," said Dannells while taking Viktor's hand and looking at him gratefully, I have been called a monster, a killer, a desperado, and even a devil, but my worst enemy never called me a hypocrite. Please believe me, Mister Serafin, you have saved my soul!"

"Under God's providence, Mister Dannells," added the old man.

"Yes, under God's providence," the convict added.

The two gentlemen left the room with the highest of hopes.

Chapter FOURTEEN

Denouncing Our Savior for His Tender Mercy

The morning after the events narrated in the previous chapter, the doctor returned to the mountain estate, bringing the necessary papers for his release into private service for Viktor Serafin.

When Doctor Sanders and Viktor Serafin went to the convict's bedside with the good news, the man warmly reached his hand out, grasped his new boss's hand, and turned a grateful glance towards the doctor. "I don't wish to knock your medical science, Doctor Sanders, but the news you bring today is more healing than any drugs you could give me."

"Glad to hear you say that, Jack. It might just save the government some money on medicines. Now, all you need to do is get well as soon as possible and start earning your keep," said the doctor.

"And, Mister Dannells, you are not being rushed. You shall get strong, and when you are ready, I have my vegetable garden that will need attending," he smiled.

"Well, Viktor, it looks like all is good here. I will take my leave now and will not return unless I am sent for." He dined with the family, bade them goodbye, and returned to Lourenco Marques.

On Monday of the following week, Jack Dannells was strong enough to go to work. Under the instructions of the head groundskeeper, Harry Todd, a gray-headed old man with more knowledge than strength, welcomed his new able-bodied assistant to relieve him.

Harry lived in a small cottage in the back grounds of the estate, which was large enough to accommodate a small family, had he had one. But the man was a bachelor with an elderly sister for a housekeeper, so he found plenty of room for Jack Dannells.

If Dannells was good enough to be received into Viktor Serafin's favor, he was good enough by the other estate servants.

Viktor ensured that Jack was provided new working clothes, books to read, and writing materials.

Many of the servants on the grounds might have thought that the old gentleman went too far in his kindness to such a well-known ruffian and convict from the penal colony outside of Lourenco Marques.

Jack Dannells was now removed from want and temptation. And he was released from the one great burden that oppressed his conscience for so, so long and made him like he was... the murder of his younger brother. He was now beginning a new life!

The converted convict was happy. He enjoyed his freedom instead of chains... cleanness instead of dirt... fragrant flowers instead of stone, and good for evil!

Everyone seemed pleased to witness his happiness.

The first smile Christian Lucas had ever seen on the beautiful face of Aurora Serafin beamed upon the convict when they came upon him working in the vegetable garden, gathering tomatoes and some flowers for the dining room table.

Christian maintained a secret he half thought he should tell the man, yet he guarded against all men with his very life.

The household of Viktor Serafin was too far removed from a church of God, and he would assemble all the family and the servants in his large parlor inside the home, where he would read and present a Christian message from the most eloquent Christian writers and pulpit orators.

This normal and quiet life went on at the mountain estate for another six weeks. Young Christian Lucas and Aurora Serafin, thrown constantly together as they were, for a strong affection for each other. However, neither of them had spoken a word of love.

Christian Lucas was a very proper and kind gentleman. Since he was received into the home by Viktor Serafin as a trusted man, almost like a son, he would not dare betray that confidence while trying to gain Aurora's love without first getting her father's consent. So, the man never breathed one word to Aurora, although he wanted to so badly. However, controlling his tone and looks was not always easily managed.

At the beginning of his seventh week, he began to feel that he was unreasonably prolonging his visit and must make up his mind to depart the home. But he wouldn't do this until he first asked permission from Mister Serafin for the hand of his daughter in marriage.

Christian did not doubt his success in wooing the young woman. He knew, without vanity, that she loved him, too. He knew that he was liked by the father of his beloved. But he also felt that he must get rid of his masquerading disguise and declare his real name and motive for having to leave and return to Black Rock Cove. It just had to be done to gain the consent of Mister Serafin.

After breakfast one morning, he was determined to drop the act and talk with Aurora's father. But suddenly, his purpose was interrupted by an unexpected event.

But, before he got up from the table to exit the parlor to talk with Mister Serafin, Harry Todd, the groundskeeper walked in and said, "If you please, Mister Serafin...."

"Yes, Harry, how are things?"

"Sir, if you please, it is Jack Dannells!" said the old man.

"Dannells! What of him?" Viktor uneasily replied.

The old man didn't answer.

"What is it, Harry? What's the matter with Jack?"

"I'm afraid, sir, that he is gone!"

"Gone!" echoed the three at the table.

Then after several seconds of surprise, Viktor again said, "Gone, did you say? Jack Dannells is gone?"

"I'm afraid so, sir," sighed Harry, sadly shaking his gray-haired head.

"When did he go," Serafin demanded.

"I don't know for sure, sir. I think it had to have been in the middle of the night. I didn't realize he was gone until I had the coffee ready and went to look for him. That is when I found he was gone."

"Poor man... poor misguided fool! I'm very sorry for him," Viktor Serafin sighed.

"So am I, sir. The lad was becoming like a son to me."

"Did you have a misunderstanding with him, Harry?"

"I'm sorry, a——."

"Did you and he quarrel," Viktor put the question to him differently.

"Oh, my God, no! He and I grew to be the best of friends. Last night at supper, he was cheerful as ever. After supper, he was working on a basket that he finished and gave to my sister. Afterward, we played a game of chess until bedtime, and both retired for the evening."

Christian said nothing and watched and listened to the narrative by Viktor and Harry Todd.

"That miserable boy!" exclaimed Viktor. "That poor fool! I suppose the doctor and minister were right. They said it was not possible to reform such a ruffian." He looked at Aurora and Christian. "I am more distressed at this all than either of the two of you can imagine."

"Yes, sir, Mister Serafin. We know that you are saddened at this."

Aurora said nothing. She appeared just as surprised and disappointed at Dannell's conduct as anyone.

"Harry, when you went to his room, did you find anything missing?" asked Viktor.

"Not a single thing, sir."

"He didn't take anything?"

"I'm sorry, I don't understand what you are asking?"

"Jack Dannells... did he take anything?"

"Jack Dannells, sir?"

"For God's sake, Harry... yes, yes... Jack Dannells!" exclaimed Serafin with impatience.

The old man fumbled with his hat and rumpled his hair in confusion. He appeared utterly perplexed.

"I don't understand what you're getting at Mister Serafin."

"Surely, Harry, I am speaking clear enough. I am asking you if Jack Dannells took anything with him when he went away," repeated Viktor.

Harry didn't say a word. Instead, he opened his eyes as wide as they would open.

"Well! Speak, man!" demanded Mister Serafin.

"I am once again sorry, Mister Serafin. Are you asking me if Jack Dannells carried anything with him when he went away?" the old groundskeeper repeated.

"Yes! That's exactly what I am asking you. Did Jack Dannells take anything with him when he left?" curtly, Serafin demanded.

"Oh, Lord, no, sir, of course, he didn't," replied Harry with an expression of amazement.

"Then why didn't you just say that before, Harry? He didn't take anything. I am thrilled to hear that."

"I am sorry, Mister Serafin. How could he, begging your pardon, sir. The Bible says that we brought nothing with us into this world, and it is certain that we can take nothing out of it. So, how could that poor lad take anything away with him?" questioned the old man.

It was now Viktor, Aurora, and Christian's time to remain silent and stare. Then Viktor said, "What? What do you mean by saying that, Harry?"

"Why, sir, I mean as he couldn't any more so than anyone else who ever departed this life!" Harry said, whose patience by now began to be sorely tried.

"Departed this life! My God in Heaven! Harry, you don't mean to tell me that Jack Dannells had departed this life?"

"Yes, sir. I'm afraid so, sir."

"But you said he had run away!"

"No, sir. I said he was gone, sir. You must have misunderstood me."

"But Harry... you told us the man had bolted," Christian added in a tone of perplexity.

"No, sir. I'm sure I didn't say that. It would never enter my mind to that, sir."

"But, Harry," said Aurora, "you surely told us that he had gone off?"

"Did I use those words, Miss?"

"Indeed. You said you went to look for him and found that he was gone... and we thought you meant Jack had run away," explained Aurora.

"I'm sorry if I confused you. If I said he had gone, I only meant that Jack had gone to his final home. That was all!"

"Come, Christian. Let's go down to Harry's cottage and see what really happened. The poor man has not run away, thank goodness. And, he can't be dead, you know. It is totally out of the question. I saw and talked with the lad yesterday afternoon at sunset. He was in excellent health."

"Oh, Father, I am so relieved to think he hasn't run off. I think I would rather hear that he is dead than betray all of us and destroy himself."

"I agree with you entirely, my dear. I hope that neither is the case." Viktor replied and then looked at Christian. "Come, my friend, let's go down and look.

The three walked down the steps to the lower tier, where the cottage was located in the middle of a bunch of shade trees next to a garden gate.

Jasmine Todd, the groundskeeper's older sister, met them at the door. She was weeping and holding her apron with butterflies embroidered to her eyes.

Viktor asked, "This is bad news, Jasmine, but I hope it is not as bad as reported. How is Jack?"

"Oh, Mister Serafin, he is gone... the poor lad. He is gone. It was so sudden," the woman said and continued weeping. "He didn't have anything wrong with him."

"That can't be true, Jasmine."

"Oh, but it is, sir. It's true. He is gone, gone, gone. His body is stiff and cold! I have just straightened it out," she added and continued sobbing.

"Let me see it, Jasmine," he said while gently pushing his way past the crying woman.

"He is upstairs on his bed. I am coming. I will show you the way."

"That's okay, Jasmine. I can find it. I know where his room is. Come on, Christian," he added while walking up some stairs.

They entered a bedroom as neat and clean as a bedroom a young girl would keep. On the bed laid the body of the young gardener.

Jasmine walked over and turned down the sheet and revealed the peaceful face of Jack Dannells, to which death had given the touch of refinement it lacked in real life.

"Poor, lad," murmured Viktor while placing his hand on the man's cold, pale brow. "And we all thought he had run away! How unjust we have been in our judgment of him. He is gone, indeed!" The old man stared down at the body for several seconds, then continued, "My God, Christian, look at his face. It is amazing how much he looks like you now!" Viktor exclaimed.

Christian didn't have a reply for the old man. He had walked over to the window and stared out over the gardens. An awful fear seized him that this sudden death of his brother might have been because of the bullet he shot through him six weeks earlier. It began to make him feel ill to think that his shooting Jack might have been what brought his death.

"I wonder what caused his death? And, suddenly too, sir?" Lucas asked.

"I can't imagine. But I will send for the doctor and the coroner, and tomorrow we will have a much better idea."

"Yes, sir, a post-mortem examination is necessary," Christian replied. He knew that such an examination would show the cause of death and end all his suspense and worries that he could long endure.

"Harry, hasten to Smitty and tell him to go into the city and fetch the coroner and the doctor."

Jasmine pulled a chair up and remained by Jack's bedside.

Harry was on his way to give the message to Smitty.

When Christian returned to the house, Aurora asked, "What do you think was the cause of his death?"

"No one knows yet. We all heard the same thing. Jack went to bed in good health and spirits. This morning he was found dead in his bed, apparently dying peacefully in his sleep."

"It is so strange," said Aurora.

Some movement was seen coming from the hallway. She walked over and stepped out. Smitty grabbed his hat as he was about to depart to the city to get the coroner and doctor.

"Father, is there anything I can do?" asked Aurora.

"In what way, sweetheart?"

"At the cottage."

"Oh, no, my dear... nothing as yet. Nothing needs to be disturbed until the coroner has had an opportunity to examine the body. Why don't you and Christian go for a walk and get away from here for a little while? It is a beautiful sunny day."

"Christian, I don't wish to go far. And, not into the gardens this morning. Take me to Sheol," she said as she passed her hand through his arm.

"Sheol!" he echoed.

"Yes. It is way back on the plateau and under the mountain's shadow. I call it Sheol. I like to go there sometimes, as the Jews would call it the "Chamber of Desolation," she explained.

"Well, Aurora, lead the way to Sheol. With you beside me, it will be paradise," he whispered.

They began walking, and it wasn't long before he could have bitten his damn tongue off for making such a stupid and frivolous speech.

Aurora began to lead Christian into a thicket in the far grounds under the eyes of an immense abyss. It was gloomy, with millions of jagged rocks thrown up in piles after piles, any of which could rip a tear in one's flesh. There were deep clefts and some pretty mean holes where there were bushes with huge thorns and thistles. There were long and noxious weeds alongside a trail from which was the smell of pungent odors, and about which crept, no doubt, venomous reptiles unseen.

So much for paradise!

"Come, Aurora, let's not stay here. This whole place is repulsive, and God only knows how unsafe it is here."

"Yes, I know. I call it Sheol!" she replied.

"Come, let's go back to the gardens and the estate. Why would you even come here?"

"It suits my mood, Christian."

"Your mood! Jesus Christ, Aurora, there must be some venomous reptile hiding in this high grass. And out of all those bugs I see flying, there has got to be terrible sickening insects."

"Christian, I have never been hurt by either. However, you might be less fortunate. Therefore, I beg you to leave me and return to the house. I will be back in a while."

"Yeah, right! Like I am going back to the house and leave you out here."

"But this place is just as familiar to me as the benches in the gardens at the house. I come here often."

"Not alone, I hope."

There was a slight hesitation in Aurora's response. Then she answered, "No, not quite alone. I never come here alone. I always bring... Elise Austin."

"Good God, Aurora!" exclaimed the young man.

"What? Has a snake bitten you? Did a bee sting you?" she asked with just a bit of sarcasm in her voice.

"No, it is your words that have stung me."

"Why should they?"

"Because they present to me a horrible picture! The picture of such a horrible girl with you in this place."

"Christian, you are so unjust and cruel in your judgment of that poor girl."

"I don't judge her. I don't wish to get near enough to that baby killer, even in thought, for that matter. I would never trouble myself about her if she didn't affect your life so badly. You must know that her connection to you can be deadly."

"Well, one thing is for sure."

"And that is?"

"I can't get rid of her."

"She takes you way back into this awful place where there is danger at every turn... noxious weeds and snakes longer than I am tall!"

"Yes, she does," sighed Aurora.

"Aurora, please forgive me for what may appear to be criticism, but my deep interest in your safety urges me to say that—-."

"To say what? You were about to say, my poor old father. He can't help what he does, Christian. But, if you please, let's not talk any more about Elise Austin. Please, let me try to forget her for a while. Come up here on this pile of rocks where we can sit and await the biting insects or the venomous reptiles," she said while climbing to the top of the jagged rocks with the agility of a young girl and sat down.

Christian did not climb the rocks quite as fast. But, when he reached the top of the pile, he said with a smile, "I'm not a mountain climber, but if you wish to go to the beach, I can surf a mile without falling."

"Here," she patted the rock, "sit here beside me. From here, we can see so much desolation for as far as our eyes can see. It is all around us. See," she continued, "over there is the Valley of the Shadow of Death. It stretches for miles and miles. The horror of misery is all around us!"

Christian didn't know what to say. He didn't reply but thought, "This poor girl's mind had been destroyed by her association with that baby killer. But never mind, I will take you away from all of this in a short while."

There was total silence for almost fifteen minutes. No words were exchanged. Then, suddenly, Aurora stood up and said, "Let's go home. It's wrong for me to leave my father for so long."

Early in the afternoon, Smitty returned with the Coroner, Doctor Sanders, and the prison physician. The men were conducted to the cottage and left in the bedchamber to complete their examination.

It wasn't more than two hours, and the men returned to the house with their findings. Jack Dannells had died from natural causes. There was no foul play. Moreover, his death was not accelerated because of his recent gunshot wound six weeks earlier.

Two days later, the body of Jack Dannells was taken to the only cemetery in Lourenco Marques, Lakeside, and laid to rest. It was located under the shade of a great oak tree.

Life back at the mountain estate returned to its calm monotony.

Directly following the funeral, Christian Lucas felt that it was time that he gave an explanation to Mister Serafin and took his leave. First, however, he made a second attempt to talk privately about his intentions with Aurora.

The following day after breakfast, he said, "Mister Serafin, may I speak to you alone for a few minutes?"

"Why, of course, lad." He replied, lifting his eyebrows with a look of some surprise. "Come, let's go to the library. We can have a good cigar together, and my daughter won't shout at me that they are going to kill me," he said, laughing gently. "Now, Mister Lucas, I am quite at your orders."

"Sir," began Christian, "I came into your home as a perfect stranger, without any letter of introduction—-."

"But, bringing my daughter to me unharmed who you rescued from violence. What better letter of introduction could you possibly need than that?"

"Any man would have done the same thing, sir."

"But you are not just any man, Christian. You have laid me under an infinite obligation, my young man!"

"Very well, sir. I have been your guest for going on seven weeks now. You have treated me kindly and like a father would treat a beloved son of the house, not as a stranger. For that, I thank you," said the young man.

"I know, Christian, your interests and your duty somewhere calls. I hope it is later... and very much later. I shall mourn the day that takes you from us, Mister Lucas."

"Oh, sir, it rests with your own will to me, a son of the house."

"I am afraid I am confused and don't understand you, my dear friend. You are my son in affection. You might be so really if, instead of being rich and powerful, as I somewhat suspect, you might also be poor and friendless as many gentlemen are so often."

"Mister Serafin, I am neither poor nor friendless. In fact, I am the heir to a large estate in the States and have plenty of wealth to support your daughter. Sir, I love Aurora."

"Dear me, young man... dear me!" sighed the old gentleman, with a look of dismay.

Christian perceived the old man's disturbance and quickly added, "If I can prove to you that I am worthy of Aurora in wealth, position, and character, may I hope for your approval, sir."

Oh, God... Dear me! I don't know—-." He mournfully repeated his words and stopped.

"Why do you act disturbed, sir, on this subject?"

"Have you spoken to my daughter on this subject?" asked Mister Serafin in a voice of distress.

"Certainly not, sir. I would not do so without your approval," replied Lucas.

"Then, sir, do not speak to her of this. Mister Lucas... Aurora Serafin can never marry!"

Chapter FIFTEEN
A Look of Sad Sarcasm

The young man gazed at the old gentleman with an incredulous surprise for a moment. Then, he said, "I beg your pardon, sir. I don't believe I understood what you said. You surely didn't mean to tell me—-."

"That my daughter must never marry! Yes, Mister Lucas, that is exactly what I was saying. But, oh, for God's sake!" exclaimed the old man at the end of his words.

"But sir, surely that's a cruel fate to doom your daughter. Miss Aurora has youth, health, and a whole lot of beauty. Why shouldn't she marry if the man asking her can prove acceptable and worthy of her? I'm very sorry, Mister Serafin, but my heart is deeply interested in this question for me to sit here and keep silent."

"Oh, God! I'm sorry, my young friend, for this. I hope... I hope that Aurora's heart is not equally interested."

"Mister Serafin, I told you that I hadn't mentioned a word one of my love to Miss Aurora and that I could never have done so without first getting your consent. However, I must admit here and now that she has read my heart, not by my words but by my actions. We have been associated with each other daily since my arrival. We talk and laugh together. Because of our constant association, there is no way we can conceal our feelings for one another.

"Oh, God, look down upon me and bless my soul! I wouldn't have had this happen for the world! I might have known it. Oh, I should have guarded against it. All of the fault is mine. It is mine, do you hear?" moaned the old man shaking his gray head.

"You receive me here, a nameless stranger without any credentials. Who knows, maybe I was a convict, too. But still, you received me here because I was so fortunate as to rescue Aurora from terrible danger. You admitted me unquestioned into your home... to your table and friendship. But, sir, this is where your complacency ends. You do not, and you ought not, to admit me for your daughter's hand until I have brought you some credentials that prove me worthy."

"No... my friend. You are mistaken," interrupted Viktor.

"No, sir... please... hear me out," persisted Christian. "It's kind of you to speak as you do. I understand. I can prove to you my wealth and, even more important, my personal character to not be unworthy of your daughter's hand in marriage."

"But, Mister Lucas, my dear sir," the old man added deprecatingly.

"Wait, sir. Listen a bit longer to what I have to say. I'm going to tell you a secret I had intended to keep as I had good and worthy reasons to keep it longer. However, I tell you now because of necessity. My name is not Christian Lucas. It is Samuel Knight, the Earl of Knighwood, back in Oregon. I'm traveling under an assumed name for privacy reasons. I respectfully ask you to promise me to agree to my marriage with your daughter as soon as I shall prove to your satisfaction that I'm, in reality, everything I claim to be."

"First, Mister Lucas or Mister Knight, I thank you for giving me a chance to finally slip in a few words edgewise at last. And now, I wish to repeat that you are utterly and entirely mistaken in your premises. Not one time have I ever doubted your respectability or your worthiness for the hand of the young lady who you have set your affections on. Strange as it is for a man who places so much emphasis on a man's credentials... I've never doubted you one time. Now to make my concerns more specific. My objections don't lie against you... Samuel, but against marriage. Again, I am sorry, but my daughter must not marry!"

"Please, Mister Serafin, will you at least tell me why?"

"Say no more on this subject, sir."

"You must at least give me a reason for so strange a determination."

"Unfortunately," Viktor hesitated, "I can't do so!"

"Good God, man! My dear Mister Serafin, please—-."

"My good friend, our discussion is finished. This subject shall never be renewed. That is my final word!" exclaimed the old man, standing up with an air of dignity.

"Fine, sir. I've nothing to do but bid you farewell and give thanks for your wonderful hospitality. I leave for Black Rock Cove today," replied the young man.

"No, you must not do that. Don't you see that it rested solely with me I would give my daughter to you with delight, knowing that I would be securing her future happiness? But, Samuel, it doesn't rest with me to give you my daughter," said Viktor mournfully.

"My God, if not with you, her own father, then who in the name of Heaven does the permission rest with if it doesn't rest with you," demanded the young lover.

"Fate, my friend," the father answered solemnly. "Stay to the end of the week, at least. You and Aurora are friends. Continue to be her friend. But, do not seek anything more than that."

"Very well, I will. But I cannot leave your home without speaking my mind about my feelings for her. I must have my understanding with her, sir."

"Very well, Samuel, my young friend! I would willingly have spared you both the pain of such a discussion... but go on and take the consequences!"

"I can wait forever. Therefore, I will offer my hand to Aurora and beg her to accept my pledge to wait for her and remain faithful to her until a time comes in the future that we obtain your consent to our union."

"Samuel, I will repeat for you. I do not withhold my consent to your marriage. It is not I who is the one who is separating you two. It is FATE! And one more thing, Samuel. I feel safe in telling you this, young man. If you go and talk to my daughter and gain my daughter's consent to you two getting married, then you shall have mine! Is that fair enough?"

Thank you! Thank you! Thank you! I shall indeed!" exclaimed the lover, getting up to depart in delight.

"But, Samuel! This is the last time I will repeat myself. Do not count on her consent. You can never get her consent!" sighed the father.

"When may I speak to Aurora, Mister Serafin?"

"Now. You will find her in the gardens this time of day."

Samuel departed to go and talk with Aurora. He knew that the mystery in the existence of Elise Austin, the murderess, would soon be unveiled. It had to as she must be in near relations with the Serafins... maybe a niece, a cousin... who knows.

The young man hastened to the gardens.

He saw her sitting on a bench and went and sat down. "You appear very interested in your work, Aurora.."

"I do?" she murmured. It is one pair of gloves I am knitting for my father. I make him a half dozen or so each summer, and he wears all of them all winter."

"Please go on knitting. I can talk while you are doing so."

She put down her needle and thread. "Oh, it doesn't matter. I was just thinking how tired I am at knitting today and wanted to have someone to talk to. Your timing is great."

"Aurora, the happiest part of my stay here over these last six weeks has been spending with you and your father. I have been so happy that even now, when I feel it is time for me to go away, I seize the slightest pretext to stay on."

"Oh, you must not go yet, Christian. You really must not leave us for a long time to come. You said you have given yourself a year away from home on your adventure, and you still have a few months yet, right?"

"Aurora, it was of you and you alone and your beauty to which it is my highest ambition and fondest hope to take you back to the states with me."

The young woman was seized with a sudden tremor. She reached up and covered her face with her hands.

"Aurora," he said.

"Oh, don't! Please!" she pleaded with a voice of agony.

"But, my dear—-."

"Hush, please! You don't know what you are saying! You don't know what you are doing!"

"Aurora, I must speak. Your father has given me permission to speak to you on this matter which is so near to my heart and my whole life's happiness. Your father has given me permission to speak with you."

"My father... my father, has done this? Oh, God, how could he have done so?" she rocked back and forth on the bench in great anxiety.

"Why not? I gave him my secret that demonstrated that I am worthy of becoming your——." He said and was interrupted by Aurora.

"Oh, God, it is not that! It is no question of your worthiness, Christian. Oh, I don't understand! Why did my father send you to me knowing what my answer would be? I don't understand."

The young man reached over and gently took her hands, leaving her pallid face exposed, and he said, "I love you, Aurora! I love you... You are the first woman I have ever spoken such words... and you will be the last and only one I will ever speak them. Do they have any worth to you?"

The beautiful young woman looked down on her lover with a wistful and mournful expression in her blue eyes. "Have those words no worth to me? Oh, they have inestimable value, Christian. They are precious beyond any price! The memory of your words will keep me from dying on the lonely life path that stretches out in front of me. God knows how much I thank you for saying them! And, Christian... I bless you for them!"

"But, you do not love me for them, Aurora? Love is all I want," the man pleaded.

"Oh, yes, I love you for your words. I loved you before you spoke them. You know that, Christian. But... that is all that I can do!"

"Then may I call you my wife?" he whispered tenderly.

"Christian, you may call me anything but that. Anything! You must never call me that!"

"My dearest, Aurora. Your father hinted that some obstacle exists to you getting married. Is that true?"

Yes, my love! An insurmountable obstacle," she replied with a sign of profound regret.

"There is no obstacle that I can't surmount to win your heart!" he answered. But, in the back of his mind, he knew that Elise Austin was the probable obstacle she spoke of.

Aurora remained silent.

"Did you hear me, my love say that there is no possible obstacle I would not challenge for you to win your heart? I mean anything, of course, except an existing previous marriage which of course would be an unsurmountable challenge."

"Do you mean on my part, Christian?"

"Yes, I mean on your part, of course. What else should I mean, my love?"

"Fate," she answered.

"That is precisely what your father told me. He said that it was FATE that divided us. I told him that I would not allow FATE to divide us.

Since I adore you and since you love me... since your father approves me, since there was no prior marriage, FATE shall not have any power to divide you and me. Therefore, if you accept me, Aurora, for your husband, I will make you my wife and take you with me back to Black Rock Cove despite FATE!" he exclaimed.

Aurora didn't say a word and had an expression that was a bitter smile. "I will tell you probably what my father told you. I would give my consent, but that consent would only mock you by its uselessness. You can't marry me, and you can't take me home with you to Black Rock Cove... not even if we all wished it. Not if I consented ever so eagerly. We couldn't even get married, Christian, if all of our lives depended on you doing it! I tell you, Christian... FATE... inexorable FATE... immutable FATE... it divides us now and will divide us forever!

"Finally! I think I know the name of that FATE!" said the young man. "Her name is Elise Austin! But, I will not let her divide us, Aurora!"

Aurora lowered her face into the palms of her hands and wept.

"There! I knew it! I knew that Elise Austin was the obstacle. Your father has sacrificed himself and his daughter in sacrifice to this Elise Austin! And I ask, is she worth it?"

"She is innocent, Christian," moaned the young woman.

"You say so, Aurora. Your father thinks so. But why should you and your father be sacrificed for her? What is she to you?"

"Don't ask me that question!"

"Is she a relative of yours?"

"She is a relative to my father," the girl murmured with pallid lips.

"I say to you right now, Aurora, that neither you nor your father is responsible for the evil deeds this Elise Austin did. You shouldn't feel obliged to suffer for them. You should not permit the facts to hinder you from accepting my hand in marriage."

"Would you... would you really wish to marry a woman who was connected to this evil person called Elise Austin?"

"I wish to marry you, Aurora. I love you. I don't care whatsoever who you are connected to, no matter who it might be."

"What if I were Elise Austin's sister?"

"Yes, even if she was your sister. It still would not be your fault."

"So, Christian Lucas, you would really marry a sister of Elise Austin?"

"Yes, even if you were her sister."

"I will take you far away from here and to Black Rock Cove, where the name of Elise Austin is forgotten and where it never shall be mentioned in your presence again. But, you remember I kept up with the papers. So, I already know that you are not her sister. Elise Austin was an only child. She was an orphan.

Again, my dear, will you now be my wife and return with me to Black Rock Cove?"

"But your family?" she said.

"I have no family. I am all alone in this world. And now, thank God, I have no one to interfere with me. My nearest relative is a distant cousin with whom I have an inheritance feud in the works. Come, Aurora put your hand in mine in token of your acceptance." He held out his hand to Aurora.

"No! It can't be."

"What can't be?"

"Our marriage can never be, Christian!"

"Then you do not care for me, my love?"

"Oh, yes, I care for you more than any man in the world. Only Heaven knows how much. The thought of parting from you is more awful to me than death."

"Then why do you give me up, my love?"

"Because I can't help it. I really, really can't help it!"

"Very well. Christian, you have a right to know the entire truth, even if it breaks my heart to tell it. It is your right. Enough is enough."

"I'm listening. Speak, my dear. Tell me at once your secret."

"Ahhh, Christian, not now or here. I could never tell you my story face to face. Some time ago, at a time in my life, I thought I would die. I wrote out everything for my friends who loved me. I have that writing with me now, Christian.

Not now, but when you are about to leave us, I will give it to you. When you read it, you will see how absolutely impossible it is that I should ever find genuine happiness in being your wife... or even returning to my native country.

Forgive me, my love, for me being a coward from telling you face to face."

"I will restrain all of my impatience until I am holding your writing in my hand. Then, I will judge for myself. At that time, I will return and claim your hand in marriage. Doing this, you know, is only setting up an obstacle for me to defeat... for me to overthrow, love!"

"You think so, Christian!" She seemed to feel her entire body fatigued from the conversation and stood up. "Let's return to the house."

Aurora returned to her room and awaited the time for supper to return. On the other hand, Christian went down the hallway and into the library where Mister Serafin was reading in his armchair.

"Well, my young friend, I see you have spoken to my daughter?"

"Yes, sir, I have spoken to her," replied Samuel as he sank into the chair next to the old man.

"And what did she say?"

"Just about everything you said... that there is an obstacle. I don't know what the obstacle is, but since it is not disapproved by you, nor her dislike, if it's not a prior marriage or engagement. Then by God, I mean to overthrow that obstacle!"

"Ahhh, my young Don Quixote de la Black Rock Cove, there are giants out there that not even your lance can ever overthrow," sighed the old man.

"We will see, sir... we will see," said Christian Lucas.

He would have sat there and had a conversation with Aurora's father regarding Elise Austin, but he remembered the promise he made the woman he loved some weeks before... never to mention that name in the presence of her father.

"I leave to go down into the city tomorrow morning. However, with your permission Mister Serafin, I shall come back and see you in three days."

"I will always be pleased to see you, Mister Lucas. Your visit has been a big lift to us here," cordially replied Viktor.

Christian began to rise. "Oh, son, no rush. It's still an hour before lunch. The newspapers from Lourenco Marques have just been delivered. Why not sit there and catch up on what's happening back home. There's one from the Portland News and the Black Rock Cove News."

Samuel looked across the main headline and saw that the paper was dated several weeks earlier. Then, what appeared as an accident, his eyes passed the column listing 'Marriages, Births and Deaths.' The first on the list caught his eye. *'On Monday last, the Lady of Knightwood welcomed a son and heir.'*

Under his breath, he said to himself, *"Indeed! Who in the Hell is the Lady of Knightwood. So, I suppose, even in the great USA, Oliver Courbis thinks himself to be an Earl. He has taken a wife and now has provided himself with a son and an heir to the estate. I hope the Lady of Knightwood and the child are well. Will there not be another disagreeable surprise somewhere on the first of September this year when*

I return. Several months still need to pass. Somebody might die or get shipwrecked on his way home to Black Rock Cove." He kept reading.

There was complete silence in the library while Viktor Serafin read his book and appeared to be entirely absorbed in it.

Christian Lucas, with his eyes still fixed on the paragraph he had just read, brooded over it.

"I wonder what woman Oliver Courbis found who was an idiot enough to marry him? Oh, that's right, he was the new heir to the estate... an Earl in America. I suppose some women will sell their souls to have a spot by his side. I am sorry for the totally innocent child! That child may be my heir, after all, for if Aurora doesn't marry me... well. I will, however, endeavor to outlive Oliver Courbis, if only to keep him from the estate... but I may die a bachelor and let that baby succeed me."

He continued reading down the column.

He came to the death list. He whispered aloud. "At Knightwood, on Tuesday, the third, Alyssa Nicole Courbis of Knightwood, in the twenty-first year of age."

"Oh, poor woman," said Christian compassionately. "Alyssa. Alyssa Nicole? That had to be the Alyssa Nicole Reynolds, the beautiful green-eyed blonde I waltzed the night away at my birthday party whom I could have easily fallen in love with... what a beauty. I would have thought she would have been smarter than that to marry my cousin."

He continued to read on. "What is this? Whoa! Death has been busy at Knightwood. His eyes had fallen on a short paragraph immediately following the death of Alyssa Nicole Reynolds Courbis. It was, "At Knightwood on Tuesday, the third, Anthony Thomas Courbis, age one day, infant son and heir of Oliver Courbis, passed away."

"Poor Child. Poor Mother. I suppose there is one blessing in all of this. Alyssa Nicole died young, and the baby at one year. It may have been better that they die than live under the control of Oliver

Courbis, my backstabbing cousin. I must return to Black Rock Cove before my cousin can attract another young woman using his false title to the estate and all of his... or my wealth.

So profoundly was Christian in thought he didn't care to read any more of the paper. Instead, he sat and stared out the window in serious thought until lunch was announced.

"Oh, dear me, how time flies!" exclaimed Mister Serafin while laying down his book and setting his reading glasses on the table next to him.

After lunch, the day passed quietly. Then, in the evening, they bade each other goodnight and went to their bedrooms.

Christian Lucas passed a sleepless night. He was bothered with doubts and fears relating to the revelation that was promised him by Aurora Serafin.

Again and again, he thought to himself that there would be nothing in that revelation that would forbid his marriage to the woman he loved.

He thought, "Since the father approves me, and the daughter loves me, and there has been no prior marriage or engagement, there can't be any possible block on our uniting our love in marriage."

He tossed and turned in bed with his thoughts keeping him awake off and on during the night. Elise Austin was not a relative to them. The convicted young woman was an only child and an orphan. She didn't have a mother or father... a sister or brother, and could only be a possible niece to Mister Serafin and a cousin of Aurora. I will defeat this obstacle. I will make Aurora my wife and Lady of Knightwood. I will take her home with me where the people will adore her for the goodness in her, not to mention her radiant beauty. I will never permit the name or existence of Elise Austin to be uttered in my home... ever! Aurora must forget that there was such a person as Elise Austin." He sat up, threw his pillow over, and crunched it under his head. He tossed and turned. The thought of Elise Austin sat in his mind like a nightmare.

The sun came up. It found Christian Lucas wide awake.

The young man got up and freshened up to prepare for going into Lourenco Marques right after breakfast.

He went to the garages and found Smitty inside polishing up a four-by-four jeep. He asked him for a ride into town.

"Are you leaving us, Mister Lucas?"

"Only for a day or two, Smitty. I will be back and forth often," pleasantly replied Christian.

"I hope so, sir. This place is always brighter when you are here."

"That's kind to say, Smitty. Thank you."

"I will be back after breakfast and would appreciate being dropped off in town."

"No need, sir. If you are coming back, take the jeep for as long as you need it. We have others if we need them."

Christian walked back up to the piazza and seated himself, leaving the French doors open so he might see Aurora when she came down the stairs for breakfast.

It wasn't long, and he perceived the approach of Aurora. He walked inside and met her at the base of the stairs. She was pale, and her eyes tired as if she had also passed a sleepless night.

"Christian, before breakfast, come back to the patio and sit down."

Once seated, she drew a small envelope with the manuscript she had written and handed it to him. "This, my love, will give you the entire truth. I don't know how you will react to it. I have suffered so badly, and for so long already, it doesn't hurt any more or less. I am so inured to pain that whatever the end might be... believe me, I can bear it and still live!"

"Aurora, I will tell you what the end will be. Tomorrow morning will find me beside you again, from which I will never arise until I have your promise to become my wife."

Viktor stuck his head out the door. "Come, everyone, the coffee will get cold. Give her your arm Mister Lucas and let's go eat."

Christian stood up. "Thank you so much, Mister Serafin," he said while glancing at Aurora. "I will return in a very short time."

"The sooner, the better, young man," replied Mister Serafin.

Smitty stood in front of the jeep with the keys in his hand. He handed them to Christian. "Sir, I hope to see you back often."

He drove down the convict-built road and into Lourenco Marques. After searching for a while, he reached the Ocean View Hotel, parked the jeep, and entered the front lobby. He engaged a suite of rooms on the top floor, including a parlor, a bedroom, and a bath. He rushed to the room, closed and locked the door, and threw himself into a wingback chair next to a gentle fire in the fireplace. He drew out of his pocket the letter given to him by Aurora Serafin.

He opened the envelope and found another envelope inside. He found a pink note on the second envelope addressed specifically to him. It was stuck on the front.

Smiling gently at the thought of the small fingers that had so deftly done up the two envelopes, he opened the second envelope, unfolded the manuscript, and began to read.

"Heaven!" he shook the paper, and it fell in his lap. What in the world caused him to drop the letter like a hot potato onto his lap. It was as though something had stung him. What the Hell was it that curdled his blood in his veins? What was it that turned his cheeks to the hue of death itself?

He finally caught his breath and continued to read,

"Before you read my letter, you must know that Viktor Serafin is not my father. He is my grandfather. And... I am Elise Austin!"

The effect of this acknowledgment and the rest of the story can be found in the exciting conclusion in the Demon Gorge Trilogy found in the last novel of the Demon Gorge Trilogy, Part III of III...

To Be Continued!

| Page

Don't miss out!

Visit the website below and you can sign up to receive emails whenever Sidney St. James publishes a new book. There's no charge and no obligation.

https://books2read.com/r/B-A-HKSI-OVMCC

BOOKS 2 READ

Connecting independent readers to independent writers.

Did you love *Fate - Eventually Everything Connects*? Then you should read *Belem Towers - Only Two Will Ever Know*[1] by Sidney St. James!

Do ghosts walk through walls or do they need a doorway open to allow them to pass from one room into another? But, wait, are there really such things as ghosts?

Sophia Knight, wife of two-time Nobel Prize-Winning Physicist, Johnathan Knight lays on her death bed. There is some terrible secret she has kept from her husband the entire time they've been married. Yet, her strength is getting weak from cancer. She lays in bed and stares out over the Pacific Ocean and watches the sun go down, wondering if it will be her last sunset she will ever see.

---

1. https://books2read.com/u/mdGL8w

2. https://books2read.com/u/mdGL8w

Lacey Robinson, her caretaker, has been with her since the day she and Johnathan were married. There's no doubt she loves the Nobel Prize-winning scientist to the end of the world, but losing her strength daily has convinced her she must tell her husband of this terrible secret she has hidden for so many years. Lacey tries to convince her she should tell him in person, but she decides a letter should be written and given to him only after her death.

There's only one catch. There are only two people who know of this secret, and that's Lacey Robinson and Mrs. Knight. As the room turned dark from the setting sun, Sophia asked Lacey to turn the lamp on by the bedside. While she does as instructed, Sophia reached over and in one large gulp, swallowed an entire bottle of pain medicine.

"My God, Mrs. Knight...why! I must run and fetch Doctor West!"

Sophia replies quickly. "No, my dear, you only need to lock the door and come back and sit by me. We have a letter to write."

"No, please, let me get the doctor." A cold hand closed around her heart.

"Sit down and write!" Death hung in the air like a suffocating blanket.

Mrs. Knight dictates the letter to Lacey and with her weak and trembling hand-signed the bottom. This letter is the beginning of the end for both Sophia and Lacey.

Before the old woman passed away, Lacey was made to swear on a Bible that she would not take the letter away from the house if she were to leave, but just before she swore on the Bible to give it to Johnathan, Mrs. Knight closed her eyes one last time.

What was the twenty-eight-year-old woman to do? She was petrified that if she didn't give the letter to Johnathan, the spirit of Mrs. Knight would come back and haunt her. She decided to run away but only after locking the letter in a small jewelry box and throwing away the key in a deep well next to the Catholic Church.

Twenty years passed...

Lacey Robinson returns to Belem Towers for the first time in two decades.

Abruptly, a chill rose up her spine, making her shiver. Something was in the room with her. She could feel it. Lacey whipped around to hushed whispering that seemed to be spilling from the old wallpaper hanging from the walls. Was she going crazy? This couldn't be happening. "My God, this isn't real!" Yet, it felt nothing but real to Lacey Robinson.

A breath so hoarse and so faint echoed all around her, coming from the shadows in the corner of the room. Lacey slowly turned her head over her shoulder, and the whispering stopped. The air chilled to ice and her labored breathing became the only sound... they were hanging from the ceiling and the corners of the room and all over the hanging light fixture, crawling ever so slowly towards her, dark and brooding!

Read more at www.sidneystjames.com.

Also by Sidney St. James

Bridget Flynn Detective Series
Bridget Flynn - A Female Detective
Bridget Flynn - A Female Detective
A Prince of Their Own

Demon Gorge Trilogy
Room of Death - Here Today and Gone Tomorrow
Fate - Eventually Everything Connects
Standing in the Shadow of Death - The Sword of Damascus

Gideon Detective Series
Rosenthall - Bete Malefique des Bois
Gideon Returns - A Damsel in Distress
The Dusty Adler Murder Mystery
Phantom of Black Rock Cove
The Transformist
Ace of Spades - Volume 1
Gideon - The Final Chapter (Volume 2)
Lady in Red
Ace of Spades (Vol. 1) & Gideon - The Final Chapter (Vol. 2)

James' Recipe Series
Wild Game Recipes - Squirrels, Bullfrogs, Alligators, Rabbits, Armadillos and More
Recipes that Won Chili Cookoffs in Texas
Duck and Goose Recipes from the Wilds of Eagle Lake, Texas and the Rock Island Prairies
Grandma's Homestyle Cooking Recipes

Lincoln Assassination Series
The Lost Cause - Lincoln Assassination
Lincoln Assassination Series Box Set: Books 1 - 5
Lincoln - Pursuit and Capture of John Wilkes Booth
Lewis Thornton Powell - The Conspiracy to Kill Abraham Lincoln
The Knights of the Golden Circle
Mary Elizabeth Surratt - "Please Don't Let Me Fall!"

Love Lost Series
It Takes Two to Tango (Volume 1)
It Takes Two to Tango (Volume 2)
Tears Are Words from the Heart
Let Me Drive
Belem Towers - Only Two Will Ever Know
The Curse of Knight's Island
Norderney Island
The Winds of Destiny

Omega Chronicles
Omega - The Lost City of Altinova
Nevaeh - The Lost City of Nemea
Crux Ansata - The Lost City of Ankara
Nevaeh & Crux Ansata Part 1 & 2 Anthology in the Omega
Chronicles
Omega Chronicles Books 1 - 3 - An Anthology

Texas Outlaw Series
Sam Bass - A Dead Man's Hand, Aces and Eights

The Faith Chronicles
The Rose of Brays Bayou - The Runaway Scrape
Adversity - Keeping the Faith
Faith - Seventy Times Seven
Genesis - Stepping Onto the Shore and Finding It is Heaven
Hallelujah - He is not Here; He Has Risen (Luke 24: 6)
Seeing the Power of God
Living in God's Word
The Faith Chronicles: Books 1 - 3: An Anthology
The Faith Chronicles Box Set: Books 4-6

The Storm Lord Trilogy Series
The Flaming Blue Sword
Nine Months Will Tell
The Three Keys to Armageddon

The Storm Lord Trilogy Box Set: Books 1 - 3 An Anthology

The Whodunnit Series
Murder in Horseshoe Bay - Death Comes Quietly
Jaded Lover - Things Are Getting Heavy
Under Cover Queen - Sequel to Jaded Lover
The Amaryllis Murder Mystery
Murder at Morgan Park
Checker Cab Murder Mystery
Destiny Waits - Murder at the Lakeside Museum

Victorian Mystery Series
This Old House - A Lily Blooms in the Jaws of Hell
I Am Woman - I Am Invincible

Victorian Romance Series
I Am Woman - Hear Me Roar

Standalone
True Love Ways
I Go to Pieces - Part 2: Sequel to True Love Ways
Guitar

Watch for more at www.sidneystjames.com.

About the Author

Sidney St. James began writing his first novel, *In the Face of Adversity* in the spring of 1995. It was the beginning of four books in his Faith Chronicles Series following a family from Oldenburg, Germany traveling to Texas in 1845 and face many adversities along the way to establish a new life in a new country, TEXAS. His second in the series was *The Rose of Brays Bayou,* a true story written from the memoirs of Dilue Rose Harris of the Runaway Scrape in Texas. His third in the series is *Faith – Seventy Times Seven,* a true story about the first ordained woman minister in the State of Louisiana and how she found forgiveness for twenty years from an abusive and alcoholic husband. His fourth in the series, *Seeing the Power of God,* is a story about a young man who fell from the sky fully grown and has trouble finding Christianity when the only book he has ever read is one based on Hinduism. Thirty-six more novels follow his first series in Science Fiction, Creative Nonfiction, Romance Suspense and Thrillers, and Religious genres.

He also loves to play matchmaker in his paranormal romances and young adult series, transporting readers to a place where the bold heroes have endearing flaws, the women are smarter than they lead on, the land is lush and untamed, and chivalry is alive and well.

He lives near Sun City in Georgetown, Texas with his wife Barbara and a cat named "Fluffy" and he can occasionally be found wearing a tie... and I do mean "occasionally." His latest release "LET ME DRIVE" is his 38th novel.

You can connect with Sidney St. James on Facebook at facebook.com/authorsidneystjames or on Twitter @SidneyStJames3 or on Instagram at SidneySt.James. You can also visit his website, sidneystjames.com to sign up for emails about new releases and a chance to win signed copies of his latest releases. And, catch some cinematic video trailers of his former #1 selling Christian genre, FAITH – SEVENTY TIMES SEVEN.

James writes sweet, fun and action-packed detective mystery books with two super exciting detectives, Vincent Gideon, and Bridget Flynn. They both are smart and fearless.

Read more at www.sidneystjames.com.

About the Publisher

BeeBop Publishing Group Established 1972 College Station, Texas

The **BeeBop Publishing Group** is an associated service for helping you understand the ins and outs of how to publish your first book. We are here to offer literary assistance and professional consultations to help **publish your novel**. Whether you're looking to top the best-sellers list or publish for a niche market, we can help you **establish relationships** with distributors and bring your manuscript to life.

Learn about the publishing process and get information on timeline, pricing, marketing and royalties. **Remain in control** of your manuscript and simply receive support for your book. With so many literary agents and publishing companies out there, it can be challenging to choose between them all. We are here to help the indie author navigate the industry and answer any questions both new authors and veteran writers may have as we have done for Sandra Landers, Sean E. Jacobs, Robert Sanders and, of course, award-winning author Sidney St. James... to name just a few.

It is the dream of many writers to hold a copy of their own book - the ultimate realization of all that hard work. **Create your own book** in whatever form you wish: from self-publishing to digital eBooks, paperback to hardcover... there is a literary agent for every situation. No matter what your aspirations or goals may be, **we can help you** become a published author and make your book a reality just as we have helped Sidney St. James become an award winning and best-selling author.

CPSIA information can be obtained
at www.ICGtesting.com
Printed in the USA
BVHW091202141122
651890BV00016BA/328